LOVE ON THE BORDERS

LOVE ON THE BORDERS

MARTIN BAX

seren

Seren is the book imprint of
Poetry Wales Press Ltd
Nolton Street, Bridgend, CF31 3BN, Wales
www.seren-books.com

ISBN 1-85411-389-5

Sections of this novel have appeared in *Ambit,*
and *New Writing 5* (Vintage, 1996), edited by
Christopher Hope & Peter Porter.

A CIP record for this title is available from
the British Library

The publisher works with the financial assistance of
the Welsh Books Council.

Printed in Plantin, by Bell & Bain Ltd, Glasgow.

Contents

The texts which appear in this book should not be regarded as quotations; rather they are like musical phrases, borrowed from one work by another composer and used as an integral part of his work. See p228 for a full list of acknowledgments.

There is the locked door,
white sheets upon
a single bed,
fireglow and footprints
in the snow all over Europe

as though crossing these frontiers
this touching overcomes
inheritance and language.

from 'That Beauty, This Beast'
Edwin Brock

Call All My Lovers

Raymond (bless him) drove her to the station. The train north had businessmen (the dowdier sort because she was travelling standard class) who eyed her silently; the labouring lads drank cans of beer and showed a tendency towards the not-at-all oblique remark, but she kept her eyes down turning the pages of (although not actually reading) *Pride and Prejudice*, the only novel she had allowed herself, desperately trying to keep her rucksack light. She had walked up to the front of the train thinking the carriages would be emptier there but inadvertently got into a smoking car. There was no chance of moving – the train was full of people and this bit with beer and smoke as well, a strange start to her health-enhancing holiday.

But it all changed when she changed at Chester. Here there was a little train which was full of grandads and grandmums taking their grandchildren out for the day. They were mostly down from Liverpool and were giving their out-of-work sons and daughters a day off at home – grandparent money for use on an outing that their children couldn't have afforded to take. The younger kids – the threes and fours – were mostly quiet, staring amazedly out of the windows, maybe never having been on a train before, certainly never like this one, alongside the Dee Estuary. The middle age of childhood – the sevens, eights and nines – were wildly excited, hard for the old folk to contain. But the next age, the pre-teens, they were already preening themselves, having whispered conversations and going off into fits of giggles after some overloud remark – '... *what* she thinks she's wearing...' The old folk bore up as well as they could. 'Nare then,' said the men, but the women were more agitated: 'You shan't come again' and 'I've told you before' or 'I've told your mother before I don't like your language and if you're out with me...'

Prestatyn. Ann Llewelyn had said it was an awful place. This had put her off staying the night there, which she had originally planned so that she could have started the walk early in the morning. Off the train she thought I must start properly from the sea itself, so she walked the quarter mile north (south for the sun was what she wanted). She passed beyond the pile of rocks with its plaque designating the Northern End of the walk, crossed the sand and managed, without getting too much salt water on her walking boots, to dabble a hand in the sea, startling two small children as she chanted, "The Sea, The Sea".

The town was rather 'sweet' – a Victorian Watering Place, was how she described it to herself. The public lavatory which she used was of course disgusting. A strange graffiti on the wall outside: 'Suck cock and go to hell'. And underneath: 'Do you want to watch eight and nine year olds fucking', with a number to call and after it in another hand: 'Yes Yes'. But in a little shop they were very attentive to finding her a missing map and helped stow it into the map pocket of her new smart blue rucksack. Briskly on up the road, getting already slightly lost on the turns at the top of town, but negotiating the 'hairpin' bend round a small carpark and picnic site. '100 yards from hairpin turn R into *path* at concrete O.D. sign.' (Celestine's italics). She was on Offa's Dyke Path.

In 1926 Fox (later Sir Cyril*) started his work. 'The travelling earthwork known as Offa's Dyke, between Wales and Mercia, is generally believed to have extended from the estuary of the Dee near Prestatyn in the N. to the estuary of the Severn near Chepstow in the S.'

* Fox, Sir Cyril, was born of Hampshire stock, always a countryman at heart; his thesis, a landmark in archeological thinking, *The Archeology of the Cambridge Region*; Fellow of the Society of Antiquaries of London; work on the Cambridge Dykes led to the full field survey of Offa's Dyke. Fox saw the past as a continuum leading into the present. There is an ink drawing in private hands.

'*Rex nomine Offa*', recorded Bishop Asser in *De Rebus Gesti Elfredi*; '*qui vallum mornum inter Britannium atque Merciam de mari usque ad mare facere imperavit*' (J. would call that a bit of a macaronic, a poem in a foreign tongue that doesn't need translation). And wasn't it funny that it was Wales that was 'Britain', Mercia simply Middle England? The Welsh might think (*infra vide*) that they had won – after all they pushed old Offa back, or at least caused his bones to be carried into England.

West of the Dyke he was killed in 796. Maybe this northern end of his great earth wall was still not decided. Certainly now the archaeologists aren't sure. He was out there bashing in a few Welsh heads in some minor flurry when he got separated from his men: hewn with axes, blood and a sudden end. His followers getting his body, carrying the Great King home. He who sent Charlemagne twelve woollen cloaks and the Emperor wrote that they were too long (were scissors in short supply?). Offa won the South by a simple trick of offering his daughter's hand in marriage to a foolish Wessex King who came for his wedding ceremony only for Offa to cut his head off the night before.

Up; up; up; steep the Dyke walk, and it shows you at its start how it means to go on. Not surprising, then, those clusters of people where it crosses the road at beauty points, but in-between, hours when you get no-one. Celestine walked alone with the Dyke – or on the Dyke path at least – and her own head for company. And in your head, what company! All those people, men who you were arranging to meet nightly, but who were men, all of them, who had left you or you had run from, and so you were walking alone, which maybe you liked; but in the end, human beings, did they or didn't they want to live alone? Certainly she had sought for company.

Rory was meeting her tonight. He was, had been, her first companion. Her first lover and yet of all the twelve lovers she was to see she wondered why she had bothered to summon him – why not put him out of her mind, put other people in? They needn't even be real people need they? The heroines of fiction were in her head, like Elizabeth Bennet, who had made in the end a fine marriage, but one never knew how it had been sustained. Anyway why should she be in such exalted company as Elizabeth Bennet? She might as well stay in the company of *Dallas* – like all those little kids from Zimbabwe, believing that was the life they wanted to lead (*infra vide*).

Anyhow you climbed the first pitch and could stroll a bit among the gorse: 'Fine views of the sea, and on a clear day' – which it was – 'Liverpool' (Centre of the human universe, Celestine added). With her visit to the sea, the map buying, the steep slope, she was already late; she cut her lunch-rest to twenty minutes. She had only bought a small bottle of mineral water; it wasn't going to be nearly enough, but surely at a road-crossing she would be able to buy a drink. She drank it all. Looking at fine views, views towards a beach.

I first met Mr Lewis Carroll on the seashore at Sandown in the Isle of Wight, in the summer of 1875, when I was quite a little child. We had all been taken there for a change of air, and next door there was an old gentleman – to me at any rate he seemed old – who interested me immensely. He would come on to his balcony, which joined ours, sniffing the air with his head thrown back, and would walk right down the steps on to the beach with his chin in the air, drinking in the fresh breeze as if he could never have enough. I do not know why this excited such curiosity on my part but I remember well that whenever I heard his footstep I flew out to see his coming and when one day he spoke to me my joy was complete. Thus we made friends.

Mutual attraction. An affection that continued into adult life, though he wrote, 'like a dream of fifty years ago [is the] little bare-legged girl in a sailor's jersey.' Many girls he lost interest in as they got older, although he longed to photo them; he was allowed to photo the young innocents – the sevens and eights on the Prestatyn train – but around about ten he was forced to stop. He caused great offence to a lady by asking permission to rephotograph her ten-year-old daughter whose naked body he had explored – with his camera – at an early age. Maybe he never knew much about that future for his little girls; perhaps he was as innocent as poor Ruskin.

Our English Cousins

In these troublous times
one wonders whether (of

course making allowance
for inflation) the expres-

sion tuppeny upright is
still current in Charing

Cross Road and do the
"family values" of good

Mr Gladstone still per-
sist and who was the emi-

nent Victorian who only
having seen the female

form in the marbles of
museums was horrified to

discover on the wedding
night that his bride had

pubic hair what a shock!

The shock that little Gertrude Chataway received was an inscription: 'to a dear child; in memory of golden summer hours and whispers of a summer sea'; and some of the worst lines in the language:

Chat on, sweet Maid and rescue from annoy
Hearts that by wiser talk are unbeguiled.
Ah, happy he who owns that tenderest joy,
The heart-love of a child!

But what followed was the incomparable journey. The company of the Baker on the Dyke would have required a train of mules to carry the 42 boxes he had, all carefully packed, with his name painted clearly on each; on Carroll's journey, however, they were all left behind on the beach (*infra vide*). Celestine got up, threw away a crust of bread – a gift to the local animals – took a last look at the sea and turned inland, bound south for the sea at Sedbury.

On the Beach at Sandown

"Of course in my childhood, Mr Quareine, we went every summer to Sandown. My father took a house and we children loved it." Celestine had never seen the beach at Sandown but she rather thought those beaches – and she couldn't remember the names even – which they were on in Kenya were rather bigger and better than Sandown beach. But Mrs Boniface, on those occasions when Celestine's father was on the beach, made the comparison regularly, and Sandown always came out ahead.

Celestine thought her father had tolerated Mrs Boniface because Mrs Boniface had a daughter whom, he hoped, Celestine would play with; but she didn't of course, she only played with the Cook's children, although it wasn't really allowed. And all this was after the Ayah had gone. Celestine couldn't remember the Ayah, she could only remember calling and calling for her: 'I want the Ayah', 'Where is the Ayah?' And screaming in her father's arms, 'The Ayah, the Ayah, the Ayah.'

The Ayah had come with them from India, when Father had been transferred there; just three years after his wife had died; just three years after Celestine had been born. "Poor fellow, bound to be broody here," his seniors said, "wife dead and all that. New country, new job; good at the job anyway, new responsibility, perk him up no end. Find a new wife, wouldn't doubt. Good thing for the little girl too, nobody will know about the mother and there will be no _ _ _ _ to find out about." So to Kenya they had gone, taking the Ayah with them.

But the Ayah didn't like Kenya. 'The Blackies' – all the other servants were 'Blackies', and she didn't care to mix with them, but had to because she was only a servant – a privileged one of course, because she looked after Celestine, always had, even for that brief six months when Celestine's mother had been alive. She liked Celestine, sent postcards to her from Delhi when she got back, but not enough to stay on in Kenya. She wanted her home, and back she went.

Poor Mr Quareine never really cheered up either. At least, Celestine thought of him as having always being sad. Just working, working, working at the law – which was all he loved, that and his daughter, for whose sake he put up occasionally with the appalling Mrs Boniface:

"I suppose you'll send her home to be educated, Mr Quareine, you can't really compare with what's here."

"I suppose I shall Mrs Boniface."

Mrs Boniface had come into Celestine's mind as she calculated the miles to Bodfari – fair of face and fair of body – not that Bodfari would have anything to do with that piece of amateur linguistics; it would have some deep Welsh meaning which she was not going to attempt to plumb. Marian Mill sounded hopeful for water, or certainly four miles further at Rhuallt, where a bracketed note said (shop, Smithy Arms).

The laces on her new boots were rather too long and she disliked their bright red colour and had thought of smearing mud over them. The boots she had got in one of those camping shops six weeks ago, and she had been wearing them solidly for the last six weekends in the house and tramping round Hampstead Heath. They were very comfortable but stepping up on to that last rather steep stile her second foot had come down on the lace and thus untied it.

The boots were, she admitted, proving their worth in terms of comfort as she sat on the stile re-ordering the lace. Her new jeans too were OK; she usually bought jeans to fit very tight but she had allowed herself a little more over her hips so she could move freely. She had better keep moving.

She was going to go down the Dyke in twelve days, whereas the old Fox (Sir Cyril) spent five *years* deviling it day by day, field by field – a man for detail. Now he was a mile or two off her, the path deviating from the actual line of the earthwork. Fox and Mr Arnold Taylor were struggling with another macaronic*, this time in the Norman French: "*Ce est le droit Robert Banastre al maner de Prestatun od les appurtennaunces en Englefield... le ancestre cestie Robert vyent en Engleterre od le cunquerer... Robert Banastre pardi sa tere en Wales a cel heure, e amena tut sa gent de Prestatun od le Deke en contrie de Lancastre.*" They were arguing whether '*Prestatun*' simply stood for the little town that now existed or for a larger area.

The Mill was charming with its ruined wheel but the water beside it was certainly not drinkable and the way on was up Marian Cym. She thought of the weight of her waterproof clothing and the August heat. Her breasts were damp; they were big, as many a man had told her, and somehow she never got bras that stopped there being skin contact under the breasts, and there the sweat was forming. She undid her shirt, what the hell, she had still seen no-one and here she was going steeply down into the wood and would meet no-one climbing up. The path actually came out by the Smithy Arms. She could see umbrellas on their lawn through the trees so she stopped and buttoned her blouse and strode out and hurried to an umbrella, pulling off the rucksack and realising how wet

---

* I'm not too sure about this macaronic stuff. I looked it up in the dictionary and the word is used "to designate a burlesque form of verse in which vernacular words are introduced into a Latin context with Latin terminations and Latin constructions. Also applied to similar verse the basis of which is Greek instead of Latin and loosely to any form of verse in which two or more languages are mingled together." But my basis is that you don't need to know the language to understand them. Any rate it is good to know the word relates to macaroni.

her back was. It was half-past three and the Smithy Arms was shut. Oh well, the shop. She risked leaving her possessions under a table and guessed the shop would be down to the right (the Dyke path being up to the left).

Why did she decide to set out on a Wednesday – early closing day, she remembered, throughout the Welsh borders? The shop – with cars roaring by, in August – kept its routine, and the garage opposite too (mostly agricultural repairs, she guessed) was firmly shut. She looked around for a water tap but it must be inside the big gates. All there was by the petrol pump was a watering-can with a little oily water in it. She wasn't that thirsty, she decided, and went and rested under the umbrella and ate an apple.

She went on more slowly up the track opposite to find a huge new road being built – a swath through the country, obliterating the path – but fairly kind notices led her across; she had to climb a barbed-wire fence – that was when you wanted a companion to hold it down, although she liked to feel a firm pressure (in her crotch) as long as the barbs did not tear her new jeans (Rory would like them, she knew).

It was up, and down again. Tomorrow maybe she'd wear a bikini top although she supposed her shirt at least absorbed some of the sweat on her back. She was going to make tonight's target OK, but would Rory? But here suddenly popping up over a fence, a man; she pulled her shirt together, fumbling with a button, amazed at the physiognomy that looked her up and down: Chinese.

The Message Friar William of Rubruck brought home from the Great Mongke (Mangu) Khan

Why did Louis IX dispatch William to the court of the Great Khan? William was not an envoy, he was a missionary, sent to tell the Khan the good news about Christ the Son. Mongols and Christians could (did the message imply?) live side by side, friendly with each other, relating to each other in a Christian way if possible, but at least living in amity. Was that all Louis' aim? What did he really want?

And there were reports that some Mongol princes had indeed converted. Was not Sartaq a great grandson of the great Chinggis, cousin to the ruling Mangu, himself a grandson of Chinggis?

We have heard it said of your lord Sartaq in the Holy Land that he was a Christian and at this the Christians are overjoyed, and especially the most Christian Lord, the King of the French, who is on pilgrimage there and is making war on the Saracens in order to wrest from their hands the Holy Places. For this reason I wish to go to Sartaq...

Nowhere have they any 'lasting city' and of the 'one to come' they have no knowledge. The next day we encountered M's wagons loaded with dwellings and I felt as if a great city was on the move towards me. We met up with Sartaq, then, three days journey from Etilia. His camp struck us as extremely large, since he had six wives and his eldest son who is with him, two or three, and to each woman belongs a large dwelling and possibly, two hundred wagons. He was seated on a couch with a guitar in his hand and his wife beside him. I was really under the impression that she had amputated the bridge of her nose so as to be snub-nosed, for she had no trace of a nose there, and she had smeared that spot and her eyebrows as well with some black ointment which to us looked thoroughly dreadful. The women are astonishingly fat. The less nose one has, the more beautiful she is considered and they disfigure themselves, moreover, by painting their faces. They never lie down in bed when giving birth.

Mangu's Court. They were amazed and kept repeating constantly "Why have you come since you did not come to make peace?" For they have already reached such a level of arrogance that they believe the whole world is longing to make peace with them. Certainly for my own part I would, if permitted, preach war against them, to the best of my ability throughout the world. "Just as the sun spread its rays in all directions, so my power and that of Baatu (his cousin) are spread to every quarter." Up to this point I understood my interpreter but beyond this I was unable to grasp a single complete sentence, which brought it home to me that he was drunk. And Mangu Khan too struck me as tipsy.*

You have been here a long time; it is my wish that you go back. This is the order of the everlasting God in heaven, there is only one God, and on earth there is only one Lord, Chinggis Khan. Whosoever you are and wherever ear is capable of hearing and wherever a horse is able to tread there make it heard and understood. From the moment they hear my order and understand it, but if they place no credence in it and wish to make war against us, you will hear and see that though they have eyes they will be without sight; and when they would hold anything they shall have no hands; and when they would walk they shall have no feet. This, the order of the everlasting God.

Thus was the Franciscan Friar able to live in amity with Mangu Khan, although often admitting he was extremely angry (he kept his head, however, and got back to Acre to write his report to his king). He advised that no further Friars should travel to the Tartars; only the Head of all Christendom could give answer to the absurdities they have written three times to the Franks. Thus they made peace by staying away from each other's borders.

Celestine became aware that the Chinese man in front of her was finding it hard to keep smiling at her. How to explain her early years in publishing as an assistant to the Hakluyt Society, and her close association with the printing and production of *The Mission of Friar William of Rubruck*? An alternative explanation of her solid examination of him seemed sensible.

* Carpini observes that the Mongols regard drunkenness as an honourable condition and that they continue drinking even once it has caused them to vomit. They are delighted when foreign guests behave disgracefully through drinking to excess and take it as a sign that guests feel at ease with them!

"Oh," she said, "I'm so surprised. I have been walking all day and I have met no-one and now you are here. And you have come all the way from China."

"Not today from China and not from China. I come from Hong Kong. I write a thesis," he said, "for my PhD on Boundary Walls, like the Great Wall you know. But where is Offa's Dyke?"

As far as Celestine could make out he had arrived at Heathrow the day before, hired a car and driven in a North-westerly direction looking for the Dyke. He must, she thought, come from an extremely wealthy and possibly rather stupid Hong Kong family. Somehow he had got onto the A541 and slowing down at Bodfari had seen the signpost with the Offa's Dyke label on it. So in his neat grey suit and well-polished shoes he had started up the path. Celestine explained to him that the Dyke here was a way off. She had looked over towards it, she explained, from the top of the Cwm she was just descending, but it was not visible. He had only a hazy idea of what he was looking for but he was deter-mined to go and look. She could at least advise him about the Offa's Dyke Society and their base in Knighton. He got out a little computerised memo pad and typed in the address. Then made her a little bow and passed on up the path.

It was after 6.30 when she hit the little metalled road which led down into Bodfari and she had told Rory six o'clock. Of course he'd be late. As she came down to the bottom of the lane, a stoutish lady with white hair, leaning over the gate of her cottage, interrupted her,

"I thought there was going to be two of you."

"Mrs Beamish?" asked Celestine.

"Oh, you're for her are you then? Ooh, you've a little step to go yet then. Other side of the valley 'tis."

"I'm meeting someone at the Downing Arms."

"Just across the road then."

There was a pub with a car-park beside it but no bloody Rory. Well that was alright, she could get in the pub and at least have some fluid. But the door to the pub was shut and there were no lights on. This is insane, thought Celestine, to die of thirst in the Welsh borders. The lady from the cottage had followed her down to the road. Celestine shouted across at her, as cars passed them, "The pub's shut," but she couldn't catch the reply so she waited for a gap in the stream of cars to recross.

"The pub's shut."

"Oh, he's only interested in his dinners these days. Dinners he does for the campers, see. Doesn't serve 'til eight o'clock, so he doesn't bother opening 'til half seven these days."

"My friend hasn't come and I said we'd be at Mrs Beamish's by half past six."

"Give a ring on my phone and welcome."

Mrs Beamish sounded cool and sensible. She had been the same last night when Celestine had rung to make the booking. She even offered to run down in her car and pick Celestine up but Celestine said she'd hang on and ring again if her friend with the car didn't appear. But then with a roar and a flash of red, Rory in a sports car was in the pub car-park. "Sorry, old thing, bit of traffic. Got your parcel though, bottle of bubbly too. Want a drink in the pub first?"

She could still see in Rory what she had seen on their first day at college. He was bronzed then and had a smooth brown cheek, a sort of square jaw she supposed – all women's magazine stuff, she knew, but it was true. She didn't know then of the curious roughness when you ran your hand or placed your cheek against those smooth looking cheeks, that curious roughness. He was wearing a light brown tweed jacket and cavalry twill trousers, which was just right that year. And eyes pale blue looking at you giving no messages. It was the new students' get-together and she couldn't resist going over to him – they were supposed to introduce themselves – and putting her hand on his upper arm, and he looked at her, still noncommittal, and she said "I'm Celestine." "Oh, my name's Rory." And it was easy to tell him all about school, the exams, and he said the same sort of things back only, she realised afterwards, a bit vaguely. "Games – squash? Tennis?" "I thought I might play a bit of rugger."

Then when they walked out to the refectory, that jacket she loved and their hands just touched and then they held hands. Which was all it was for weeks. Celestine organising them to films, local theatre; Rory, yes, he'd come. 'He's sweet,' she remembered thinking and already that first linguistics lecture from Crystal: "What do words mean? Where did they come from? Where are they going? Go and look up a word and see."

Sweet. Ten meanings in the OED, and tenth was 'a: to behave affectionately or gallantly towards; b: to have a particular fondness or affection for (one of the opposite sex), to be enamoured or smitten with.' And it had been in every language: Old English '*swete*', Old Friserian '*swet*', old Teutonic '*swootja*', and on and on.★ She loved being beside him and his quietness, his occasional contribution to her chatter.

Then the surprise, after six or seven weeks of the term, when he said he was in the second rugger team: would she come and watch him? Well, she was playing squash with a girlfriend. "Come to the pub afterwards, anyway." She got there a bit late and Rory shouting "fucking *awful*, they were" and abruptly cutting his voice down, but red, sweaty, beery, kissing her. And all second and third year men coming over to her and hearing them say, "Look what Rory's bought."

And the next day Rory a bit shy of her. He still looked sweet, but became his usual inarticulate self. Out to a film, or to a club, and trying to dance with him, both a bit clumsy. They had kissed always but now more insistence until one night, "Come into my room," blurting out, "I bought a rubber."

And he was her sweet. So she went in shaking but when he was undressed he was uneasy and looked beautiful and she touched him and suddenly he was erect and pulling on the rubber and looking down on her, but it was alright because

★ The old doctor was more direct: Sweet: (1) pleasing to any sense, (2) luscious to the taste, (3) fragrant to the smell, (4) melodious to the ear, (5) beautiful to the eye.

she was wet, wet there and he pushed, was in her and in a moment he gasped and pulled out of her. Got up, "Did I lock the door?" and could he smoke. He didn't turn the light on but smoked and she could see him in the firelight. And when he finished the cigarette she was still on the bed and she said, "Come back here, Rory," and this time he was in and in her and she didn't want it to stop. *Sweet swete swootcha.*

Next day Rory was high – high with her, high with everybody. Very keen he should take her to the pub – the rugger pub – and keen there on touching her, letting people *see* him touch her, and then very determinedly saying, "We must go. Sorry folks, we – kids having to be getting along, see you then, see you." And laughs. And Celestine knew that the mates had pushed him into getting his end away. And that was why he'd done it. Not really for her, but to be in with his mates. Yet she still wanted to touch him.

In the summer they went on holiday together, Celestine arranged a Greek island, just themselves, she said. Rory would probably have liked a crowd. He couldn't talk to many people, he had no languages, so he became the quiet Rory again, didn't read many of her books, went into the taverna earlier than her, drinking the ouzo. Sometimes they didn't fuck when they got too drunk, just slept; but then they had fucked all afternoon anyway. And Rory could swim – he taught her to snorkel, which she found difficult at first, going too deep and water pouring down the tube, but Rory was patient with her; they floated over the rocks, holding hands again, and then going back to their little studio. Celestine's father had provided most of the money for the holiday; Rory seemed to have spent all the money his parents had put up for his share of the trip before they left.

So in their second year they shared a flat with another couple. They were all to participate in the daily chores, the shopping, keeping the place fairly clean. Only at once, Rory, who swore he would do his share, didn't. Could you shop today, lover-girl, I've got this class, this paper, or this rugger... Yes, yes, I'll be in to eat at eight but then not there 'til ten. Beery. "Sorry, love, got stuck in the pub – you know how it goes."

How it went was that his work was not going well, Physics with Chemistry – somehow he thought he was reading the wrong subject. Anyway, his exams went wrong and he really wanted to earn some money. So this man who'd left (he'd been Captain of rugger their first year) was saying he could get Rory a job. Something with the car trade, for God's sake. You get a car with it too. So Rory left the university and was surprised that Celestine wouldn't come with him. "Staying on at this place... let's go to town. Tony says there's this flat. Well we'll set up together when you've got your degree."

And he was her first great love. Here he was as large as life, with a car that would kill him one day. The first of the lovers she had summoned so that she could see why she was alone again. Why had she not gone to town as Rory had suggested and fulfilled her life with him? She knew of course, as they bundled her rucksack into the car and set off to Mrs Beamish's.

Why had she bothered, then, to summon Rory to Mrs Beamish's? In the parcel she had, for old times' sake, a black blouse, lacy at the top; low bra, garter belt, black stockings, silk shirt. Rory would like all that. And she could remember his whispered appeal to her, *Wear black stockings*, it was a real communication from him. He was lying still inserted into her in bed and she realised he really wanted her to do it. Perhaps it was a bit tarty, but why not if it made him really want her, turned him onto her – away from his mates. But then, of course, it was partly because his mates admired girls in black stockings that he wanted her in them. Where did his desires come from? She wanted them to come from her alone. She wanted him to want her in black stockings because that was how he felt she should be, an idea rising directly in his mind out of what she was. It was all more complicated than anything poor old Rory could work out. On then to Mrs Beamish's.

Sheep & Lambs

Celestine had had visions of Mrs Beamish's old Welsh farmhouse but it was not to be; it was a rather poorly-built thirties house but there was a small but reasonable bedroom with your 'own' bathroom next door. Mrs Beamish showed them proudly in, "Make yourselves comfortable." Rory, who had come all this way for one purpose only, was ready to get it away at once, but Celestine wanted a drink (there was a tea-maker in the room so she boiled a cup up) and a bath. The bathroom was a bit strange, there were leaks round the base of the loo so the fitted carpet was soggy and slightly smelly, but there was hot water. So she lay there watching the time – dinner at eight. I'll have to give it to Rory first, he's driven all this way! And she knew what was in store for him: changing jobs, a marriage to a secretary in one of his firms, kids, bitching with his wife, short of money, then wrapping himself and a car round a tree. She'd been to the funeral and his wife had said: "Rory often talked about you. Said you were one of those 'clever girls'." So yield once more, deep deep, sweet sweet, and then put on the stockings and skirt and go down to dinner to drink champagne, but mostly, more, more water. Rory would finish the bottle of champagne, she would half listen to his conversation incessant about this, that deal, or the way old Tony or old John or old Joe had gone on about this or that. And by the end of dinner to see Rory as something hazy, ephemeral and perhaps not really mattering at all.

Mrs Beamish and her family, poor Welsh sheep farmers, were off themselves to the Denbigh Show. "Could you be gone by 8.30?" Rory: "Goodbye, old thing, should let me drive you, but I know you, you'll walk." So off in a roar in his over-priced car. But Mrs Beamish did do sandwiches and yes, there was a good plastic litre orange bottle she could let Celestine have and fill with water. Celestine thought perhaps she ought to go back to the Downing Arms at Bodfari because she would miss out half a mile of the Dyke path, but Mrs Beamish knew a track round the contour so that she didn't have to go down again, and Celestine gratefully accepted the compromise. The silent Mr Beamish even walked with her a hundred yards to see she didn't miss the turn beyond the barn – a rather overgrown track used by sheep but not by humans, so she had to crouch, her rucksack catching on the boughs above her. But then she was out of the wood and there in front of her was the familiar signpost of the Dyke – turn left and go up.

Very steep at once and some of the fields were very broad. She was glad she had bought her binoculars (a present from her father); with them she scanned the opposite hedge for the Offa's Dyke Path posts with their acorn plaques on them, or for a stile. Plenty of water today though, and it was a luxury to stop and take sips of it. People, for the first time (except for her Chinese man): coming down towards her were four real back-packers. They had camped near a ruined farm. How had they managed for water? she didn't ask, but they looked bedraggled and asked her about breakfast in Bodfari. She wondered if Mr Owen Evans – his name had been over the door – did breakfasts at the Downing Arms. She rather thought he might not, but she didn't depress them, full as she was of Mrs Beamish's good porridge and bacon and eggs.

It was funny that she had liked, enjoyed them. After the Ayah had gone, what did she have for breakfast? Cornflakes, she guessed, and certainly some fruit. The first fried egg she remembered was at the 'Sally' school in Nairobi – St Aloysius, but all the children called it 'The Sally'. During her first term, her father had to go away and he thought that it was not really suitable to leave his daughter alone with only the 'Blackies' to look after her. But she loved black cook, a big fat lady who would take her on her knee and hold her when she cried, and what she remembered her saying sounded in her head like a Southern Negro from the States but that was probably from listening to Mahalia Jackson later. Any rate, cook was friendly, school was not, and after the first disaster, her father was not keen to repeat the experience.

Happily, he had got back on the Friday, so unlike the permanent full-time boarders, at least she didn't have to face Sally for long boring weekends. But there was horror for her and embarrassment for Mr Quareine when he did come to pick her up. Waiting, longing, at the gate and sobbing in his arms. Then the porter, "Mistah Quareine, Headmistress, she like a word with you." The two of them, she trying to control her sobs, taken to the terrifying Head's study.

"Mr Quareine, you didn't tell us she wet the bed."

"She doesn't."

"Every night, Mr Quareine. Parents must supply their own rubber undersheets. She must come with her own if she's to board again. And there will be a small extra charge for laundry. And all the extra work that matron has had to do."

"Of course, Miss Cox." Waiting perhaps for some other remark but none came, so, "Celestine and I will be going along home now then."

So she never had to explain the full horrors of the breakfast, because when she said in the car, "Not to stay again, Daddy, let me stay with cook if you're away", he just said, "Alright, Celestine."

At breakfast, unlike at home, you didn't run into the room and sit down and somebody poured you your milk. You had to walk quietly, stand behind your place and wait (it was not good to be late); and then Miss Cox would come and stand and say "Hands together, children" – the *menashe*, like she remembered, just, from Indian – and then she would say, "For what we are about to receive may the Lord make us truly thankful." And then, after a pause, she would say, "In silence, children, all yourselves say to God a thank you for the food you are about to eat." Celestine thought wildly, 'God, take all the food away'.

But he didn't and after Miss Cox had given permission she would sit down and this grey splodge on a plate would appear. You felt sick.

"Eat your porridge, Celestine." She would try to spread it round the plate and when Miss Cox wasn't watching one of the black maids would whisk it away but deposit in front of you the cold yellow thing with the grey border and the thin tough single rasher of back bacon. Years later in a joke shop in New York she saw the egg again, made of rubber to trick your friends with. You couldn't have tricked Celestine with a Sally egg and bacon. It was further mashing and trying to spread the yellow all over the plate so that none would have to go into your mouth. She prayed that she would be sick – that would teach them – but she never was.

Her name, why was she called Celestine? She would never ever find out. It was one of those questions her father answered with: "Your mother..." and then he would just stop and you knew it was no use asking any more. Even years later when they did talk a little about her mother (she had found out by then) she never asked why her mother chose *Celestine.* But at Sally's she hated it – almost hated that mythical mother for giving her the name. It was June, or Kate or Judith or May or Anne. So the little boys at break-time tried to form a ring around her and shout, "Celestine, Celestine, silly thing, Celestine." But now, after the other boarders had told on her they sang: "Celestine, Celestine, wets her knickers, Celestine." In that horrid boarding week, she wanted to go, and stood by her desk and suddenly she was standing in a pool. But then Miss Grey, quick as a flash, took her out to a servant, and she thought the other children hardly knew.

The whole of that first year was a misery because Miss Cox was always there. She had said to Mr Quareine: "I'm always in and out of the infant class myself to see the little ones make a good start – the start is so important." So, suddenly behind you would be this voice: "What are you doing – staring? You haven't been listening. Why isn't your pencil in your hand? What did Miss Grey just say?" How could you remember after all that battering, shouting?

So, after the first year when they got back in the Autumn: "We don't have Coxey in class any more." But they had Miss Grey still and she sat and played a sort of Snap with cards, with the writing underneath the pictures, and then covering the pictures, and suddenly you could read and you and your friend Angela were racing through *Janet and John* books. And one day she got her friends, Angela and Jane – although Jane was a bit scared – to shout at some of the taunting boys, "Poor little weeds, can't read, poor little weeds, can't read." Any rate she had longer legs than most of them and could run faster.

Long legs were good things to have, too, in the Clwydian Hills. The guide book she was having to read backwards – why did people always start in the south? But that town down there must be Denbigh, where Mrs Beamish was even now at the County Show – her daughter had been into ponies. Celestine had met Angela again ten years later and she was all ponies. James' sister was into ponies and of course so was James really. Mrs Beamish had said her daughter did really well locally (there were rosettes everywhere) but hadn't made it nationally because they couldn't afford it. James had wanted daughters, and he would have seen that they had the money to 'make it nationally' with their ponies.

A pack pony would, Celestine thought, be handy for her baggage (as well as the Baker's Boxes) although there was no way, of course, you could get a pony over all the stiles. The Offa's Dyke Path notes meant exactly what they said: 'Steep slopes up Moel Arthur.' Moel Arthur was the first of the many hill forts she would pass or walk through on the Dyke. It was small but had very steep triple banks defending the inner area. The hill forts were a-building long before Offa. Celestine loved hill forts.

In her English school days, she had visited Dale Fort in Pembroke, and then Barbary castle, which she knew well, and of course Maiden, the biggest one. One was always wondering what sort of people lived in them. Naomi Mitchison had written about Maiden but it was a story of the Romans visiting the fort, and asking an old man why it was there. But he said nothing. The Romans left baffled, as she, Celestine, did all these centuries later.

Romans visiting the castle: two men and a boy and the boy ran off and found a girl called Ygerne. He told her about Roman Dorchester, and she parried, "It may be a nice little town, but it's not on a great hill like this, straight under the sun and the stars and the lightning. This is Mai Dun." And she was going to tell him a little of why it was so called. "She did not move for a minute, seemed just to be gathering herself up into a thing with eyes and a terrible new sharp voice. She was going to speak almost at once." But then an Uncle – a benign Uncle, indeed an Uncle from Rome (*infra vide*)* – came up and she never spoke. So Maiden Castle retained its hidden secret.

You had a bit of a feel about Offa himself. He was a European, there were coins with his face on them; he was a planner, an organiser, which she supposed was what you wanted in a ruler then. Whence came his willpower to drive forward this astonishing effort by a small state of farmers and peasants? The Dyke was off five miles to the East and the old Fox was over there now, digging out a bit to see how and when it was built. Below the crest the ancient surface-soil was struck at a depth of 5ft. The core of the mound was composed of water-worn boulders. Black (charcoal stained) soil interpenetrated these and extended beyond them. Over this black soil was strong clay with dark patches here and there. A thick layer of humus covered the whole.

It was all very well to comment on the engineering but what, Celestine wondered, about the diggers? There was a post-hole and this illustrated the building method: posts were doubtless set up at convenient intervals along the line the Dyke was to occupy and removed one by one as a gang reached them. But who were in the gangs and did they appreciate the need for the labour, for which they were

* This Uncle from Rome was visiting the Border Country of Britain.

surely not paid? It was a boundary set between two peoples, but it was a peaceable thing. Although Offa was killed fighting the Welsh, he saw the need, when one people were pressing against another who pressed back, he saw the need for establishing a meeting place.

To Celestine, it was like two people meeting. And between two people did you set boundaries? When you set first to establish unions, when you *sought* intrusion, should you then set boundaries? Was that why she had failed to achieve a lover who would stay with her – because she had never been aware of where to set a boundary? And that was why she walked down this old boundary, to see how such a course was set.

Maps, you'll remember, the Bellman solved instantly:

> 'Other maps are such shapes, with their islands and capes!
> But we've got our brave Captain to thank'
> (So the crew would protest) 'that he's bought us the best –
> A perfect and absolute blank!'

Equipped with this simple guide Carroll sent his Bellman to look for the Snark whom he had dedicated to Miss Gertrude Chataway. Seeking it with him he had a crew, which was complete including a Maker of Bonnets and Hoods – as far as one can tell a masculine activity, so that the only women who intrude on the scene are the mythical figures inserted by Henry Holliday the illustrator. They are *Hope* and *Care*, who joined in with the search for the Snark:

> They sought it with thimbles and they sought it with **care**;
> They pursued it with forks and **hope**;

The Bellman's intention on this fated journey is to find a Snark but what eludes us and him is the exact characteristics of this creature. Is it human and more importantly is it female? There are some characteristics which might give us a clue, the five unmistakable marks by which you may know, wheresoever you go, the warranted genuine Snarks.

'Let us take them in order. The first is the taste,
Which is meagre and hollow, but crisp:
Like a coat which is rather too tight in the waist,
With a flavour of Will-o-the-wisp.

'Its habit of getting up late you'll agree
That it carries too far, when I say
That it frequently breakfasts at five-o-clock tea,
And dines on the following day.

'The third is its slowness in taking a jest.
Should you happen to venture on one,
It will sigh like a thing that is deeply distressed:
And it always looks grave at a pun.

'The fourth is its fondness for bathing machines,
Which it frequently carries about,
And believes that they add to the beauty of scenes –
A sentiment open to doubt.

The fifth is ambition.

Carroll suggested to Gertrude Chataway that she might spend the night in a bathing machine and he sent seven kisses (to last a week).

Celestine had twelve days to get down the Dyke and more than kisses to help her in the night as she descended its course. She had visited her old friend Henry in Liverpool before she set out and spent time as usual in the Philadelphia with him. "Offa's Dyke," he said. "I didn't know she was gay" – turning aside, as usual, from any serious discussion of her or his life. Perhaps she liked Henry because she saw he was like her: he never sustained a relationship, living alone now, bored and depressed no doubt, and when asked about his old girlfriend, just said, "I've finished with all of that."

Celestine felt there was unfinished business ahead of her. She had thought to put in her sack Flint's most famous book, *Love and its Disorders* – "It [love] shall be the cause of war and dire events," he wrote, "and start dissension..."

So maybe it was best to be alone. She had got on a bit but needed, she felt, to be beyond the pass at Bwlch-pen-Barass by lunchtime. She was now on the steep slope to Moel Famau with its curious monument which commemorates 50 years of the reign of the mad King George III. No record of why Mr Harrison of Chester (no doubt with some public support) decided to build a monument in Egyptian style to his king. It was going to be huge, 150ft high; it wasn't completed, but even the base was formidable enough. Celestine liked George III because he had wanted at a formal opening of the House of Lords to address the company as "My Lords, Ladies and Peacocks." His attendants restrained him. How, she had always wondered?

Here there was almost a crowd. Five or six picnic parties mostly with attendant noisy kids, something she'd last heard in Prestatyn. It was windy too and they had all the best sheltered spots round the monument. She almost got out a jersey but then she remembered how hot she'd been just moments before. She decided the best thing was to use the topographical plates to admire the view and then leave. Actually the view caught you not because of the famous mountains you knew – Snowdonia, Cader Idris – but because of the lovely unpronounceable Welsh names in the guide – Aran Fawddwy and Aran Benlyn. So on down to the sounding pass Bwlch-pen-Barras. Would you pronounce it Belch? No, it was more like 'o' in comb. *Bolch*, still a comic enough sound.

Here there was a car-park and a real crowd. Fifty cars on this August day, but mostly spilling their contents on the Moel Famau side of the road. They were busy around her as she crossed from the bottom of the path through the carpark. The path up to the monument was broad and well graded, gravelled with small stone designed for the car-born, but the other side you were back onto the good old Dyke path, not all that clearly marked and again very steep. She only went up about 50 yards or so, far enough to diminish the cries of the children, and then collapsed gratefully with Mrs Beamish's ham sandwiches.

Then curiously a little group crossed the road and walked up a little way towards her before spreading rugs. One of the men was actually wearing a Yasser Arafat head-dress, and the women had scarves which they could easily draw across their faces to make veils if they wanted to. Then there was a ten year old son. Celestine ate and then lay back in the heather allowing herself ten minutes doze before heading on. There were seven or eight miles to go – and not on the flat, as she could see.

She woke feeling someone was looking at her, and there was. It was the boy from the party, who had ran up the hill. He was looking down at her.

"Hello, what are you doing?" he asked in a Brum accent.

"Walking," she said.

"Why?"

"I like walking."

"We came in a car. Haven't you got a car?"

Celestine decided it was her turn to ask some questions.

"Where do you come from?"

"Birmingham. We live in Birmingham."

"Have you always lived there?"

"I was born there but my mother comes from Jerusalem and my Dad from Amman. That's my Uncle, they ('Uncle' clearly included his wife) are visiting. We are taking them for a drive. What's that?"

A sheep which had been peaceably sitting further along the hillside had got up disturbed by the conversation and headed up the hill.

"I must go," said Celestine.

"So must I," said the boy.

"What's your name?" asked Celestine.

"Saladin," said the boy and turned down the hill.

These were Muscelemen who Mangu Khan knew about and who Louis had hoped the Khan might fight against to get them away from those holy places which should be denied them. But actually most of the time they had had Jerusalem, apart from that bit of Christian kingdom. Funny that, because probably the Christians only succeeded because the Khans had done in the Caliphs in Baghdad and the Musceleman Empire was in poor shape. But then '*Sala-ad-din*' – Honouring the Faith. By race not a real Arab (who/what was a real Arab?) but an Armenian Kurd. Whose side, therefore, would he be on now? His father's name 'Ayub' meant *Joh*; what a muddle, all those Semites. So Saladin was really a Jew after all. His uncle was Shirkuh and they were sons of a certain Shaday of Ajdanakan near Davin; they were both generals in Zengi's army. Ayub received Baalbek from Zengi; he moved, on Zengi's death, to the court of Damascus. His influence secured Damascus to Nur-ed-din. Saladin was therefore educated in the most famous centre of Muslim learning and represented the best traditions of Muslim culture.

On October 2nd 1187 Saladin, after Chivalrous Clemency to the Christian inhabitants, crowned his victories by entering and purifying the holy city of Jerusalem. In June 1191, Richard of England arrived and achieved Acre and a great victory at Arsuf. But in January 1192 he acknowledged his impotence by renouncing Jerusalem to fortify Acre. Negotiations for peace accompanied these demonstrations, showing that Saladin was master of the situation. That that they pressed for hard, he gave way on. He established borders along which people could come and go.

The character of Saladin is singularly vivid. In many ways he was a typical Mohammedan, apparently fiercely hostile to unbelievers – "Let us purge the air of the air they breathe" – he was intensely devout and regular in prayers and fasting. "God reserved this triumph for Ayubites before all others." But he gave the Christians and the Jews access to their holy places, despite that stated intention of purging the air, that the demons of the cross might not breathe. He let them breathe and let them live alongside the 'true' believers in Jerusalem.

Celestine had finished her late lunch. The Arabs below here were still eating theirs. She pulled on her rucksack and climbed up to the second hill fort of the day on the top of Moel Fenlli. On the east the hill had triple defences but she took the lower western route below the ramparts, looking at the great view into the vale of Clwyd and over towards another little town, Ruthin, where there is a house built with gallows incorporated, so friendly were people to each other.

On the southern edge of the fort as she was climbing down she met two back-packers, a father aged 50 maybe, and a son aged 20. They were impressed by how far she had come that day which cheered her; they assured her she would make it to Llandegla easily by nightfall and recommended the Clwyd Gate Restaurant. They were sure that would stay open all afternoon. Celestine, who could have bought drinks from an ice cream van at Bwlch-pen-Barass, thought of yesterday, when there had been no people and no water.

She was at the Clwyd Gate surprisingly soon and found she had a good thirst. It was mid-afternoon, the bars were empty but the landlady herself appeared when she rang a bell by the bar and served her a pint of shandy. She, the landlady, had long dark hair – a beautiful face, Celestine thought. She came from Manchester – how did she end up here? – she didn't know. Some man, Celestine guessed. She had two big Alsatians; she was just going to take them for a walk. She was 'nice' but she said she did as she was told. Llandegla, she said; there's a really 'nice' hotel there. Celestine had suggested to James they go to a hotel in Llangollen but the Manchester lass recommended this other one. Elizabethan manor house, really good, she liked to be taken there.

She had promised to call James anyway and was glad she remembered. Just the sort of thing that made him cross if you forgot. She called from the bar and there he was. He loved his mobile phone, he'd have had one before anyone else, like he'd had a fax and a word-processor. And of course, he knew about this hotel – in Egon Ronay. He'd got them a room booked, see her around seven. Bye-bye to the lady with the dogs.

At the bottom of Moel y Plas she found a group of about ten walkers resting. In fact she caught up with the last two and heard a fattish man shout, "Ten minutes, just ten minutes." She said "Hello" and sped past them up the hill; she got her reward because suddenly she saw ten yards ahead of her on the path a beautiful mask – and bright eyes looking at her. They stared at each other and then the fox turned and made off back along the path which twisted a little so he was lost to sight in the depth of the heather. She hurried after him (?her) trying to move fast but quietly up the path, but it was difficult to do that and the fox suddenly jumped off the path and bounded leaping over the clumps of heather. The beautiful fur of his back and tail undulated as if he was swimming through the heather. She waited staring at the way he'd gone, willing him to come back, but of course he didn't.

The last mile or two to Llandegla were a complete change, with streams and even a little river, the Alun, to cross. On this stretch the group suddenly caught up with her. They were hurrying now because they were being picked up at Llandegla. They were walking for the heart. Celestine could have said she was walking for her heart. The teacher had a limp and an anxious young black retriever with him who couldn't manage the stiles and had to be lifted over, always seeming to be slightly panicked by the ordeal.

"Always do a charity walk every summer. Never done the Dyke before, always do the Pennine Way, but this is longer and we'll raise more money for them if we all make it."

"Are you going all the way down?" asked Celestine.

"Yes, are you?"

Celestine was not sure if she wanted to spend the next ten days with the group so she temporised.

"Not sure really," she said, "I'll see how I go. I think I'll take tomorrow morning off."

Not true, but she did start a bit later the next morning and felt they must be well ahead of her, but they were not. At Froncysyllte when she was waiting in the pub for her taxi, the landlord asked her if she'd seen the 'Heart People' because they were expected, and then all the way down the Dyke people asked, "Have you seen the cardiac group?" and she never had. They became ghosts who haunted her track ahead and behind but never present.

But they were OK anyway; two medical secretaries from a hospital in Wrexham which wasn't far off. "Dr Grant's marvellous; he's not walking himself but his sons are driving the cars to pick us up." There was a religious lady from Weymouth and a retired Bank Manager from Mansfield. They had all just written into the Heart Foundation which immediately raised some money, and there was private sponsorship which each individual had raised. And then three drug companies with money depending on how many of the group finished the walk.

Celestine found herself feeling sinful: she was walking for herself. The lady from Weymouth had heard of it in church. The collection had been for the National Heart Foundation and vicar had mentioned the walk in his sermon. "Walking for God. Jesus and Disciples, you know, walked all the time, so one feels one is with him in Palestine.

> "And did those feet in ancient time
> Walk upon England's mountains green
> And was the holy Lamb of God
> In England's pleasant pastures seen"

Any rate, their back-up organisation was highly efficient. As they stepped onto the road at Llandegla, three cars roared up and they all bundled into them and were off to their overnight accommodation. Celestine was not so lucky, there was no-one about. She went to the shop but it was shut, she looked for a phone to call the hotel but there didn't seem to be one. Finally she called to a woman who was hanging up some belated washing in a cottage garden. She came immediately and took her three hundred yards to show her a side road running east out of the village, but warned her it was a good mile.

Celestine felt distinctly bedraggled as she staggered up the drive; white doves spun about her and there was an actual peacock in the open courtyard. She felt the receptionist would dislike her muddy state but when she mentioned Mr Alderney: "Oh, yes, Mrs Alderney," (so James had kept to the old fictions). "He said you were arriving on foot. I'll just ring up to him." And there was James – charming as ever. "You must be exhausted, darling." (She was) "We have a lovely room, with a real four-poster, and dinner – Margeritte here was kind enough to show me the menu – will be delicious. And a good wine list; let me take the rucksack." And he led her up the duelling stairs to their bedroom.

He must be thinking of the first time they shared a hotel bedroom and what he did to her. Well she wasn't doing that this evening. James had sprung up in that last year at university. The authorities, having suddenly developed a conscience about the need for students to have jobs once they graduated, actually sent them off to a biscuit factory so that they could see some manufacturing 'on the ground'. The factory was part, of course, of some huge industrial complex, and Head Office had sent down a young Senior Manager to explain to the students how the particular factory fitted into the prepared food industry; how this sector of their business related to their whole conglomerate business, how they were planning to expand – were airlines a profitable venture? – and finally, of course, opportunities for Arts Graduates in Industry.

"Pointers to look for in assessing a factory." Celestine couldn't remember what they were, only the sickly smell of hot chocolate as they went round the plant and the obvious and utter boredom of the jobs that most people had there. Celestine stopped to talk to some of them, feeling it almost a duty to give them some interruption.

"Do you get bored?" she asked a girl watching the chocolate-coating machine as rows of biscuits filed out of it.

"Not really," she said. "Anyhow, people will always want biscuits, so it's steady. I'll get married soon too."

"Nice guy?"

"Oh, I don't know who to yet."

Celestine had a period so when they got round she hastily sought for the toilets. By the time she left, the other students were well down the road towards the bus stop. As she turned out of the factory gate a car pulled out and James, who was of course the bright young Senior Manager, was leaning out and offering her a lift.

"Well..."

"Come on," he said, all charm, "no trouble, jump in."

She wanted to say what about some of the others, but they swept past them as he ran her on into town and back to the university. And, of course, he wanted her phone number, and when could they have dinner...

Jean said, "Go out with a bloody accountant, not likely." But Celestine went and liked it. First of all, he was so attentive to her, sat her at table, looked at what she was wearing, said things about them. It was nice too, eating in a French restaurant where he was known; and he bought her a rose. He seemed to listen to what she said. Remembered too, the next time, what essay she had been busy writing. It was a cliché again, but he was absolutely charming. *Charm*: quality, attribute, trait, feature etc. which exerts a fascinating or attractive influence, exciting love or admiration. The derivations weren't so interesting, just Middle English '*charme*', from French '*carmen*': song, verse, oracular response, incantation.*

You couldn't help finding it nice, too, that he had money. An expensive voucher at Liberty's for your birthday – to buy a really nice skirt and silk blouse. She loved silk against her skin. She bought a green blouse and would put it on at night with nothing under it to feel the sheen on her skin. And

* Dr J. was more sinister: "Charm: words, or philtres, or characters, imagined to have some occult or unintelligible power."

scents, of course, she loved scent, and had never afforded anything but the most basic toilet water. So when he said, "Will you come away for the weekend?" she went.

Not a very expensive hotel, he wasn't that rich, but 3 Star was very nice. When they got there they showered together, lovely, and stood by the bed embracing and she was waiting for him to push her back onto it when suddenly to her surprise he pushed her shoulders hard so that she was kneeling to him and pressed his penis on her lips and she realised she had to open for him and he said, "Deep as you can", as she held him off with one hand and then he took her head and moved hard into her. And "Suck it dry, suck it dry" as he came.

She sat back on the bed, pink and flustered. I'm freaked out, she thought. He went over and washed himself, wandered round the room, pulled on some socks. Then came over to her, kissed her and looked at her proprietorially, and said, "I always like to do it that way first." After dinner, she prayed, not my mouth again; but now he was gentle, slow, told her she was more beautiful naked then clothed. Stroked her, really turned her on so that when he was in her she pulled up her legs really hard so that he was deep, deep in her.

Soon he was running her over to meet his parents. He was a single child; his father had been on the railways, no money at all. For James it had been scholarships all the way and his mother showed her the certificates from school she'd kept, and then at college how well he'd done and what the teachers said about him. The only thing was, at the end of the afternoon, his mother suddenly said to James, "You haven't seen the children for a month, James. They were over yesterday." "I'll go tomorrow, Mother, I promise."

Celestine knew about the early marriage. "I was just young," James said, "we all make mistakes. Cathy manages very well on her own." As they drove away from his parents, Celestine said, "I hope I haven't been keeping you away from your kids. I'd love to see them."

"They are alright," said James, "a bit messy that's all."

When they did meet, that was his first reaction. Pulled his little son's (only six) tie straight saying, "Look in the mirror always, Anthony" and "Your hair" to Lucy, the four year old, "can't you brush it yourself yet?" Lucy stared back at him, "Mummy brushed it, she says it's OK." They didn't say much: "Where are we going to eat? Will they have banana split?" "Have you got us presents?"

They demanded. He demanded.

"I'm sorry they are so untidy," he said when he rejoined her waiting in the car outside. "Well, kids are," she said. "Cathy said to bring you in next time." "That would be nice." Cathy was almost overweight, long blonde hair, bouncy, and not at all subdued by the new girlfriend. "James is such a fuss-pot, always wants the kids to look like dolls, wanted me to look like a doll," and laughing, "Watch it with him, Celestine, James likes dolls." James red, very, very angry. "That woman, the things she says about you."

Well, tonight, going down to dinner in Bodidris, she knew how James wanted her to behave. "Go first into the dining room," he said that very first night, and Celestine was surprised that, after holding the door for her, he wasn't immediately behind her. But he was waiting, waiting a little while. She stood with her natural composure in the middle of the room until waiters and diners had looked at her and then James would hurry in, claiming his property, and saying, "Now, where's our table?"

But he would make love well in the four-poster bed.

Duelling Stairs

"What are duelling stairs?" Celestine asked next morning – the receptionist smiling at them as they came down to breakfast.

"They have uneven treads."

"I noticed."

"The people who lived here knew about them," said the receptionist, "but enemies who fought up them would trip as they fought."

"How quaint," said James, "but I think I'd put regular treads, it would look neater."

"But they are the original stairs, James, a real antique."

"Yes, well, I would see they were preserved. They would be an interesting item in a museum."

As she sat down to breakfast, she said, "I was your duelling stairs. I have irregular treads."

"Celestine – " he was going to try again.

"It wouldn't work, James; anyhow, you are very happy where you are."

James had done well, now a Managing Director, with an apartment in the Albany full of antiques; there were chairs which had red brocade across which were too valuable to sit in.

"Why have it here, James," she had asked, "if it can't be used?"

He had gone on pursuing her seriously for over a year. But he kept, of course, dropping himself in it:

"Wouldn't you like to have children, Celestine?"

"Of course, it would be lovely. Wouldn't you love to watch me having them?"

"Be present at the birth, do you mean? No, that's disgusting."

And Celestine's vague career plans:

"Well, you wouldn't have to work if you married me. I couldn't get you into the firm anyway."

"I want to do something with what I've learnt."

"Work involving English and History! Celestine, you can't do that. You've got to get into business, earn money."

She shrugged her shoulders and he never knew why.

After breakfast, he wanted to drive her part of the way – at least down the drive of the hotel, which was a good three quarters of a mile; but having met the 'congenital hearts' Celestine was determined she would walk all the way. So she left James in their room (he thought he could make his morning calls comfortably there) and strode down the drive.

She hadn't such a long stretch today but out of Llandegla it was again up and up to the top of Llandegla Moor and then a difficult bit of route-finding, down across the moor, following white posts and a path described as clear but often muddy. She was a bit vague at first about which way to turn on the road when she reached it and almost started off the wrong way, and the route-notes just 'continue, to reach Minerva-Worlds End'. But it didn't say anything about the distance, a good mile and a half before she was at Worlds End.

How many Ends of the World were there? What would you conjure up as the end of the world? Here a turn in the road and a waterfall high up a valley. Or there an island, 'the great globe itself. Yea, all which it inherit shall dissolve and, like this insubstantial pageant faded, leave not a rock behind. We are such stuff as dreams are made on and our little life is rounded with a sleep.' That made the End of the World a personal end as much as a public one – the end of your relationships, so that when they ended you yourselves ceased to exist.

There are other places
Which also are the world's end, some at the sea jaws
Or over a dark lake, in a desert or a city –

But this in time the nearest, in place and time
Now and in England.

Well into Wales here, thought Celestine, so perhaps I will survive it all and maybe it is all those others who don't exist.

As a child, Celestine had commonly thought that she might be the sole person in a world and that the rest of the world might be a vast stage set in which she as a single person was set down to act a part. So that she ran sometimes to street corners thinking if she looked round quickly enough the street would not be there. Or that behind the house there would be a blank. And people round corners took off their garments and ceased to exist. All only existing to make her exist. The only way to prove that this was not so would be to have a real friendship – but more than friendship – with someone who was so much part of one that they couldn't be one of the insubstantial pageants which could be dismissed at the wave of a hand.

Because friends, people, did disappear, her father was here OK, but he took her from the blackies, lovely Cook, Angela, Miss Cox, all that insubstantial lot, and moved her to England. He wasn't staying in England but nor was he staying in Kenya; he had a new posting. But he acquired a small flat in London: "ours" he told Celestine, and Celestine acquired an Aunt, a Cousin and a near semi-permanent home in Bournemouth. But it all might still disappear, thought Celestine.

Still, she had learnt what you did when you went to a new school: you went quiet, you watched, you said, "Yes, it's a funny name," and embarrassed other children by saying, "My mother gave it me before she died." And at her Aunt's house, although the food was strange, it wasn't like the Sally food and you could leave it and her cousins were alright to her. Johnnie at his public school and Gilly older than her and OK. Celestine overheard her saying to her mother: "I'll take her to school as long as she isn't a nuisance." Celestine wasn't a nuisance: she walked, as prescribed, with Gilly to the school, was always ready waiting at the gate to walk back, and in the house she could lie on the floor and read books all the time. There was swimming and tennis and Celestine was tall and quite good at them and could play with her older cousin. And so then they could play all the indoor games that Celestine had never been shown by her father. Card games, snap, rummy, patience, racing demon, and then Monopoly, halma, draughts. Playing them endlessly and often collapsing with fits of giggles.

> Sudden in a shaft of sunlight
> Even while the dust moves
> There rises the hidden laughter
> Of children in the foliage
> Quick now, here, now, always –
> Ridiculous the waste sad time
> Stretching before and after.

Then after a bit, because they were sharing a room, they could talk late at night. Afterwards, it was hard to remember what they did talk about. All the teachers at school, who was her favourite – Miss Webster, did you see her skirt today? and old Mrs Coutts, fancy her wearing black stockings, and then, of course, there were things the older girls had said. The bleeding between your legs. "Mum will tell you about that soon," Gilly said, "we all do it. Bleed. The P.E. teachers tell you about it and Miss Gaunt in Biology – now she tells you about rabbits."

It was a small local school in Bournemouth, but they were good at getting you into a good school, Aunt had assured her father. Gilly was going to Malvern Girls College and Celestine's Father had been to visit Easthurst – advised by some British Council man in Kenya. He liked it and hoped Celestine would. Meanwhile, was she happy at the Aunt's? Well, she was really. Aunt was her mother's sister; and Celestine felt that because of the unmentionable things that had happened to her mother, which somehow her father was responsible for, there was some constraint whenever her father was with them. But when he was gone the Aunt relaxed and even displayed some affection for her awkward sister's awkward child.

The other good thing was the uncle. Later Celestine realised he was probably not a very good doctor, but he was kind and polite to his many elderly patients. His main occupation was books, which he collected avidly. He was very keen on bargains, so even if he didn't want a book but he reckoned it was cheap, he would buy it, and there were hundreds of old novels for Celestine to bury her head in. Uncle was good too because he would listen while she talked about the stories she had read, sitting in his chair with his funny sticking-out ears, spreading his hands as he told her how he liked Sapper too.

The Baker's Uncle sat up in bed with his arms spread out as he warned the Baker that if the Snark had a certain characteristic, the Baker would softly and silently vanish away. The Baker was the most remarkable of the Bellman's eccentric crew. He came as a Baker but admitted too late he could only bake Bride Cake – for which, I may state, no materials were to be had.

> He had forty-two boxes, all carefully packed
> With his name painted clearly on each:
> But, since he omitted to mention the fact,
> They were all left behind on the beach.
>
> The loss of his clothes hardly mattered, because
> He had seven coats on when he came,
> With three pair of boots – but the worst of it was,
> He had wholly forgotten his name.
>
> He would answer to 'Hi!' or to any loud cry,
> Such as 'Fry me!' or 'Fritter my wig!'
> To 'What-you-may-call-um!' or 'What-was-his-name!'
> But especially 'Thing-um-a-jig!'

While, for those who preferred a more forcible word,
He had different names from these:
His intimate friends called him 'Candle-ends',
And his enemies 'Toasted cheese'.

A nameless man who has no skill but the making of Bride Cake has only one destiny: he must become a bridegroom. He set out with the clear notion, which he wholly forgot to explain, that the Snark could become his wife. He strode boldly along the cliffs to meet his fate.

South of Worlds End the path tracks steeply across steep scree slopes under cliff edges. Celestine, for the first time on the walk, found herself a little alarmed and was glad of a group walking from Worlds End behind her and pleased to meet two back-packers coming her way. The track was simply, it seemed, a trodden portion of the scree and it had slid away at several points. She didn't want the sleep which rounded off her little life to be caused by a slip off a scree.

They were still miles off the Dyke, the path keeping well away from where Fox struggled through a ravaged landscape around Victorian industrial development. But the builder of the Dyke in this blighted area of the Ceiriog knew what he was doing. The alignment of the Dyke in each of the three great stretches Fox examined in 1928, though sinuous, is singularly direct. The intellectual quality, the eye for country, the intimate knowledge of the district manifested by the creation of these alignments carried out in very broken and mountainous country intersected by deep river valleys without the aid of accurate maps, is remarkable. There is an impression of a firm, undeviating will, applied to what must have been, having regard to the resources of a primitive state, an almost impossible task.

It is the feel of that *will*, that (Celestine felt) *male* pressure, on the peoples. It was the iron age but what were spades like? Were shovels wooden? Surely yes. There were those antlers. Were they used as picks? Much material must have been moved by hand or in baskets. Celestine could see men in the ditches loosening the earth with horn picks while the women, she guessed (and the children), hauled the loads up to the top of the growing Dyke. It reminded her of India, where she had seen the Untouchables carrying hods of bricks up the sides of buildings – women and men – while their children scampered round them, climbing the rickety scaffolding and sometimes falling off. They resisted even a primitive hoist because they wanted the money for the work they did. Offa's people surely did not get paid. Did they get fed? Were there falls of earth burying and killing the children? There were surely armed men seeing that the work was carried on. The Dyke created a border people. Boundaries bring people together as much as put them apart.

The scree slope and the crags above felt like mountains. Mainly the Welsh Borders were hills like the Clwydian range, steep but grassed and friendly, but when the grass went and the rock faces began you were among mountains – which were fine, often beautiful, but also held a menace; people didn't fall off hills but they did – and died – off mountains. You skied in mountains as she had done and met Carlo. Skiing was exciting but there was also in the downhill that element of fear which Carlo had almost eliminated as he patiently taught her the parallel turns. So it was good to get off the screes and even to be using, as you did for nearly three miles, a metalled road.

For the first time on the walk occasional cars passed her. One man even stopped and offered her a lift – memory of James – and seemed astonished she was walking by herself. How sexist people still were. "But you're a girl," he said, "and walking by yourself." "I'm quite alright, thank you," she said and stepped back from the car window and he drove on. There were more walkers about, some cars pulled up off the road with families and dogs. But even so, her main companions were sheep, as ever. More sheep in the Welsh borders than people. Mostly, on the open moorland, they just hurried off. Here with a firm fence on the left she had two as companions for a good half mile. The silly things ran ahead of her, and however quietly she approached they ran on again. Finally she got worried that she was driving them far from their home so when they were standing in a closed gateway to a field thirty yards ahead, but looking anxiously back, she made a massive detour, scrambling up the steep bank on the left of the road and climbing fifty feet up through the heather and then along, way above the sheep, and down again well past them. They were still safely in their gateway, looking away from her now.

For we, like sheep, were gone astray. She didn't often sing aloud but after all she was in Wales, land of hymns, and a bit of the Messiah seemed appropriate; only she couldn't remember any more of the words, so she tried the Hallelujah Chorus but then she couldn't really remember the whole melody. She disturbed some sheep on the bank and so she shouted at them "Join in, sheep, this is supposed to be a chorus," which of course astonished the sheep who bolted off up the hill.

It was a slight embarrassment to her too because round a bend in the road two men were leaning against the steep bank to ease the weight of their rucksacks and were sharing a cigarette. They must have heard her so she decided the only thing to do was to continue her extrovert behaviour.

"Hello," she shouted, "having a rest? I was singing."

"We heard you," one replied.

She was about to go on, "The Hallelujah Chorus, do you know it?" but she quickly noticed that one of the young men had that absurd little Jewish hat pinned on his head. A yashmak, she thought, and then, no, no, that's the veil the Arabs wear. What the hell is that cap, and her mind trailed off and she was thinking, I'll ask Linda, she's good on all things Jewish.* But meanwhile, the boys were going on talking,

"Would you like a cigarette?"

"You're sharing one, isn't that your last?"

"No, we've a pack, but we are trying to give it up so we

* And Linda did know, of course: it's a yarmulke.

decided to try and cut down by only having half each."

"Is it working?"

"It seems to be, we've only done three today."

She refused a cigarette but then got into the conversation you had with everyone you met who was a real walker; telling them about the next bit of the walk for them.

"Watch out for the screes. It would be awful if it rained."

It was greyer today; they all looked anxiously at the sky which, for the first time since Celestine set out, did look as if there might be rain.

"If it rains, it says to keep along the fence lower down but that looked pretty rough to me, more of a sheep-track with overhanging trees. Did you go to the castle?"

"Castell Dinas Bran. No we didn't. It's all very well these detours but we've only got two more days to get to Prestatyn."

"You'll have to move," she said.

"We know," said the Jewish boy but they didn't seem to want to hurry off. Celestine checked on her turn-off from the road, and they still lingered; she asked them where they came from. Pretty predictable, really; both North Londoners and actually bank clerks and both almost, she thought, exercise freaks despite the smoking. They were doing the walk in ten days to her twelve. Too young to be married; I'd have been married by then if Rory and James had been right. She didn't really like that thought, so she asked something else, hoping they wouldn't mind.

"Are you both Jews?"

"Certainly not. I don't have to wear David's stupid hat," and he laughed and hit at his friend's 'hat'. David didn't seem to mind joking about it, so Celestine pressed on.

"Do you mind wearing it? You somehow don't look as if you go to the synagogue much."

"I don't much, but then my parents, they do. I expect I will when I'm married. And anyhow what with all that's happening, you know, if you're a Jew, you have to say so somehow. I mean what's going on in Jerusalem and all that."

The serious note he introduced to the conversation worried him and he laughed awkwardly, standing up from where he'd been leaning against the bank easing his shoulders and started more jovially, "You heard what the lady said, Jon, we'll have to move."

Jon, Celestine thought, would have been inclined to dally longer in conversation and looked as if he didn't mind too much whether they eventually made it to Prestatyn or not. But he was obedient to his friend and shouldered his pack but needed to score off him.

"The Jews lead, we poor Gentiles follow."

"Well, bye Jew and Gentile," she said and strode away from them almost skipping (not easy to do with a backpack) down the road. Birds of a feather, she thought ironically, flock together, and suddenly birds – buzzards – came into her head, one of the thrills of the Welsh hills, and maybe they would be up there above those craggy cliffs, so she swung her binoculars up and scanned the sky above the cliffs, but no buzzards. She scanned backwards expecting to find that David and Jon had disappeared round the corner but they had not. They had taken off their packs again and were standing in their little enclave of rock tightly embracing each other. Celestine found herself focussing on their lips as they kissed each other deeply. Of course – David and Jonathan – demonstrating here, though, a love not of Jew for Jew but Gentile for Jew. She lowered the glasses.

Celestine in Jerusalem

Poor Friar William, his mission to the Mongols didn't help Louis in his battles with the Saracens, and William never got to Jerusalem – but Celestine did.

"They want to pay for a representative to go to a book fair."

"What on earth for?"

"They want you to give a talk. Could you talk on

'Combining the Oral and the Written Word in Teaching ESL'?"

"Well I could if there's a free trip to Jerusalem in it. But I can see what's in it for us if they are giving us a free stand, but what's in it for them? I mean it will just cost them money. Who's paying?"

"Some American Trust is involved. You see, they are getting all these immigrants in from Eastern Europe so there are a lot who want to learn English."

"I thought they spoke Hebrew there."

"Most higher education is in English. Anyway, you'll find out."

"I still can't guess why they want us Brits involved."

"Politics, love," said her kindly boss, Able. "They like people to go and say 'what a nice civilised community they are, not like those shifty A-rabs'. I'd go if I could."

So Celestine went.

A trip anywhere for Celestine despite her much-travelled childhood meant hours of preparation. What should she wear when she gave her talk? Should she be informal – jeans (smart ones of course and she always wore them tight) – or should she wear the suit she had bought for interviews, or her favoured loose skirts, separate top, scarf, one of her many scarves. And, by this time, all her friends – some of whom hadn't been to Jerusalem for years but still wanted to give all sorts of advice – telling her what to expect (which would turn out to be wrong and out of date). And then organising her flat and different people to water the plants. Emptying the fridge and all that.

"You are going for *five days*, Celestine," said Joan. "Why make such a big deal of it?"

"It will be different," Celestine said, "I must be ready."

It was frightening all those soldiers with guns but what was mainly amazing was not that they were fighting each other but that they were not. In fact her first difficulty was to find any Jews in the Holy City. Her father had taught her to eschew professional guides and now she didn't even have a good guide book – there had been no time to buy one. She only had a map of the old city. "You can't go round the old city without a guide," one of the Americans at the congress told her, "it's simply impossible. Pick one up at the Jaffa Gate, their prices are quite reasonable and they know their stuff."

But Celestine knew her stuff better. She told the taxi driver (Arab of course) to stop twenty yards short of the Jaffa gate, got out and paid him, turning as if to walk away along the wall; but then she suddenly spun round and ran fast – she could run fast – and shot through the gate and then the first left she came to, scuttling down the narrow street, passing startled people, then quickly realised she was not being pursued. She had lost the guides.

Where was she? Well it was clear that the people around her were Arabs and when she worked out her position on the little map she saw she was in the Arab Quarter so she might as well start here. She headed off to the Church of the Holy Sepulchre. Christians here, of course, and one Arab (*infra vide*) but of course you wouldn't expect to find Jews here, that was to be in the Jewish Quarter after lunch.

The Church of the Holy Sepulchre is rather strange. It seemed as if three rival Christian groups had each started building at once. An Orthodox group, a Coptic group and she thought a Catholic – although this was all surmise as she had no guide book. But she met different sorts of monks and priests in different bits of the building and then inside the centre of the whole structure there was a domed chapel. There was an anteroom with a showcase in it containing relics – people had kissed the glass and it was smeared with lipstick. She ignored the relics. Beyond, through a doorway, there were the remains of a cave with, as it were, a bed of rock, and here was where the body had been laid.

She peered at all this but couldn't get in because there were females there: two white-robed nuns; when she heard them speak she knew them for Irish. They were on their knees praying. Well, they were at a border, and a border-crossing at that. From here a body had been transported into another dimension, from here Christ left for heaven. She waited, thinking that at least she should go into this tomb.

Suddenly there was a commotion behind her. Stamping along, banging his stick down with each pace, came one of the Arab guides from the Jaffa Gate. He had two well-dressed ladies with him – they were even wearing hats – and when they spoke she knew where they came from too – the good old U.S. of A. They looked confused and even a little frightened.

The guide bustled through the doorway to the Sepulchre and banged his stick on the floor within this most sacred of places. "Come on, come on, they need their lunches." The nuns broke off their prayers, and saying, "We were just going," came scuttling out; but Celestine was not to be denied – she had been there first – and in she went while the guide stood banging banging behind her. There was nothing to see, only a slab of rock on which – yes – a body could have rested, but she stood for a time while the old guide whined behind her. Celestine smiled at him mischievously and then said to the ladies, "Enjoy your visit, it is the way to heaven."

After the Holy Sepulchre she found another church – its name she never discovered – and then bits of Calvary with some Stations of the Cross, but it was confusing because sometimes the road changed into an entirely Arab road with its name up in Arabic, but she got into a Franciscan monastery with a cool garden where she caught a monk taking a good big swig from a bottle of wine he had by a watering can. But no Jews.

Anyway it was lunchtime, she headed back towards the Jaffa Gate and where the Jewish Quarter starts; she had recently acquired an American Express card and she thought she would treat herself to a good lunch. Nothing too expensive of course but a restaurant where she would be served nicely with a well cooked omelette or something like that, where she could sit leisurely over half a bottle of wine, write some postcards, and generally enjoy her free trip. A well-meaning shop-keeper had been trying to sell her sandals; he spoke fair English so she asked him for a restaurant. He shrugged his shoulders. "No restaurants," he said, "but there's a café," he indicated a few yards further along the covered street. She went and looked but it was not appetising. There were cauldrons on a fire, and when she paused the proprietor lifted the lid and some sort of stew was revealed to Celestine. It seemed she was expected to eat it standing in the street. She wandered baffled along the street and her hesitancy attracted the usual young man, "You're American, I speak English, I show you round free, you come with me." Celestine explained that she wanted a restaurant; this confused the young man for a moment but then he hurried her around several corners and brought her to a rather less sordid café. There were tables and plastic chairs and a fat proprietor with a rather greasy apron who actually waved a menu. It was that or a further walk with the young man. So she sat down. He wanted to join her of course and stay to escort her round afterwards but Celestine knew how to dispose of that sort of young man easily enough.

She got her omelette and some rather greasy chips but no wine. She wrote some postcards but was not inclined to linger. She got up and asked the direction back towards the Jaffa Gate and emerged blinking into the bright sunlight of the main street and now followed it round to the right into the Jewish Quarter. One, two, three, restaurants, all with American Express card signs on the door within a quarter of a mile of where she had been asking for them. Asking Arabs!

So she had still met no Jews. Well the next thing to see was the Stables of King Solomon's Temple – they were clearly marked on her little map, on what seemed to be called the Dome of the Rock. She found there was another gate to go through, with soldiers, armed, glaring at you but not interfering, and she joined the crowds that were jostling through. She had been jostled all day. Ahead of her to her astonishment was an enormous mosque – the El Akbar Mosque – very beautiful, a site of major Muslim pilgrimage. She had never heard of it and nor apparently had the man who had made her tourist plan! Prophet Mohammed had, it seemed, arrived or left here on a flying horse borrowed perhaps from Solomon's Temple Stables. Inside the mosque was the summit of the rock and what she suspected might have had quite a lot to do in antiquity with attracting the religions here. It was a curiously pierced rock – limestone she assumed – so that you climbed down into rather spooky grottoes. She reclaimed her shoes and wandered off to look for the Stables; there were just piles of rubble, perhaps the odd wall, so she headed for a gate out.

This one took her down a narrow ramp onto a large open area while to her right under the steep side of the dome there was a fenced-off area in front of a wall. Ah – the Wailing Wall. Now she would find her Jews. And she did in a way; as she turned to walk down to the wall she found her way barred by a line of trestle tables with young soldiers behind them. Not very politely they demanded her handbag which they turned over, tipping its contents of make-up, passport, pocket book, purse, change, and about a dozen scruffed-up paper hankies onto the table. A hand rummaged around the bottom, pressed down the the lining, pressed the sides and then, contemptuously, as it seemed to Celestine, tossed the bag down on top of the contents and nodded OK.

Feeling somehow assaulted, Celestine reloaded what seemed now her somewhat sordid possessions and walked on down, allowed through the barrier to peer from behind another barrier at the Wailing Wall. The first thing she perceived was that the Wall was sexually segregated – women to the right, men to the left. Gentiles were held out by the barrier perhaps twenty yards back, and so it was hard to see what actually happened at the wall. A woman was sitting by it on a solitary wooden chair, while further over a man in those curious black skirts who had been standing still, for all the world as if he was urinating, suddenly began to oscillate from one leg to the other. With all the soldiers around Celestine thought it would be unwise to laugh and she decided to get out of the holy city.

Perhaps the Mount of Olives might be more soothing. She got out at a gate through which the ordure had once been removed and came on huge numbers of graves piled higgledy-piggledy on top of one another, lots of dead Jews. And also on the Mount of Olives in a field, scattered graves, about 24 of them, men who, an English inscription recounted, had been killed by the British during the War of Liberation. On the top of the Mount there was quite a sweet little chapel, and a camel tied to a lamp post who looked at Celestine mournfully.

She walked down the other side of the field with the graves and looked across at them. Just as she did so an Arab opened a gate on the far side – it must have been an Arab, not a Jew, and let in about 30 goats and they gambolled across the field, jumping on the tombs, nibbling at the longer grass round their edges and depositing faeces on the tombs themselves. There were no Jews present to protect their dead and clearly the Arabs regarded the land that the tombs were on as their land, whoever was buried there.

Celestine thought, I still haven't met a veritable Jew today; someone who believes this land is his by God's ordain. She hailed a taxi and headed back to the Sheraton where she was to dine with the new American friends who had sent her out so eagerly on her trip, with advice about the guides at the Jaffa Gate. Celestine joined them in their penthouse suite, marvelling at the lift which she had accidentally entered and which automatically stopped at every floor.

"It's for the Sabbath," her hostess explained, "so that you can come out without pressing a button," which their God would not allow. "How was your shopping, Celestine?" she asked.

"Oh, I wasn't shopping," said Celestine, "Sight-seeing today, tomorrow I'll shop."

"But my dear, you can't shop tomorrow, it's the Sabbath, everything will be closed."

Except in the Arab Quarter, she thought, which my hostess does not know. Of course, of course, Celestine's mind seemed to go *click*, my *hosts* are Jews. The great diaspora. They are all around me. And she remembered Father Rubrick in his letter to King Louis: "There are other barriers that shut out the Jews, about which I did not succeed in discovering anything for certain; though there are great numbers of Jews throughout all the cities of Persia."* In South Wales there was a Jewish community, but along the borders? Celestine wondered. Certainly Saxon married Briton and Norman married Welsh; border people might claim one side or the other but, of course, neither an earthwork or a holy city would in the end keep men and women apart. It might scatter them – and surely the Welsh were scattered – their diaspora extended to the Argentine – but maybe they had aboard less baggage than the Jews carry with them.

Celestine's baggage was beginning to make her shoulders ache but now she was bouncing down through a little wood. And then with a couple of swings, she was on the towpath of the Dee looking up at the great technical marvel, Telford's aqueduct of Pontcysyllte. She could have crossed on to the aqueduct itself but she preferred to stay down and look up at Telford's work. Further south there were great brick aqueducts carrying the Montgomery canal but the height here was too much for brick and Telford had built stone piers and across them laid a wrought-iron canal which has carried the water safely since 1805.

Up then to the village of Froncysyllte. She had not asked Carlo to meet her, that would have been too much for him, she knew. He was safely, she hoped, waiting for her in the hotel at Llangollen, and she had to get herself to him. She went along to a phonebox where there was no directory but she thought she would call Directory Enquiries for the local taxi number. But the machine was dead, she realised, with a coin stuck in the slot. Thank God, the pub is open, and the

* The Jewish diaspora in Persia had been greatly swollen in the Sasanian era by immigration from the territories of the East Roman/Byzantine Empire.

landlord said: "Sure, love, the number's stuck up by the phone. Have a drink while you wait." And asked her about the Cardiologists.

In Llangollen, Carlo was sitting nervously in the hallway awaiting her. He hasn't even checked in, just told them he is waiting for someone. It was really unfair of her to have asked him, but she loved him, and the last thing he had said to her was, "If you ever ask me to come to you, I'll come, whatever has happened." Carlo was corny too – a ski instructor, for God's sake! But she had had the relationship.

She was doing temporary jobs in London after college, James behind her, and Joan said come skiing, we're going to Austria in a party just after Christmas. They were high but there wasn't much snow that year and quite a lot of people gave up skiing for the social life. But Celestine wasn't like that, she skied every day, ice or no ice. Everybody had said that Carlo was such a nice boy. An immaculate skier too. He wasn't from the resort but lived some ten miles off. He had bronze medals at competitions and here he was, in his first season as an instructor.

He was shy, Celestine caught that at once, polite and end-lessly patient. He sent the other four up the lift to do the run down on their own; they were better than Celestine and he stayed with her over an hour, over and over again showing her how to do those parallel turns and finally she got it. It was all just balance and timing and once you did it right it suddenly was easy. And then they went up to the top and she skied perfectly all the way down behind him. So that when they stopped at the bottom by the ski store, she slid up beside him and grasped his arm, "Carlo, it was wonderful," and she leant her head on his shoulder.

The other instructors would have kissed her then and there and maybe there would have been an affair and maybe there wouldn't have been, but, of course, Carlo was different; he looked at her and just said, "Celestine." And then bent to take off his skis. But that night he came to the Bernehof where they danced. "Carlo's come," all the class shouted, and Celestine made sure he danced with the others first. And he was marvellous to dance with, because of that sense of rhythm; he didn't really know any dances but he could just move with you perfectly and holding you firmly. And when they sat down it was hand-holding time again, and when the place shut at midnight she held him back and then they did kiss but she realised he would never come into the hotel with her.

But every day he offered to give her an extra run at the end of the class and of course they often got back in the near dark and Carlo had to lock the store. She came in and when the skis were off they kissed. One day, she just had to have him, she unzipped him and slipped him into her standing on one leg, the other cocked round behind him as she lent back against the wall. Of course Carlo's English wasn't that good and she mostly remembered his "Celestine" whispered, as they danced, in her ear or when they stopped on a run. Of course Joan knew and suddenly said, "Why don't you stay on a week. You easily could you know, it'll be out of season. I bet they'll give you this room for almost nothing."

So she cabled her temporary employers and stayed. But Carlo still wouldn't come into the hotel. Carlo had no ski-school to teach now, so they would sit in a café most mornings drinking coffee and now Carlo did talk. His family owned a farm (of course) but he wanted to join a ski-school which his cousin ran in his own village. But they would have the farmhouse – *they*, meant him and Celestine. He could not bring himself to say what he wanted and Celestine sat beside him saying nothing.

In the end the week was up and there was a bus to the airport. He came with her and it was here he whispered, "I'll come anywhere anytime you ask, Celestine. I swear whatever happens I'll always come to you." He had spent six months since then in England working in the summer as a waiter, improving his English; but Celestine had been in Africa (*infra vide*) and they exchanged cards at Christmas and birthdays. Of course Carlo had married in his village; he wrote, 'I had to, Celestine, even though I love you.'

About 'Nice'

Yes, Carlo was the nice one. Nice: 17 meanings, some frankly contradictory, like wanton, loose, mannered, lascivious (perhaps that applied to her). Carlo was agreeable, that one derives pleasure or satisfaction from. Its diversity made the writer nervous, 'The precise development of the very divergent senses which this word has acquired in English are not altogether clear.' There were 'nice' variants: *nyce, nycy, niece, nysa* – and a Latin origin, *nescius*. 'It is often used,' writes the doctor, 'to express culpable delicacy.'

Was she nice to him? She hadn't stayed when he'd wanted her to. And the next year, when she'd sworn she'd come back to ski again, she had written to explain about Africa. And he still had her skis there – she'd bought them in the end, she'd skied so well on them, and they stayed there in the shop year after year. They sent a bill every year, £5 or something silly, and she paid, while hiring different skis in France, Norway, America, Spain. But kept them because she'd sworn she'd go back. The skis, kept there, meant she would return, but now he had come to her as he'd promised.

She had summoned him. On what excuse had he got away to England? But here he was and she signed him in and she could talk easily to him about the walk, something he understood, and his work, but didn't embarrass him about his wife. That night he was too shy to make love. Celestine did not mind, she slept easily from exhaustion but woke beside him in the morning aware that he was awake and tense, so she just slid him into her arms and thought, I'm doing all this and I want to. And slept again.

Border Castle

She wasn't obsessed (as American women are) about her fitness and figure. She was indulging in the luxury of staying in hotels and having eggs and bacon for breakfast. After all she was burning up energy during the day alright. She had fifteen miles to do today and she realised she was already thinking of the route. She had forgotten Carlo. He was sitting opposite her looking at her just as he'd looked at her all those years ago in Austria.

She could have spent years of breakfasts with that look. She would have, by now, three children. They would have been carefully planned. She was sure, too, that they would have been admirable children, calm, well-behaved, even when she herself got excited, irritable. She knew she would find children irritating. They *were* irritating. Once the children were at school, Carlo gone to work, she would have driven off to the nearest town where she would have taught English at a school. Not full-time, she thought – three days a week, with plenty of time to shop and cook more interesting meals than that heavy, boring, Austrian food. Carlo was endlessly patient, always loving, adoring her. She had stayed with him an extra week but said no to the lifetime.

She could remember she had sat on the aeroplane, her face towards the window – luckily she had a window seat – crying, not sobbing hard, but just tears which she allowed to fall down her face as she thought of the days she had spent sitting with Carlo in the café. They had done nothing but she had not been bored. It was not the thought of boredom exactly that drove her away. The life would have been busy; so why hadn't she surrendered to those tears? It was something to think about on the Dyke.

She had already fixed the bill telling Carlo she was phoning for the taxi which actually she'd organised the night before with the man who drove her here. When he demurred about the payment she consoled him by saying he could pay for the taxi which would drop her back on the Dyke at Froncysyllte then take him on to Wrexham and the train back to London. He had now, these years later, contacts with travel firms and his trip to London was not unuseful to him. He got out of the taxi with Celestine and embraced her for the last time and got back into the taxi, his one adultery completed.

The path went for a mile along the towpath of the Ellesmere or Shropshire Union Canal bringing Denbighshire coal over to the Midland plains. All shut now, just leaving the mess of old mines, but the canal was peaceful; one motor boat shunted towards her and there was a silent fisherman. "What are you catching?" Celestine asked. "Not much," was the reply and Celestine felt that there was an implication that her presence was discouraging the fish. Great bit of dialogue, she thought, for the start of the day. There was a nice brick bridge to cross to get to the south side of the canal. It was the 'Irish Bridge' which seemed strange on the Welsh borders, but neither of her books offered an explanation; Irish navvies building the canal, she guessed.

And at last, too, the Dyke was really with her. She rather regretted that the path had not followed it through those sordid industrial bits. On the other hand she had marched, she thought, with the Welsh all these miles over those splendid Clwydian Hills and she was still deciding whose side she was on.

When she crossed the Dyke near Plas Offa House she knelt down and patted it. It was going to be a good friend, that she knew already, and she wanted to welcome that friendship. It was silent, the Dyke, it didn't speak back but it breathed of a permanent relationship between two people that had lasted over a millennium. Williams thought that it was the coming of the Romans that really brought Wales into Europe, but she thought that it was Offa. The Romans weren't really Europeans, they were a Mediterranean culture. But Offa spoke with Charlemagne – surely the first European ruler – and Offa spoke to Wales.

We've been Europeans for a millennium
And where's it got us? Doing piece work
By strip lighting in Waco, Texas.

Damn the Americans, she thought, one can't help having them around but do they have to come in now? I want them in a later, much later, chapter of my life. But then she remembered Don tonight. She was going to meet her 'first' American and he was still the American she loved the most.

The underlying rocks here are millstone grit. Grit, she thought to herself; maleness; don't be a girl; she had practised taking long strides and she could walk as fast she thought as any man. At all those early schools, the boys were always trying to be in charge; they had gangs in Bournemouth and the girls had never been the bosses. "I'm the leader," said Alfred, "and you can be the secretary." "Why can't I be head?" "Girls are secretaries, men are bosses." Alfred and Peter had agreed to form gangs so that they could have disputes and fights about this and that. Elaborate written messages containing hidden threats were passed to and fro between Alfred's classroom base in Room 3 and Peter's in Room 4. Then Celestine's list of their gang was found in her English book by the teacher and there was a row. Gangs were forbidden. Gangs were things boys had and they were seen to be bad, but to Celestine they seemed good.

But at twelve and a half she was suddenly off to Easthurst. Memories of boarding at Sally's filled her mind as she sat shyly on a train travelling down there. But there weren't those hideous big dormitories. Little bedrooms you shared with one or two other girls; one who was your 'sister' when you arrived; she'd been at Easthurst a year and the first thing she said was,

"Celestine is such a lovely name, I was longing to meet you," so that all the things that had worried her – finding the lavatories, having to ask to go and all that – didn't happen. Jill showed her everything at once. And the other girl in the room was nice to her, her father worked abroad. They were soon into the long night talks about 'everything'.

She didn't know it but she had actually arrived at a reasonably competent school. Of course, there were all sorts of ideas about girls being 'nice' – one of the other meanings. There was a Head who was always talking in assembly about manners but there were teachers who really seemed to like teaching.

She met, not realising it, her first 'scholar', teaching Biology at Easthurst. Easthurst was renowned because of this little lady who was passionately interested in water-lilies and spiders. She owned two great volumes published by the Ray Society on the *Arachnidee*, in which there were corrections pencilled-in in her own hand. She had actually published papers herself in the *Proceedings* put out by the Natural History Museum in London. She would give you a copy of the paper if you asked. Celestine liked her, so feigned an interest in the spiders, which she didn't like. Then there were the natural history outings. "Wellies, girls, wellies, and all on to the bus."

They went over to the Devizes Canal – the famous 18-lock stretch – and studied the side-pools, their flora and fauna. That was the idea and one had to keep finding something to show Miss Parsons but really it was the outing, scurrying up and down the stretch of canal, wading into pools with nets, scooping up a frog and yes, getting some idea how water affected the way things live. Easy, friends to be with, sandwiches, orange juice. It was like the beach, the beach at Sandown, on which she had never bathed.

The Bellman landed them on the beach, his enigmatic crew included all the people in the world the world doesn't need; they were all, except perhaps for the Boots and Maker of Bonnets and Bows, people who did no real work. A

Billiard Marker whose skill was immense. But what of a Barrister brought to arrange their disputes and a Broker to value their goods. These people were useless, unable to contribute except perhaps cash; and a Banker, engaged at enormous expense, had the whole of their cash in his care.

The Broker, she supposed, was an accountant. Law, accounting, banking, the parasites of civilisation; men – and it had been men, but women had now joined them. It was a man's idea, Celestine bet. Anyway at least the Banker had a thoroughly bad time, attacked by a Bandersnatch.

> He was black in the face and they scarcely could trace
> The least likeness to what he had been:
> While so great was his fright that his waistcoat turned white
> A wonderful thing to be seen!
>
> To the horror of all whom were present that day,
> He uprose in full evening dress,
> And with senseless grimaces endeavoured to say
> What his tongue could no longer express.
>
> Down he sank in a chair – ran his hands through his hair –
> And chanted in mimsiest tones
> Words whose utter inanity proved his insanity,
> While he rattled a couple of bones.

The Bellman had no time for failed companions. He was some sort of captain of industry. A Rupert Murdoch or a Robert Maxwell character. The Bellman dismissed the Banker: "Leave him to his fate – it is getting so late." Presumably the Banker spent the remainder of his life on that dismal strand rattling his bones.

The way-marking was poor on this part of the path. Celestine missed a field entry when she was on a small road. It was a track up opposite Caeau Gwynion but the Offa's Dyke post with the sign was buried in the hedge. She must have walked on a good mile because she suddenly came to a barred back-entry to Chirk Castle and realised from her map she must be wrong. Even with this detour, she was making much better time today. It was no use working things out in straight miles, she realised – you needed to watch for the rise and fall of the land. This afternoon might not be so good but she would have time, she thought, to visit Chirk Castle, which she began to see as she crossed fields above Caeau Gwynion – now back on the right route.

All the details of the route occupied your mind when you had thought your mind would be free all the time. Of course, you looked at all the scenery but Celestine had thought she would each day come clearer in her mind about her clumsy life. Her failed relationships. She sat on a stile and looked at Chirk. Other women had been on journeys and talked about their lovers rather freely and spoke of 'the woe that is in marriage'. Celestine had married, it had not exactly been woe (*infra vide*) but she had left. Maybe if she could have been widowed five times naturally she would not have had these worries about her future and her past. And that Lady of Bath was jealous of King Solomon who had many wives. The Lady 'wished God it were lawful unto me, To be refreshed half as oft as he.' Celestine had enjoyed her lovers; she wondered, apart from husbands, how many lovers the Wife of Bath had had.

Poor Elizabeth Bennet, fated to be married to one man. Not very much fun, particularly if all you did was marriage. Celestine had a new job to go to and she was good at her work. She had somehow found a curious career teaching the world English, both writing texts and publishing them. New York. She had friends there now, thank God. Don lived on the West Coast now, and Celestine thought unfaithfully that she was actually looking forward to the possibility of a new love in New York – but would it be that final permanent relationship she thought she wanted? (It struck her then that maybe she should look for impermanence in relationships – that could be achieved by standing in a shop window in Amsterdam.)

As she swung her foot up onto the first step of the stile to go into Chirk Park she saw bright eyes looking at her; they were low down in the grass and, as she stepped down, a rabbit hopped out of the long grass and scurried across the track to crouch down again in some long grass. Celestine crept after it; it had lovely brown fur and limpid eyes. She guessed it was a young one as it didn't seem to know whether to run again and tried to settle deeper in the grass when she approached. She had got out her camera and hoped to get a snap-shot of the animal. It didn't come out when she developed the film.

Suddenly it was like the Bwlch-pen-Barrass pass, only much more so. There must have been 300 cars in the car-park in front of the castle. She found the end of a trestle table which she shared with a family from Edinburgh. Mum, Dad, boy, girl, proper picnic, hardboiled eggs, salt in a twist. She should be on a picnic with two kids and she thought if she had met Don before his wife had, that would be just what she would be doing. The Llangollen Hotel ham sandwiches were not that good. She longed for a hardboiled egg.

The Scots did not offer her one but they helped her, offering to put her backpack into their car, while she went round the castle. The family had been round the castle before their lunch. 'Mum' was going to sleep in the car while the Dad and children played some sort of ball game in the field by the car-park. Mum put Celestine's pack on the seat behind the driver and then pressed her button and allowed the front seat to go back so she was almost flat. She smiled at Celestine, who peered down at her eyes looking up at her, then shutting her eyes seemed immediately asleep. Celestine stayed for a moment to look down at the fully clothed body which she had not considered before.

She had to queue to get in, and there were some moments when you were just in line walking past ancient artifacts, beds, pictures of course. The courtyard was fine and as usual she liked the domestic bits best – the kitchen had had a clear hierarchy of servants, the most junior sitting nearest to the door, getting cold and obeying all sorts of rules.

Rules to be Observed Here

That every servant must

Take off his hat on entering here
Sit in his proper place at table
Keep himself clean becoming
of his station
Drink in his turn
Be diligent in his business
Shut the door after him

That no servant be guilty of

Cursing or swearing
Telling tales
Speaking disrespectfully of
anyone
Breeding any quarrel
Wasting meat or drink
Intermeddling with any
other's business unless
requested to assist

N.B. The person offending to be deprived of his allowance of beer – for the first offence, one day, and for the second offence, one whole week, for the third offence, his behaviour to be laid before Mr Myddleton.

All these border castles have been built, of course, because of the Welsh. But all the fighting had been because it was a stronghold. Fought over in the Wars of the Roses and even besieged by its owner in the civil wars when it had fallen into the hands of the other side. That was all castles did: cause people to fight over them. That was why the Dyke was so great; it was indefensible. It might have stopped them rustling cattle where it had steep sides originally, but it wasn't a fortification, it was a boundary.

The gardens outside were splendid and she would have wandered longer but she was worried that the family with her rucksack might want to go. Any rate it was half past one and there was ten miles to go and a lot up-hill so she scampered round the garden and hurried back to the car-park. She needn't have worried about the car party, the wife was sound asleep and she had to find her husband for him to open the back seat and help her out with her rucksack. Onto her back and away to Chirk Mill.

And the Dyke had been actually under the castle walls; they had buried some of it in their artificial lake. But as it leaves the immediate castle grounds it rises to its full height, up to 14ft and here Fox says its crest is marked by stag-headed oak trees. She was waiting for those broad open areas which she knew were to come in the middle of the border. Fox had some curious detail here; he had detail again and again, that was what she liked about him. But the detail, 'The Dyke now follows the eastern flank of a small N. and S. re-entrant, the ditch at one point coinciding with the streamlet which created the re-entrant'!

What was a re-entrant? Someone who was gone and come again. (Certainly true of the Dyke as it disappeared completely down near Chirk Mill.) A re-entrant – someone who came back, a certain and sure part of your life; friends were like that. Joan was like that. They had met in that silly first job working for Electrical Industries which sold radios, record players (back before CDs) and all sorts of other elec-trical equipment; all the sold equipment had had their guarantee cards put into filing drawers especially made for them – little postcard-sized drawers – but they had been placed in no order at all; some manager must have been for the chop. Celestine had got her degree and had just started real job-hunting. But took this temporary job and found Joan.

Joan was just back from Australia also job-hunting – older than Celestine – going to get back to being a copywriter. Joan taught her to swear and taught her – when she thought about it – how to be an 'independent' girl. At the end of their morning, dumped by this manager in a tiny room full of these hundreds of cards, she suddenly exploded: "This is the most fucking, fucking, fucking stupid cunt-ridden job I've ever done. Come on, Cel, whatever our little runt manager thinks, you and I are going out for an early lunch and we're coming back from a late one having had too much to drink."

Celestine hated people who shortened her name – she wanted to be called Celestine. But somehow with Joan it suited: "Hi, Cel," she'd shout across the street. She wasn't going to marry, she was going to live alone in London: "Get the sex on the side, they always want it." She was constant in advice to Celestine about Celestine's troubles, "James – he sounds a real wanker. Be good and vulgar, that'll get rid of James." Celestine wasn't even sure whether she wanted to, at that point, but when she did it was Joan who came up with what she should say to him. One night when he had driven her back to her flat and wanted to come in, she'd said: "Go away, James, all I want to do to you is fart in your face." And he hadn't rung Celestine for three months.

She would tell Joan she was a re-entrant, she'd like that. Some enter by the portals, some do not. "Vulgarity," said Joan, "is great but don't have too much of it." Men had male friends: there was the fiction they spent their whole time in bars telling dirty jokes. Where were girls? In tea shops simpering. Rory, she supposed, when he was alive actually did do bars a lot. It was her friend Posy who told Celestine the best dirty jokes, though mostly they were recounted to Celestine via Bernard. Still, what could you talk about? Anything, she supposed, but men surely talked about women and women about men. So what was the difference? Feelings, she supposed; she could say something to Joan and Joan knew how she felt at once. When the two of you were talking, and then the men came, there was that change in the level of intimacy. She'd have to ask Joan, the re-entrant, if she felt the same.

Up and down, good to get to the long flat bit by the old Oswestry racecourse. Too much road-work too, before that. You could vaguely see where the horses once ran. There was a possibility of dreaming the scene that had been. One could dream of the past and dream of the future and dream of the present. One could have the anxious dream which was required of one on some nights, but Celestine prayed that she could assign nights to other dreams.

Some minor roads ran up here from Oswestry and there were several cars parked with parties venturing 20 or 30 yards from them to scan the great views of the Berwyns on one side and Shropshire on the other. She avoided them carefully but further on near a monument there were some wooden seats and she took a rest and ate an apple. Only to find a man approach her:

"Have you seen a lady with a dog?" It wasn't a pick-up, he was genuinely asking.

"Well, I think there's a lady by the wood there."

"Oh, thank you, that's her, my niece. I'll just wait here 'til she gets back." He sat down along the bench from Celestine.

He certainly didn't look a great walker but she had also caught the accent. Unmistakable if you'd been in Zimbabwe, and Celestine was too vain not to tempt fate and enquire.

"You know the country, you've been there! Where did you stay there then?" He was off at once: "'Course, the country's not what it was," and he was into what Doris Lessing called The Monologue, about the horrors of the new Zimbabwe:

"They have all this money, they build themselves houses that would be seen as shocking taste even by Thatcher's *nouveau riche*. You simply wouldn't believe what they are building, nothing to do with the country or the climate. Stupid little windows, a mincing suburban refinement, but boastful and ostentatious at the same time. They fill their houses with furniture that no one would be seen dead with in Britain. There isn't one thing in their house that isn't hideous..."

But she had been there, she knew how to deal with the Monologue, at least she knew how to get round it. Back to the past, then you heard what he saw as his life and what he thought he had achieved.

The Bush War

We thought they looked suspicious, probably spies for the 'terrs'. You acquire an instinct after a bit of practice. We took them prisoner. They didn't mind going along with us a bit. We didn't even have to tie their hands. They had no spirit, those chaps, poor buggers, government forces or the 'terrs' they got it in the neck either way. We usually had someone with us who could tell us what the drums were saying, but not that trip. But the 'terrs' wouldn't have been singing their heads off if they knew we were half a mile away. We left the prisoners with two guards. One was shitting his pants with fear. That is what is meant by the smell of fear.

We were watching the leaders going in and out of a hut where we were sure a girl was. They were having a good time with her. We could hear her laugh. The ones who made the longest and most fiery speeches got most time in the hut. I had given orders no one should open fire until I did. I knew they were itching to let go, with all those drunk 'terrs' reeling about. I waited until the girl came out of the hut to have a pee. Then we all threw our bombs into the hut. Girls were screaming, and I realised there were other girls in there. There was general firing for about a minute. The 'terrs' ran away into the bush. They didn't know how many soldiers were out there in the dark. One of us was hit by a ricocheting bullet.

When the light came, there were several dead, including civilians, lying on the earth between the huts and in the huts where I thought there was only one girl, were several dead 'terrs' and three dead girls. The girl who had come out to have a pee had a smashed hip. We gave her morphine and called in the choppers.

I followed the girl's progress. It turned out she was three months pregnant. We gave her a new hip and she kept the baby. I visited her in hospital. She had already got herself engaged and she's had another baby since. Our wounded chap, the choppers took him to the hospital but he was as good as gone by then. In the *Herald* next week it said "One member of the security forces dead. Five civilians, eleven Terrorists."

Celestine noted the white skin with grey brown blotches on it. It was no use letting him talk on about the war. It had ended, that was what interested Celestine. At that time there were, theoretically, blacks and whites in Zimbabwe living together (there were still barriers at the club but, like the Dyke, they were penetrable). What made that possible? And here was a man who survived there, but she could ask him nothing of it. It was best to ask him about the old country, Rhodesia, in which he still lived. It was because of the land that he stayed and related to those blacks (those blacks who build themselves houses... the Monologue was turned on again).

The land mediated some sort of relationship for the white man with the black man, even though they related really in no other way. Early one morning you can imagine them singing; they left the river and journeyed through a region, the scenery of which was exceedingly pretty – more picturesque than any they have ever seen. Hills and valleys, spruits and rivers, grass and trees – all combined to present a most charming variety of landscape views.

The Africans did not know they were about to lose their country. They easily signed away their land when asked, for it was not part of their thinking that land, the earth our mother, can belong to one person rather than another. The anxious dream follows. Night after night I wept in my sleep and woke knowing I was excluded from my own best self – Southern Rhodesia. I dreamed I was in the bush but I was there illegally without papers. 'My' people, that is whites, were coming to escort me out of the country while to 'my' people, the blacks, amiable multitudes, I was invisible.

Some words the whites learnt include *musasa*, the most common tree in Mashonaland. *Guti* – mist. *Mudzimo* – a spirit or soul. And what you saw: duiker, bush buck, wild pig, wild cats, porcupines; koodoo stood on the ant heaps; eland went about in groups like cattle. That was what the oldish man on Oswestry Racecourse knew about. And here was the niece, who had married a farmer who farmed nearby, coming back from exercising the poodle.

The walk down through the woods to Llanforda Mill holds a good bit of the magic of the Dyke. She is beside you some of the way and some Victorians built a little grotto here.

Curious curved roof with stone seats inside like a bit of a set of a pantomime. But, miles from anywhere (Celestine had long lost the walkers from the cars at the racecourse), who would have walked and stopped here to sit in the shade of the great trees? The Dyke divides them with beech below and newly-planted pine above. One glimpses through the trees the alternate hillside fields and farms peacefully lying there. One could come here to make a marriage. Up the hill from Llanforda Mill one again hits the Dyke, a splendid section which one walks along before gently crossing some fields, losing the Dyke to a track leading into Trefonen.

There was Don walking up in the evening sun to meet her.

"I couldn't really believe that you wanted me to come, Celestine."

"You wrote you were going to be in England so... I couldn't resist asking you."

"I wish I could do the whole walk with you."

"No, I'm limiting myself just to tonight."

After all Don was only another affair – a second ski-instructor? No, more than that. Once you had been to one meeting it seemed you got to more. Any rate, the Chicago annual get-together of all English-as-a-Second-Language-teachers from the whole world was something no self-respecting University publisher could neglect; so there she was, sent to Chicago. And at a good time of year too, the fall temperature just right, good weather to walk by the lake.

Any rate to the meeting – vast Sheraton – the usual opening reception. She only had one complimentary wine ticket and she was saying to the barman, "How much for another glass, it can't be $3?" when this man – 'Don' – said, "Here, let me, I stole a packet of them." So that was a nice introduction and they wandered together, fortunately sitting near the back, into the vast ballroom for the opening ceremony. But who had the idea of inviting the President (was that what he was?) of the American Library Association to make the opening speech? Five minutes drone – ten more –

Celestine looked at Don, he nodded his head towards the door, she nodded in confirmation and then he took her hand and, keeping half stooped, they crept out.

"Did you eat?"

"No."

"Well, let's go."

"Providing we go Dutch."

"OK, if you say so." Then, "You like to dance?" Celestine nodded. "Well it's a strange joint but last time I was here we went to this place with a three-man jazz group and OK food."

So they went, luckily they got a table in an alcove against the wall, otherwise talking would have been impossible. Dancing was very crowded but there was an hour's intermission which started soon after they arrived.

Celestine's first classification of Americans had been on Graham Greene's line: 'loud' and 'quiet'. Don was quiet, not that pushing talk, that "Everything here is just so wonderful" over-enthusiastic style so you never knew if they liked anything. No, he could have been an academic (but blessedly wasn't), he'd done a post-grad thesis on the Cambridge songs and he knew all those old German poems.

Hear me, prelate most discreet,
For indulgence crying
Deadly sin I find so sweet
I'm in love with dying.
Every pretty girl I meet
Sets my heart a sighing.
Hands off! Oh, but in conceit.
In her arms I'm lying.

Much too hard it is, I find
So to change my essence
As to keep a virgin mind
In a virgin's presence.
Rigid laws can never bind
You to acquiescence
Light o' loves must seek their kind
Bodies take their pleasance.

Don was pleasant. He was pleasure too and Celestine liked him. He was excited by many things, but not with that gushing enthusiasm. Straight liking of things he knew about.

Pleasant, was that too mild a word to describe Don? Not really; she knew that was a biblical use she was half-recalling. Weren't David and Jonathan pleasing to each other before Jonathan exceeded himself. Pleasant: agreeable to the mind, feeling, or senses. Coming, of course, from *please*, to give satisfaction; gentle, mild, peaceful. Don was those despite his firm love-making. Middle English *plaise, pleise* or *plese* and also old French *plais-is*. Pleasant. Johnson rejected the verb 'to pleasure' (to please or gratify): 'this word, though supported by good authority is, I think, inelegant.'

Back at the hotel she had a hard time saying no but he accepted it. But rang her room in twenty minutes because he had her purse which she'd taken out of her bag and asked him to keep in his pocket while they danced. Couldn't he deliver it? No, but she wouldn't deny the invitation the following night. She had planned to spend two days in New York whereas he was going. But some deft phoning on his part and they had two more days and nights together.

He worked in publishing too, for the new press that Stanford had set up. He skied every winter, he loved olives. In the five days they were together he seemed to have everything; but there was one whole topic they couldn't mention: he also had a wife and two kids. He didn't say too much about his wife, she wasn't that sympathetic to my interests, books you know, she thinks I buy too many. But... she's good with the kids. He showed her photos of them. Don was not going to leave those kids.

Which was a pity. The third night in Chicago, they had dinner in her room. Some really gross sparkling Italian wine and early to bed. And his hands were all over her, probing her, into her bum. She'd never had that and she said, "Don't do that, I don't like it." But the next night she suddenly wanted him to touch her there and he did. The sailor's way, he joked, and it was quite different. Something you wanted and didn't want at the same time.

And Celestine thought with this guy I really could live – and we would travel, we wouldn't be stuck in Austria, in England. She would be moving the way her father had taught her. But he, of course, couldn't ask her to stay. He didn't think he would visit England that year but he would try, but whatever happened they would both be in Chicago next year.

Here, ten years later, they were in Trefonen. "I don't think the food will be great," Celestine warned, "but there is a shower in our room, and I think they'll be good locals in the bar afterwards." All her predictions were entirely right, she didn't have to organise the evening at all. She could leave it to him, that was also good. She could give up being independent tonight. Celestine knew he liked being a bit dominating, which he was, and had been as he made love to her. She was his but he wasn't hers. That was the trouble with affairs.

Also, of course, she hadn't, despite promises, promises, promises, she had not gone to Chicago the next year. She had been in Rhodesia by then, but she could have gone. He had written; she had not replied until after the meeting.

"The hotel must have thought me mad," he said. "I was sure you'd make it, I rang the desk 'til four in the morning, when they said, 'Sir, no-one is going to check in at this time of night.' Then I knew you'd checked out on me."

"Sorry," said Celestine.

The Camp at Buttington

Celestine was prepared, in the morning, to let Don walk along with her, and he came as far as the start of the steep climb up Llanymynech Hill, so that he could see and touch the Dyke – which he did. She could see him immediately beginning to share her fascination with the old earthwork. When she told him about Fox's great book he was eagerly asking where he could obtain a copy and she suggested he stopped in Shrewsbury for lunch, telling him of the old town and detailing its three good bookshops.

He was eager to continue with her and he was sure he could stay an extra day. But at the bottom of the hill she gently turned him back. His car, she reminded him, was at Trefonen and he was supposed to be consulting fellow editors in London. They either had to walk together (which she had decided they could not do) or they had to walk apart. Celestine set off up the hill alone.

The Dyke was simply a western ditch from which the main material had been thrown up to build a slope while the eastern side of the bank was allowed to slope easily away in many parts. The ditch itself Fox had studied in detail in this area. Back in Caeau Gwynion he had sought permission for his investigations from Colonel Myddleton, owner of the land; the Myddletons were the family who had bought Chirk Castle from the Crown in 1595. The previous owner had got involved with the Perkin Warbeck plot and had the misfortune to be beheaded. The tenant of the farm who also gave permission for the dig was Mr Evan Evans. The ditch was flat-bottomed, six and a half feet at the bottom and eighteen feet in breadth at ground level. The depth of the silting varied from three foot nine inches to four foot ten inches and this detail allowed Fox to fix within narrow limits of error an original depth of seven feet and seven inches.

But here in Treflach Wood some quarrying had exposed an excellent cross-section of the bank. Here the bank is composed of gravel and clayey sand in diagonal layers. The nucleus of the bank was, it is evident, cast on to the edge of the (W) ditch. Full size was achieved by adding material to the reverse slope and the crest.* This was all very well but how had the diagonal layers been constructed? One lot of villeins standing around with the clay and another lot with the gravel? Any rate Fox seems sure of the height here, seven feet above the ground, giving fourteen feet and seven inches, if Celestine was adding correctly, as the overall height of the Dyke from the ditch bottom to the crest of the bank.

The bank here was a repository of beautiful rich clay. Better stuff to have in a bank than money, Celestine thought; she might take a pot of earth from the Dyke and ask her bank to keep some as a deposit against the loan she'd need to get her to New York. She could point out that it had kept the Welsh and English apart for over a millennium and that even a part of it was worth much more than any gold she could deposit with them. She would challenge the bank's right not to accept it as a valuable deposit which when redeemed she would intend to return to the site from which she took it. The bank would probably seek a legal opinion.

With the Banker out of the way senselessly rattling his bones, it was time to dispose of the law and the barristers. It was good that the barrister went under following an anxiety dream.

> But the Barrister, weary of proving in vain
> That the Beaver's lace-making was wrong,
> Fell asleep, and in dreams saw the creature quite plain
> That his fancy had dwelt on so long.

---

*An excellent Fox footnote: 'This is the usual method of making such earthworks: the only bank known to me which was constructed on the opposite plan, that of placing primary deposits at a point furthest away from the ditch inwards, is the Devil's Dyke, Cambridgeshire.' (Camb. Antiq. Soc. XXVI p.90)

He dreamed that he stood in a shadowy Court,
Where the Snark, with a glass in its eye,
Dressed in gown, bands, and wig, was defending a pig
On the charge of deserting its sty.

What was offensive to the Barrister was the fact that the Snark made the whole of the legal procedure look ridiculous.

The Jury had each formed a different view
(Long before the indictment was read),
And they all spoke at once, so that none of them knew
One word that the others had said.

As for the judge when he attempted to explain something the Snark interrupted rudely with "Fudge" and subsequently took over both summing-up and pronouncing the verdict and sentencing the pig. This strenuous defence lawyer, who had spoken for at least three hours in sorting out what the indictment was, became spent with the toils of the day. But it found the pig guilty and arranged for it to be transported for life and then to be fined forty pounds.

The whole legal process, as so often, proved quite point-less, as the pig had been dead for some years.

The Judge left the Court, looking deeply disgusted:
But the Snark, though a little aghast,
As the lawyer to whom the defence was entrusted,
Went bellowing on to the last.

The Barrister awoke from this nightmarish attack on the whole legal profession to the sound of a knell of a furious bell which the Bellman rang close to his ear. He makes no further appearance in the tale and it is fair to assume that the knell he heard was his own. Thus end all law and lawyers.

It was strange that Celestine had always hated the law when her father, whom she loved, had, as far as she could tell, been an ornament to his profession. A judge who had worked all over what was left of the British Empire had an experience somewhat different to that of his better-known and better-rewarded colleagues, who had practised all their lives in British Courts. Celestine assumed his meticulous interest in detail (which she had not, at least not fully, inherited) was one reason for his exceptional acclaim from his colleagues.

After they left Kenya and her years in Bournemouth, the Judge had decided that he and his daughter ought to have their own base. For years they were there barely two or three weeks in the year because, with the Judge abroad, if she didn't join him for holidays, Celestine would go to the Aunt in Bournemouth. But it was their flat; in a splendid position, 100 Carlisle Mansions, just near Westminster Cathedral; and it was large and spacious. It was marvellous for her when she eventually came to work in London. All her friends were struggling in poor rented accommodation and she had this splendid flat at her disposal. Joan said, "Don't you feel you should leave the parental home?"

"The opposite," Celestine replied, "I want to really live here. It's not my mother and father's house. It's mine and my father's, we got it together. It's not a parental home, it's my home which my father shares with me."

"OK," said Joan, surprised by the passion which Celestine displayed.

In school holidays, there were two alternatives. Either she went to the Judge or he came over to join her in Europe. Going to him could be alright although it was often lonely. There was that period when he was in the Caribbean, based on one of the smaller islands. He had a house, and his excited thirteen-year-old daughter discovered there were six servants; but none stayed the night – in fact they had dinner (as the Judge liked to call it) at seven, so the staff could be gone by eight and then the two of them were alone in the great house.

Her father would play a game with her, halma was her favourite. There are no really good two-handed card games, and some of her other early favourites like Monopoly now seemed rather silly. But then in an embarrassed way, her father would say he had to go and work and he would disappear to his study. There seemed to be no way she could make friends with any of the local children. She was white and the daughter of the Judge. She couldn't go on the beach unless one of the house-staff accompanied her; the days were long. "Never swim out of your depth."

She wasn't long alone because her Aunt and her cousins arrived for their summer holidays, and after their three weeks she went back to Bournemouth with them. But that first week her father had probably hoped somehow he would get to know his leggy daughter better. Better than from those weekly letters she wrote him. 'This week we beat Roedean at hockey. I was top in an English essay on Rhythm. All my friends have colds but I haven't.' How was the Judge to reply? He took to writing little character sketches of witnesses who amused him, telling Celestine how easy it was to tell when they were lying.

But the next year he had 'home' leave so after a week at the London flat and a visit to Bournemouth, they went off together to France. Here it was she learnt how meticulous her father was. He had the most enormously detailed guidebooks and once in the Louvre they passed slowly from painting to painting while he read her out, *sotto voce*, so as to not disturb others, a detailed art-critic's account of the painting in front of them. Finally she had to say "Father" – she called him 'Father', not 'Dad' (why and when had that change occurred?) – "let me just look." And they had to arrange to meet at a specific point in the entrance. She could see he was hurt that he didn't go round with her, but she just couldn't go on like that.

It was better when they went down to the Loire. It was impossible to avoid going round in guided groups. Her father grumbled that most guides were totally ignorant and was always trying to peer at his guide books, but Celestine allowed herself to be swept along by the crowd. She loved the Loire, they would picnic by it each day as they drove slowly along, stopping a night here, a night there. It was the view of the great river that remained with her far more than the castles along the bank.

Her memory was all of the great breadth of the river. She never knew where it was that they crossed a bridge and stopped on an island. She walked along the shingle and saw those blue-grey poplars, trees – what were they? – willows, on the other bank, the brilliant blue sky and mounds of shingle emerging and disappearing in the midst of the stream. And a fisherman with a rather complicated arrangement of two boats, one of which seemed to be permanently moored and from which he hung a line dangling while he rowed along in another towing a line behind him.

Celestine became an expert map reader. She liked to get her father to talk about their mutual past. And he would answer her questions ("What was Cookie really like?") with tales of disastrous gastronomic attempts, and the awful Mrs Boniface. But if she said, "What was it like in India?" he would just fall silent, pour himself some more wine and look abstractedly away for several minutes before re-entering the conversation with a: "Where did we say we would go tomorrow?" Aunt had been very noncommittal when Celestine had finally asked her about her mother. "She was killed rather tragically in India. I don't know the details, you'll have to ask your father." Her cousins knew nothing; Johnnie, now a rather pleasing seventeen year old, said, "All our mother will say is she was killed under unfortunate circumstances." There were strange fantasies for Celestine to think about sleepless in her bed in the nice hotel overlooking the Loire near Chinon. Outside, their car was being broken into and Celestine's birthday present – a camera – was being stolen.

At the top of Llanymynech Hill there is a golf course. The route-notes enjoin you to keep close to – but not on – the golf course. Celestine wondered 'why not?' as she wandered out onto the well-cropped grass – perhaps the Oswestry Golf Course was managed by some ex-Rhodey who didn't like scruffy walkers. But it was more likely to be obsessional concern that you might stray from the route.

Celestine did not get lost and was soon in Llanymynech. Ice-cream time. From Llanymynech the Dyke goes down, the road crosses into fields and eventually ends at the Severn. For five miles the river patrols the border until at Buttington the Dyke starts again and sets off down through eastern Montgomeryshire. You can walk the main road to start with on the Dyke but Celestine, having observed the holiday traffic going North and South, was happy to abandon her friend for a time and take the alternative route along the canal.

The Montgomery Canal here is especially fine, blocked catastrophically by a road built through it at one point, but there is another remarkable aqueduct to enjoy, stone-pillared and crossing the Vrynwy river. Just past the aqueduct, Celestine began to meet groups of Boy Scouts. She was struck at once by the varying accents and indeed shades of skin. On the bridge which crosses the canal, she found three of them leaning over, peering into the water. She stopped and asked them first where their camp was.

"By the fields at Buttington," said a boy with an Australian accent.

"Doesn't sound as if you've been around these parts before."

"No, we're all Internationals. We've representatives of fifty different countries."

"Are there still Scouts in all that number of countries?" Celestine realised she had said this in a tone of implied criticism. "How absolutely splendid that is," she hurried on, "where do you come from?"

"Zimbabwe," said another boy, flashing her a great white-toothed smile.

Another Zimbabwean, thought Celestine.

"It's the first time you've been abroad then."

"Yes, we flew here from Johannesburg."

"That must have been fun. And what are you doing now?"

"We are looking at the canal. We had a talk on it this morning."

"Was that good?"

"It was alright," the boys shrugged. "We're supposed to go to see the viaduct."

"You could do with some of this water in Zimbabwe."

"Sure could," said the Zimbabwean.

It was 1890 when that first white column of settlers – the Pioneer Column – hit the lands that belonged to the Mashona and the Matabele. The Matabele were invaders in the early 1800s, a split-off from the Zulu peoples further south. The Mashona – a name that others gave them; like the Mois of Vietnam, or the Brazilian rainforests tribes, why should you have a name for yourself? You are the people. Nor do they have written records, so what is written down is the pioneers' descriptions.

All the tribes of the Mashona have similar customs, which are different to the Matabele's. Their huts are circular, with a wall a foot or two high made of poles and daga mud mounted by a conical thatched roof, differing also from the beehive huts of the Zulu. All the family live in the hut which, on the inside (a grudging compliment this) are kept clean. Grain is stored in granaries on rocks or on stakes to keep out the white ant. The Mashona amuse themselves by making earthenware pots which are very soft and easily broken, though in the South they are quite clever at making water-tight baskets from rushes grown in the Sabi river.

The Matabele, or rather the Amandabele, are the descendants of Zulus who trekked under the leadership of the famous Musilikatze up through the Transvaal from which they were driven by the Boers.

Well, that's enough of where the Scout came from; now he must be a son of one of those 'trough feeders' (the whites' description) – the corrupt administrators who rule the roost in Harare. He would hardly come from what were the old 'native' reserves where so many still lived. Mugabe got all sorts of advice, "don't throw out the whites, you'll ruin the economy," and (Chissano to Mugabe) "You were lucky to have the British, at least they leave behind a decent infrastructure."

Infrastructure. Youth – this one a top Scout; then that other one who got down from a truck at a desolate crossroads in Zimbabwe, opened the door of the car and got in, bending away from me in a disconsolate curve, his hands limp between his thin knees. He was trembling in spasms. He began a dreary and hopeless sobbing. It was clear he had been doing a lot of crying.

"Please tell me what is the matter. Perhaps I can help?"

"No one can help. I lost my job this week. They said I am not good enough. I got my certificate but they said I'm no good."

To get a job in the big city is the goal of every young person. His big city had not even been the metropolis, Harare, but Marondera.

"It is because all the white people are going. They are taking all the jobs with them. The whites are cleverer than us, we need them to stay and give us jobs."

In Makondi, close to the Mozambique borders, the women are famed for their skills in love-making. Mention them to any black man in Central and East Africa and his face will put on the look of one who has to pay tribute. But just ask what those skills are – for after all they might contribute to the joy and well-being of human kind – and nothing more is forthcoming. One man said that the women scar their stomachs. Alright, fine: but so far that's it, that's all we know.

Jobs from the whites. But what else do they think of the whites, those whites sitting on the verandah talking their Monologues about how it was? Nothing! They are not thinking about those whites at all. So they don't want to relate to those whites, but they do want to relate to some whites. In the districts – the old native reserves – they walked miles to watch television, one set to three hundred. 'And what came ye forth for to see.' White men, of course, with maybe a coloured servant, in *Dallas*. Not Dallas, Texas, where

Kennedy was shot but *Dallas*, the end-of-the-world show on every television station.

Dallas was Offa's Dyke, standing as a boundary between the black Zimbabweans and not the white Zimbabweans but between black and the world they dreamed of.

Boundary: that which serves to indicate the bounds or limits of anything, whether material or immaterial; also the limit itself. A good boundary sets limits but allows people to cross, mix and mell at the boundary. It creates borderers; but the flickering image as a boundary allows only one-way transmission. You see them, they never see you; they can never walk into your world, you can never walk into theirs.

Maybe when it was seven to ten feet from the bottom of the ditch to the crest you needed a shoulder to punt you up here. Maybe cattle (cows and sheep) had problems crossing, but you crossed. Of course, the formal crossings were few. Fox considered that, like the Devil's Fleam and Bran Ditches in East Anglia, the Dyke was intended to present a barrier *almost* complete, legitimate traffic being limited to defined routes. (Celestine inserted the italic all her life.) Such a legitimate crossing Celestine had passed today. Up on to the highest and most western point on the plateau west of Selattyn Hill. Here there is a slight hollow on the line of the ditch. The opening is not now in use and there is no indication on the rough moorland pasture which adjoins it on the East of any trackway having formerly existed. The opening is therefore ancient.

Just past Pool Quay you cross the main road and get into the water meadows beside the Severn. Celestine immediately had thoughts of Jonathan and herself, arms around each other, crossing water meadows; not here, somewhere else: she would have to ask him the name of the place. It was in some part of the south country, Sussex, maybe, but she had no memory of the name of the village.

At Buttington Bridge, she crossed the Severn River and assured herself of the route she would be setting off on in the morning when she came back here. She had thought she would walk into Welshpool where she was to spend the night with Jonathan, but the traffic on the road put her off and she didn't fancy having to inhale those fumes. She saw where the Offa's Dyke path took off over the railway line but herself wandered onto the small hamlet at Buttington where she found an unvandalised public phone. She guessed she was not the first exhausted walker who had stumbled into the phone booth, because she was delighted by a card which proclaimed 'Welshpool Taxis'.

"You wait where you are, Miss, we'll be there to pick you up in five minutes." They were too: "Royal Oak, Miss? And welcome." She liked being 'Miss' again, particularly as she was just about to meet her husband. "But I won't take you back along the main road, dreadful jam there is. We'll take you back round by Leighton. It's a bit longer but it will be far quicker." Celestine didn't understand any of this geography but liked all this solicitation for her. Her busy driver filled her in with a constant flow of information about the local roads and he was soon striding into the car-park at the back of the hotel. "I'll drop you here Miss, instead of at the front. Then I can hop out the side and get round the traffic at the cross-roads. August, Miss – always the same. But we're going to have a by-pass. Thank you very much, Miss. Did you want to go out in the morning, Miss? Very good; give us a call when you're ready. Here's our card." Celestine liked the 'we' of his speech. In England the singular use of the plural 'we' was of course restricted to the Queen who spoke as the nation. Mrs Thatcher had sometimes slipped into a royal 'we'. This taxi driver was a Queen or a Prime Minister.

The driver had vaguely indicated a passage; "That'll take you through to the front." She plunged into it, there was a turn to the left which she considered but went straight through and bumped into a short, suited man who was coming from her right. Mutual apologies.

"I'm looking for the reception," Celestine said.

"I'm the Manager here, Ma'am, let me take you along."

"You don't sound Welsh."

"No," he said, "I'm Italian," ushering Celestine through the front door of the Royal Oak, and indicating the reception desk. "A guest."

"Certainly, Mr Bernadini."

What on earth was an Italian doing mixed up with these borderers? Border country, of course, though, that was just right for Italians. And she thought that's where all strangers belong, in border country. Later at dinner she found him serving her. And mixing in and helping out with his staff, among whom she thought she detected one other Italian – but were mostly locals, she guessed. Not like a snooty English manager, she thought, who'd stand and direct, push the waiters about and swear at them. Lasagne on the menu. She wondered whether the chef was Italian.

It was comic also to find herself addressed as 'Mrs Jones' which made her sound like a local. She had not held onto the title and had reverted to her family name as soon as she and Jonathan had split up. But it amused Jonathan (and her) when she suggested this tryst, to come together for one more night of married love. "Mr Jones got here an hour ago, I think he's up in your room." Scramble up the old stairs to Mr Jones.

She had been 'Miss' to the taxi driver, 'Ma'am' to the polite Mr Bernadini, but Jonathan was 'Mr Jones'. Jonathan Presant Jones, do you take Celestine May Quareine to be your lawful wedded wife? And then it had been her turn to affirm, and then it had been their turn to begin perfect happiness. Their manners were mild and their principles steady. 'The bells rang and everyone smiled and this happened within a twelve month of their meeting, it will not appear that they were in a way hurt by delays.'

Well it had been a little more than a twelve month, and that had been chiefly due to Celestine changing her mind more than once. Had she been worried about Jonathan, or the process of marriage – she wasn't sure now – but she had alarmed the Aunt to whom the arrangement had fallen by the number of times the marriage was on and off.

Jonathan was lying on the bed reading. "Hello, old thing,

how's tricks? Tired?" And he tossed the book he was reading (*Northanger Abbey*) and jumped up to embrace her. Celestine had always thought he was really the wrong shape for her to love: he was a little shorter than her and as a young man, right from the start, you could really only call him paunchy. He was not tidy, his shirt crumpled now, no doubt, from lying on the bed. Somehow it was never tucked in properly. He always wore those thick woollen socks, surely in this weather he'd have come in sandals; but he wasn't a sandal man. He just pulled on a pair of jeans, shirt and the same jersey he had taken off the night before.

She was always giving him jerseys because that was what he seemed to like to wear. He would put the new one on to please her but then he'd just wear it and wear it, never thinking to select a different one. He had drawerfuls by the time they split up but he always wore one he had taken off the night before.

"Why don't you choose?" she'd cry out and he'd smile and started riffling through the drawer.

"How should I choose?"

"Well, some are thicker than others. Then the colours. Who are you going to see? You must be able to choose."

"You choose for me, old thing." Not that that had made her give him up, no it had rather endeared him to her. She was his old thing – he was a dear! That was his word, he was a *dear*.

'Dear'; nice, old English: *dieru, diorie* or old high German, *diure*. The first meaning was a bit over the top for Jonathan. *Glorious, noble, honourable, worthy*. Not that he wasn't all those things, but better really for her was to see him regarded with *personal feelings of high esteem or affection; held in deep and tender esteem, beloved, loved*. Endearment, wrote Johnson, the cause of love. One day she must write and complain to David Crystal that his introductory Linguistics lecture had led to her compulsion to study all her lovers using the dictionary.

She had met Jonathan at some hall student party she'd got involved in. Someone who her father had asked her to help had come to London from the Islands, to study Biology at University College, so she had put him up in the flat for a while and helped him to sort out his accommodation. And in gratitude she had found herself being invited to a party in a large rambling house in Muswell Hill. Mostly students, she found; how old she felt compared to them.

Jonathan was a tutor to a group of them and his essential amiableness had brought him along. He was a lecturer in genetics and she found herself standing beside him while he had conversations which were totally meaningless to her. But she got to rather like the language.

"The Southern blot technique! Jesus, what's that, Jonathan? It sounds like something to do with blotting paper."

"Well, it is in a way. Writers give up blotting paper because of all their machines and scientists start using it to fix things up."

"Genes aren't the same as Jeans."

"No," said Jonathan, "they are not."

But when they started going out together, she found she rather liked being with somebody who did something so completely different from her and which, without excluding other interests, really deeply obsessed him. He was trying to locate the gene for a rare disease – Schie's disease, or Hurler-Schie's disease or was it Hurler's disease? "Well, they're the same biochemically but morphologically they are quite different." He was disorganised about his work, not seeming to apply for renewals of his grant in time, so that he seemed always as if he might be going to lose his job.

She met his Professor. "You'll never be a Professor, will you Jonathan?" "Don't want to be – too much admin – never get any real work done." All this serious science and disorganisation made her wonder what his family was like. When she asked, he suddenly said, "Getting curious about me are you?" It was about their third or fourth meeting and that night he suddenly said as they finished dinner: "Come to my place tonight then and I'll tell you about the family."

Once he started love-making she called him the satyr because he was so easy to re-arouse. He loved her kneeling to him and she loved that too, putting her hands back to pull him harder into her, and when he'd burst into her he'd collapse on the bed as if he was so exhausted he'd never ever be able to do anything, certainly not make love again. Celestine threw herself beside him and drew her body half over his which he'd accept in a moment or two (she always wanted to hold a man after he had made love to her). She'd find that holding him he quickly became aroused again and if she wasn't prepared for a prolonged bout, she had to lie away from him or even get up. But then other days he'd come home with some great piles of work and be bashing away at his computer all evening, hardly speaking to her and now collapsing into their bed without even reaching out to touch her.

"Well, do you want to know who my father is? Guess."

"A member of the mafia."

"Not far out, he's a retired General."

"General! He can't be!"

"Well he is, we'll go and see them this weekend."

The 'General' hadn't planned to be a soldier but he'd gone into the Army during the Second World War and he'd been a good soldier. So after the war he'd stayed and become a soldier-diplomat – military attache in Washington and all that.

Now they lived in a manor house in Wiltshire. The general was now largely a gardener and his wife doing what is still described as Good Works. Celestine found herself liking them a lot. They were very solicitous. "You Londoners work so hard, you mustn't help in the house at all." Next visit: "I remember last time you were here you liked my sponge cake. I made one for you to take back to town."

To her surprise Jonathan had certain very practical skills, helping his father with jobs the older man found difficult, like pruning trees, offering to mow lawns and behaving with an affection to his parents she liked. She could contrast James' cold acceptance of his parents' adoration compared to the settled companionship in Jonathan's family.

Celestine lived with Jonathan for more than a year without any real discussion of any more permanent relationship. Her father's return for three months precipitated perhaps Jonathan's sudden and overwhelming demand that they should get married. He was suddenly talking about their having children. They had not been on Celestine's agenda.

It may have been that part of his agenda that made her so ambivalent about the marriage. Her father liked him a lot and her Aunt and cousins all approved. The judge and the general and his wife were rapidly good friends. Her Aunt, who had organised Gilly's wedding, was all for a repeat of the same scene for Celestine. That, too, may have been what put Celestine off. The invitations were suddenly all printed when she told Jonathan she wanted to wait a bit. "Of course, old thing," he said, and the church was cancelled and all the invitations binned.

Suddenly three months later she thought, 'I was silly. I do want Jonathan. I could have his children.' His compliance with her changing moods made him more endearing, and she said suddenly: "I will marry you Jonathan. But not all that big wedding stuff. Let's do it small and quick here in London." Nevertheless her father flew in, the cousins all assembled, and Jonathan and Celestine spent a week in that southern county, and one afternoon after a drive, walked through those delicious water-meadows.

She realised that Jonathan wanted to go on with the package straight away. So she said, "I'm not getting pregnant for at least three years"; and of course, he argued. "I want to really get somewhere in my job." Which she was, the press suddenly asking her if she would go and work in their New York office for three months. That interfered with settled domesticity although Jonathan came over for a month. And they were happy together. Was it her own recklessness that broke the marriage or was it just Jonathan and his continuous, "Alright, old thing?"?

There he sat, across from her in the oak-beamed dining

room, in the Royal Oak in Welshpool looking as cherubic as ever but there was grey in his sideburns. He had moved to the University of Surrey, seemed almost to have become Head of a department, lived in a rambling old rectory with a huge garden which she knew he spent hours in. A second wife and two children and yet he'd agreed to come and see her; that was some compliment.

Suddenly he said:

"You know, old thing, I don't know how much we are going to sleep."

"We are going to be busy are we?" said Celestine, smiling.

"Oh, I wasn't thinking of that," smiling back. "I was thinking of cattle. Tomorrow is market day and Welshpool is perhaps the biggest cattle market in Britain. And I guess they start pretty early."

Behind the hotel there is a huge area that looks like a car-park but is actually the cattle market.

Border country. 'Gateway to Wales', they call Welshpool (Lloyd George called it 'Gateway to Paradise'). Welsh cattle from all over Wales, bought by butchers to be trucked all over England. Celestine heard French voices in the morning (that would cause trouble with the French farmers). The Dyke had been built partly perhaps to stop the Welsh stealing Saxon cattle. Now the Saxons came to buy the Welsh cattle right on the border.

The Long Mountain

The Royal Oak was cozy and despite Jonathan's prognostications, quiet. The cattle market in the morning was irresistible. Obviously much of the selling had taken place already when they walked around there at nine o'clock; but there was still selling going on. Young cows – heifers, Celestine supposed – driven into a ring and a man immediately shouting: "What am I bid, what am I bid? Fifty, I'm bid, fifty I'm bid. What am I bid, what am I bid? Sixty, I'm bid, sixty I'm bid. Sixty-five, I'm bid, seventy. Seventy, seventy. I'm bid seventy. Seventy-five I'm bid." And suddenly, knowing instinctively (or rather from experience) that that was it, *bang*, down with his board onto a fence post and the next animal would be in the ring.

The farmers wore brown suits, not very tweedy as Celestine thought they might have been. Good solid cloth. There were many cloth caps too and quite a few had sticks, long sticks with a forked top. Celestine felt she wanted one to walk with but realised it would only be an encumbrance for her – but she felt it would look good. "They're for dividing sheep with, not for walking with. I'll buy you a real walking-stick if you like," Jonathan offered.

Jonathan would have detained her longer. He wanted her to walk over to Powis Castle. "The tallest tree in the country and I've heard the terraced gardens are amazing. They still have seven gardeners, my dad is always coming here but I've never seen it." But Celestine was looking – was she? – for a new marriage and had guilt in her mind about a marriage which perhaps she had destroyed. "Write and tell me about it. I must get back to Buttington." She found Mr Bernadini in the hall and was able to bid him a fond farewell while his receptionist rang for a taxi. "No, no trouble at all," said Mr Bernadini, "a pleasure."

But she had not finished with Jonathan even when she got back to Buttington. She was dropped the Welsh side of the Severn and she walked over the Bridge looking back at the water meadows; she remembered she had never asked Jonathan the name of the village where they'd walked over the meadows just after their wedding when they were staying at that town in the southern country. Water meadows feel lush, feel friendly. That day she had thought: "This is OK. I've made a marriage and it's going to work."

They'd entered the meadow through a kissing gate. So, of course, they'd kissed and Jonathan had not let her through until they French kissed deep. So Celestine said the next fence we cross it's my turn for a forfeit. There she slid her hand into his shirt and erected his nipples, a touch-up he was extremely sensitive to and found so arousing he could hardly bear it. So at the next stile, he took his revenge, feeling her up deep. So it went on, at a little bridge she made him bare his buttocks and beat him across the stream with some willow twigs. It was one of those bright sunny early October days but it was past holiday time, there was no-one about and in the end Celestine was walking bare-breasted through the meadows before she was pulled to the ground. So why did she let the marriage fail? Something to do with work perhaps.

Meanwhile here you were at Buttington. This was one of the real gateways to Wales, the other upstream at Forden. They were the two fords across the Severn, one either side of Welshpool where the two bridges were. There was fighting on the border of course, at Buttington. One hundred years after the Dyke was built the Saxons caught the Vikings at Buttington and there they fought. The old English did not really make a macaronic although said aloud, it sounded nice: *pa nie pa geguderode waeron pa offord nie here hindan ae Buttingtone.** The site marked for the battle is East of the river, opposite those water meadows through which she had just re-walked with Jonathan. Presumably the Danes chose not to be caught mid-stream wading the river (it must have

* From the Saxon Chronicles.

been quite deep) but rather stood just north of the ford to fight. If they won well and good they could cross the ford at their ease. If they lost they would be crossing a deeper river. They stood beside the river waiting to fight the Saxons. What was it like, the battle? You could read the results but how did you mark up the score? It is reported that battles with sword and axe sounded like pots and pans being banged and rattled together. Some of the warriors may have had chain-mail, that also would clash as it was struck. But your aim was not to strike the sword or the armour of your opponent but to strike him. Get past his shield (there is an iron-age shield in the Welshpool museum) and get into his flesh. That must have been accompanied by almost no noise at all or at least some sort of dull thud. And then blood, blood on the sword, blood on the body, blood on the ground. And finally more on one side than on the other would be lying bloody on the ground and you would give ground, retreat.

The story, which Celestine looked up when she got home was a bit more complicated. The Danes had actually been camped on an island, now no longer extant, in the middle of the river. Presumably they had been planning a sortie into Wales but when the Saxons arrived the Danes crossed back to the English bank to fight them. The Saxons reported they won the battle but the Danes were able to march on, they occupied the old Roman fort at Chester and wintered there, cold and hungry, returning in the spring to East Anglia from whence they had come.

The battle was on Offa's boundary but it did not involve the Welsh Borderers, they stayed home. Celestine slipped across the road-bridge eliding the memory of the water meadows and the battle. Fighting warriors rising out of the mist with her lost husband. Better to get on with the serious business of finding the Dyke where it restarts again five miles beyond the river forming the boundary. The North/South Offa's Dyke Notes give no indication of the climb you are in for. Admittedly, it is not as steep as on the Clwydian Hills but this climb up the Long Mountain is long and is up over 750 feet. Offa's engineer had a task to solve and looking at the contours one can but admire his achievement. Visual control of the Powys valley is cleverly maintained without any alteration of alignment. Unquestionably this was taken into consideration when the line was staked out.

The path here does even more than the Dyke because it climbs right up to the top of Long Mountain which has a height of 1,338 ft; Celestine realised she had climbed 1000 ft. There are two features of the top of the hill, the first is an iron age hill fort. The second is a wireless station and also possibly some secret Ministry of Defence surveillance system which kept and keeps watch across the flat plains of the middle of England across to the North Sea, to Northern Europe. Anyway Keep Out if you don't want to be arrested. But walking round the hill fort raises no objections from the old inhabitants.

Fox knows all about re-entrants. Celestine still wished she did. Offa's chief engineer is predictable. When proceeding along a hillside in broken country (such as this) small lateral re-entrants are crossed in a direct manner, the Dyke dipping to the floor of the little valley and up again the other side. In the case of a larger re-entrant the Dyke swings inward for a moderate distance, dips slightly to cross the valley at the higher level thus attained, and then swings outwards to regain the correct alignment.

Celestine wished the path-makers had kept to the Dyke as she climbed on up the slope of this Long Mountain. Halfway up she was glad of the distraction of a farmer stood on the hillside watching his two dogs who were working the sheep against a fence below him. One dog sat about ten yards from the fence while another ran around behind the herd of sheep who, frightened by the sitting dog, occasionally made a dash past him, in which case they seemed free to wander in the field as before. The line of the Dyke Path actually passed in front of the stationary farmer. Celestine had the notion that maybe farmers didn't like the walkers but she was puzzled by the apparently purposeless activity. So she stood still and finally dared ask,

"What are you doing?"

"Counting," said the farmer, continuing to stare at his sheep and dogs.

"Counting?"

"Yes, see, you've got to know you've got all your sheep, haven't you then. Cos, see, I picks up the lame ones later."

"How often do you count them?"

"Most days, see, sheep's worth money, I don't want to be losing any. So I counts."

Celestine watched the counting concluded and then the farmer whistled his dogs up to them. Both nuzzled up to Celestine.

"Do you mind people walking the Dyke?" Celestine asked.

"No, I likes it."

"Good. Why?"

"Well, looking after sheep, it's a boring job, see; you're out here all day, see, with the sheep and the dogs. So walkers like you, I can have a talk, pass the time of day."

Given this encouragement they talked – dogs, sheep. Yes, he sold them in Welshpool. Prices were bad too, Common Market, the French.

"Where are you going then?"

"I hope to get beyond Montgomery by tonight."

"Oh, I mustn't keep you then. My wife says I should be in parliament, see, because I'm always talking."

"Better talk than you get in parliament," said Celestine, wanting to pat him like she did his dogs before she headed on up to the hill fort on Long Mountain.

The views from the top, of course, were 'fine', and the hill fort with its interior packed with small beech trees – little gnome-like people she saw them as, and perhaps they had grown out of all the bones of Celts who must be buried there; that was good, but she resented now those bits of the walk when the comforting rise of the Dyke was not beside her or under her as she walked.

The Dyke was home. Home was something that other people had but she hadn't. There was the Victoria flat (but that was later), there were things of hers in Bournemouth but after her Father had had to leave for his job in the islands, Celestine longed to get back to school. It was where she spent most of her time, it was where things were most safe for her. When she got back after holidays her friends would say, "Where have you been?" She would tell them she'd flown here or there or stayed in the London flat and she would ask, "What did you do?" "Oh, just mucked about at home." Celestine wanted to say, "That sounds wonderful," but knew her friends would be mystified. She also wondered what you did when you 'mucked about'.

There was so much time at school, time which was, of course, formally occupied, but in which you could still laze. You could sink into a daydream in a lesson and mostly nobody noticed. The day was structured for you, too – what to do, all that detail. Once you knew how to work the system, it was good knowing what you had to do. Matron's careful talks about washing: "You must strip-wash every morning. Pay particular attention to the area under your breasts and between your legs. Soap them well. Once you get the habit you'll do it every day." Celestine still did, although there was now no need to strip in front of a little tiny washbasin. One could have a shower. Showers hadn't got into Easthurst in her day. There were three baths allowed a week, otherwise it was strip-washing.

Breakfast, when you knew each day exactly what was to be put before you (porridge on five days in winter, cereal on two days and in the summer the reverse, cereal five days, porridge on two). Toast, marmalade, school marmalade which came out of huge stone jars and was scooped onto a plate. Twenty years later, you could conjure up in your mouth the taste of that marmalade distinct and unique. Between breakfast and first lesson there was time, time to begin to look at newspapers. Tidying one's room, of course, had to be done.

Friends occurred naturally, spontaneously. You didn't have to make relationships. They just occurred. And talking was easy. (She would remember this later at dinner parties she so carefully planned, when nobody spoke, and she'd think, why isn't it like school?) School-work, of course, and school activities – "Are you going to be in the play?" "Who's in the hockey team?" All the endless chat about the stars, their personal idiosyncracies repeatedly observed. And then themselves – families, brothers, sisters a bit, but mostly themselves. Who had 'a crush' on who. Celestine never really had a crush on anyone and was unaware of anyone being excited by her.

One felt one's body. First the funny soft downy hair and then firmer rather coarse hair growing on her mound. And breasts – how were your breasts going to be, yours and your friends? Buying a first bra, with the Aunt. The Aunt had been very good at all that, telling you about periods and what to do. And, of course, as soon as you got to Easthurst, Matron talked to you in groups of four or five, and then in Biology more talks about bodily parts. People kept telling you how your body was changing, but not what you did with it when it had changed.

It changed too, as you got older, thought Celestine as she shouldered her pack with some fatigue to press on south from the old Beacon Ring hill fort (Cefyn Digoll). Now she was into Leighton Woods. With her fascination with things Victorian, Celestine would have loved to spend time looking at Leighton House – a Victorian Banker's Gothic reprise to the flaunted established wealth of Powis Castle across the valley. He planted trees from all over the world, there are even great Californian Redwoods lower down. But Celestine had to content herself with Monkey Puzzle trees – the trees on one side of her, the Dyke on the other.

Aristocratic rivalries. All along the border there were knights and lords involved. Chester, Powys, the Mortimers and the Welsh princes. A motley company indeed. The only aristocrat clearly discernible in Carroll's motley crew is the poor Baker's Uncle, a man who probably died just as the party set off on their historic search or hunting. On arrival, the Baker had fainted away during the Bellman's speech.

> They roused him with muffins – they roused him with ice –
> They roused him with mustard and cress –
> They roused him with jam and judicious advice –
> They set him conundrums to guess.

The Baker's Father and Mother were honest though poor and the Baker was named after his Uncle, clearly a substantial man with whom the parents sought to curry favour. They did successfully, hence the 42 boxes (*supra vide*) so carefully packed with his extensive wardrobe. Although he called himself a baker, he couldn't bake, as we know, but what he had done was things like hunt – hence his eagerness to join this hunt. He had experience with wild animals:

> 'His form is ungainly – his intellect small – '
> (So the Bellman would often remark)
> 'But his courage is perfect! And that, after all,
> Is the thing that one needs with a Snark.'

> He would joke with hyenas, returning their stare
> With an impudent wag of the head:
> And he once went a walk, paw-in-paw, with a bear,
> 'Just to keep up its spirits,' he said.

Sheep and cows, the occasional sheep dog and occasional distant farm dog who'd barked at her; but she had seen no real wild animals since the fox, was it two days back now? In Leighton woods you felt you might meet something. Naylor (the builder of Leighton) is said to have had bison and kangaroo released in his woods, but all she met coming along a path was four or five horsemen. She was a bit puzzled by this as there were notices saying no riding in the woods, but the first rider, a woman, gave her good-day and had an air of someone who would not take too much notice of any woodman who tried to turn her off. She was followed by a man in his fifties who nodded but didn't speak and then a boy, maybe fourteen, and a slightly older girl who had a crop which she raised politely and said, "Good afternoon."

Celestine realised she had not yet eaten her sandwich. She hoped to be off the Long Mountain before she stopped. Just then the path left the Leighton Estate and struck down a hollow way which runs beside the Dyke.

It is the earliest evidence that people used the Dyke as a passageway, walking along beside it to one of the few carefully placed gaps. Or more likely simply using it as a North/South track cut through difficult and often heavily-wooded country. Fox measured the depth of the hollow way and assumed that people had walked it for eleven hundred years, calculating that that passage of people had sunk the path by one foot every 64 years.

Further down as the way flattened out, an elderly man had just driven a tractor and cart into a field. Celestine arrived as he was getting down off his tractor now and re-shutting the gate. More confident of the kindness of the borderers, she hailed a good afternoon and asked him what he was doing.

"Hay to pick up," he said, but not in the soft Welsh burr she had been expecting.

"You're not Welsh" she said.

"Not originally."

"Where do you come from?"

"I'm a German."

"How did you end up here?"

He explained that he'd been captured in 1944 and then offered the chance of working on the land. He'd worked here ever since.

"Do you go back?"

"I still have family who live near Mainz."

Mainz, another boundary town on that great natural boundary, the Rhine. Travelling downstream you passed the famous *Lorelei*, the sirens who had lured men onto the rocks – Rhine-maidens. All that stuff of Wagnerian opera had always seemed pretty silly to Celestine and any rate, on this outing from the Frankfurt Book Fair, it wasn't necessary to listen too hard to the details of the scenery.

At the first halt, a fat little man in what looked like a Franciscan tunic had got on the boat. He was some local Bacchus and he sang songs accompanying himself on an accordion. They were German drinking songs and Celestine found herself condemning German drinking songs along with Wagnerian opera. But she couldn't complain about the quality of the six wines they were being offered and she realised her early childhood feelings about the war coloured her feelings about the Germans. Now Germans were people who you could get drunk with on a boat on their borders.

Teutonic peoples, different to the Celtic Welsh but just like the Saxons – Offa's people. The Teutonic peoples appear to have been pressing the Celtic peoples across the Rhine and were only stopped by Julius Caesar and held there by the Romans. But the pressure was formidable in the second century, Teutons were pressing on to the Danube to which the campaigns of Marcus Aurelius gave temporary relief. The Vandals overran Gaul and Spain, with the Franks being pushed westward by the Saxons and on their tails Huns and Goths. The last of the great Teutonic migratory movements were those of Langobardi and Avars who combine to crush the Gepidae. The Gepidae went off to Italy but the Avars remained.

All these Teutonic peoples, Jutes, Saxon and Angles from Denmark pushed into Britain. School-book stuff this, but the pushing of the migrations ended in 794 when they decided, those Teutonic people, to push no more and built what Celestine was standing on while she talked to her German; they built the Dyke, a boundary that recognised they had come to an end. Oh of course, people crossed it, tried to eliminate the Welsh, but they didn't succeed and there they are, still babbling on in that language of theirs, this millennium later.

On the occasion of the enthronement of Charles as Prince of Wales

We have
Given
The Welsh
A nice
Day out
And now
We don't
Want to
Hear any
More of the
Welsh
For years
And years
And years
And
Never
In Welsh.

Still on the Rhine, the well-organised little villages with their clean, tidy houses: these were where the pushy people came from. Those people who combined the mediaeval passion for adventure with the intellectual culture of a modern gentleman. A lover of poetry, of art and of science (we are talking of Frederic Hohenstaufen, a great statesman). He knew how to adapt his policy to changing circumstances and how to move men by appealing at one time to their selfishness and weakness and at another time to the noble qualities of human nature. For outward splendour his position was never surpassed, and before he died he possessed the crowns of Germany, Sicily, Lombardy, Burgundy and Jerusalem (*supra vide*). But of course what he achieved was a negotiated treaty, like Richard before him, to allow the pilgrims peaceful access to Jerusalem.

Dropping the Pilot

Bismarck had long been dissatisfied with his position. The Alliance with the Liberals had always been half-hearted, and he wished to regain his full freedom of action; he regarded as an uncontrollable bondage all support that was not given unconditionally. It was a part of the new policy not only to combat Social Democracy with repression, but to win the confidence of the working men by extending to them the direct protection of the state. The old guilds had been destroyed, compulsory apprenticeship had ceased; little protection was given to working men and the restriction of the employment of women and children were of little use. A few days after the election Bismarck was dismissed from office. The difference of opinion between him and the Emperor was not confined to social reform; beyond this was the more serious question as to whether the Chancellor or the Emperor was to direct the course of government.

With such antecedents, it could be said that the complicated Germans have two very distinct sides to their nature. On the one hand they are powerfully drawn to the rich interior life, to the world of emotion, idealism, privacy, depth and sensitivity – and friendship belongs to this. On the other hand, they are very practical and ambitious admirers of efficiency, order and authority. The two do not easily fit together.

But Hans, as Celestine quickly recognised, was a re-entrant. Hans was keener to tell her about the problems of farming in the border country where he had been born. He had some cousins there but his parents had been killed in the Hamburg raids. But he seemed to bear his adoptive country no grudge for this murder. Any rate he had a Welsh wife.

"Which side of the border do you live?" asked Celestine.

"In Wales," said Hans.

"Do your children speak Welsh then?"

"They learn it at school now."

"I know, but you don't speak it?"

"No."

"That's alright, you're a borderer, you live on the edges."

Hans looked slightly puzzled and they parted company.

Straight back from Mainz, still swilling with wine, and her boss said we need someone to go over to the New York office and get them really sorted out on all this ESL stuff. It's big business.

"Would you like to go? You might have to stay there months."

"Of course, I'd love it."

"Jonathan won't mind?" He had been at their wedding.

"I expect he'll be able to squeeze a month and we can be together."

"Culture shock," they all said. "You've never been to America, you'll get culture shock."

"What's that? Anyhow, I've been in Manhattan on my way to the islands with my father."

"This is living there and you'll find it different. The Americans are just different."

"How? – Like?"

"Well..." But nobody could say quite.

And when you got there, well, into a whirl. Into the office straight away. Fixing up appointments with academics, the first tentative approach to the UN (her idea, they must want ESL) – and is the apartment we found OK? And they were all over her too,

"You're wonderful."

"That's the best publicity idea I've heard this year."

"You put things so concisely."

"You can say things so clearly."

"It's really great to have you here."

"And Friday night Joe's having a party, so you can meet people."

On Saturday collapsing in her apartment. Thank God, it did have what they called a tub. Too short of course, but she could lie in it that morning and pick up the novel, Margaret Drabble's latest, which she'd started on the plane coming over and it was about a different world. The Americans spoke the same language (nearly) but their messages, their body language, was unapproachable. Did they really think she was *great*? Did they like her? Did they mean the things they said? Italians, French, even Germans, you didn't speak their language but you followed their feelings; not this lot.

What did it feel like? She had had the feeling before and as she raked through her memories, it came back to her. It was way back when she was nine arriving in England for the first time and going on a train with her father and silent and uncommunicative Aunt, who was, after all, his wife's sister, and getting to Bournemouth and the cousins, and her father going the next day.

And those people, they were not the same as the people you knew. They were not the same as fat Cook who said: "Sure, you have a biscuit Miss Celly," and those first days at that school in the west country. Of course it had been like Sally's – or rather Sally's had been trying to be like it – but what messages were the other children giving her? They had confused her, but that was because she had nothing to compare them with.

'What it was,' thought Celestine, hotting up the 'tub' with the oceans of simply boiling water Manhattan apartments have, '– or *is*, is it that I don't really have the culture shock they describe, because I was born out of a culture, in a no-man's land. My only culture is my father, restrained, far away, not saying anything much, not expecting to give anyone any messages at all. Except he always gave me a message – he loved me, I knew that, but he was the only one (maybe the Ayah).'

The Dyke passed through a little bit of Forden that was almost suburban, cottages either side and some new bunga-lows – that one was really called *Mon Repose* – but then you were out on great bits of Dyke walking along it. Except for that bloody bit where the landlord refused permission and you had to turn down to a road for three fields, but then you were back on the Dyke. As soon as she was clear of the houses, she stopped for what was by this time her very late lunch. And then strode on to Hem Hill.

The alignment of the Dyke in general may not represent, as I have been disposed to hold, the free choice of a conquering race but a boundary defined by treaty or agreement between the men of the hills and the men of the lowlands. The latter, one would say, although clearly the dominant, did not have matters all their own way. At Leighton, the King of Powys demanded and received a large part of the westward-facing slopes of the Long Mountain.

The afternoon was easier than she thought, the steep slopes ended when you came down off Hem Hill and, although there was probably a slight gradient up to Lymore Park, and down again afterwards to the Bluebell, you felt you were walking on the flat. So she was able to make good time, which was reassuring because tonight was Rupert and Rupert would be ill at ease, awaiting her as he was, far away in Shrewsbury.

Rupert had come to her indirectly from the UN contact. Rupert was at Columbia doing a Master's degree, something to do with the need for English teaching in East Africa. He was a Kenyan, a Masai – tall, big, huge shoulders. The word for Rupert she got at once when she first saw him: he looked *noble*. And when she got to know him, she used the word again about him with a different meaning. He looked noble, he was a noble person.

Noble – *nobyl*, *nobylle*, *nobel*, *nowble*. French: *noble*; Latin: *nobilis*. And for her first (she could have had any one of nine meanings, excluding the tenth – a coin) he was distinguished by splendour, magnificence or stateliness of appearance, of imposing or impressive proportions or dimension. In his grey suits, his body burst through them, you could see the huge solid chest, the great muscles of his shoulders, the strong thighs but also the slenderness he maintained by running. But, until you got to know him, he was 'having qualities or properties of a very high or admirable kind', he was (Dr J.) 'sublime.'

He knew all about the corruption – President Moi's one party state – what had happened to political opponents, the butchering that had gone on. And he could have decided to stay away. But no, he was going back to his country. He, as a black man, was going to work at the Nairobi University. He was going to teach, to administrate, to establish real standards. He despised friends who had settled for an easier option. He had been offered fellowships in Schools of African Studies in Berkeley, Minnesota, Princeton, all across America. If you're a bright, well-educated African they want you. They don't want you if you're a poor benighted sod with AIDS from the shanties around Nairobi. "Bring me to America, help me, but make me go back to Africa," was Rupert's cry.

There was almost something religious in his determination – and, of course, there was: his education had been started by the white fathers and he had been brought up a Catholic but had later vigorously rejected Catholicism. First they colonised us, shopkeepers who wanted to make money out of us, rip us off, and then they said sorry – sorry about colonialism, that was wrong, but our society, our politics, our religion, our whole civilisation is superior to yours, so you must learn from our Marx now, our Nietzsche, our Christ, our Washington, our Lincoln, our United Nations, because we are the cats who know how to get the world working. Well there is something to learn but – shit on them. They shouldn't assume.

And talking, talking, talking that first night with him, there was another assumption that Celestine's warmth, interest, admiration of him was such that she would come back to bed with him. So back she went and there was a moment of controlled tenderness when he said she was beautiful, sensitive, intelligent, and can we make love. But when she said yes, his huge, powerful body overwhelmed her, tearing at her clothes, picking her up naked, lifting her in his arms up high and carrying her to his bed and submerging himself in her, rolling off her and falling at once deeply asleep. While

Celestine lay beside him stroking and feeling the beautiful, firm, dark skin.

It was not good that Jonathan was arriving the week after she had first met Rupert, to spend the middle month of her three months in New York with her. Rupert and Jonathan met at lunch, Celestine had begged Rupert to be sensitive to Jonathan but Rupert couldn't listen or understand anything Jonathan told him about his work. Rupert asked Celestine to go with him to a UN reception that evening and snorted when she said she was sorry she was spending the evening with her husband.

She rang Rupert and said she couldn't see him while Jonathan was in New York and they didn't meet but Rupert rang her daily to talk about African events and despite her instructions only to call her at work, he sometimes rang her apartment. Jonathan stated to her flatly one evening, "You've slept with him," and she did not deny it. Jonathan was not able to make love to her for the rest of his stay. Celestine wept continuously and confusedly and sought relief in working longer and longer hours.

Once you passed Rownal Covert and crossed the Chirbury road the Dyke was level for maybe three fields and then sloped gently down to the Bluebell Inn. Rownal Covert. Here was one of the possible old openings in the Dyke, not as good as the one at Hope which sadly the path by-passed when it went up to Long Mountain. The difficulty of identifying original passageways through the Dyke is that evidences of contemporaneity are entirely destroyed by long-continued use. But at Hope a new cut was made, deflecting the traffic before the original opening was damaged; the flanking terminals are cut back to widen the gap or dug into for material to fill the wheel-ruts; carts then passed to and fro through the Dyke. Tomorrow she must be careful not to miss the opening adjacent to Yr Hen Ffordd, on the Kerry Ridgeway.

On through to the Bluebell. Rupert was not waiting but the Welshpool taxi driver was. Celestine had set up the whole trip to accommodate Rupert, knowing he was at an African Studies meeting at the Commonwealth Institute, but she knew it would occasion too much comment for him to take if she'd made a too-local arrangement. He needed a big hotel and anonymity. So the taxi was to run her all the 20 miles to Shrewsbury. She had even booked two separate rooms because Rupert, with all his arrogance, was still subdued by the forms of the civilisation he affected to despise, not that Celestine had any intention of sleeping alone. Jonathan, when she was back in London, once and once only lost his temper and swore at her, "You're really only a little slut." Celestine had wept again but now she sat in the taxi and smiled and thought maybe I'll leave in my Will an instruction to have that carved on my tombstone: "She was *only* a *little* slut."

The taxi went via Montgomery; it would really have been nice to stay there. She got the driver to swing her through the Georgian Square, picking up the blocked window of the Queen Anne house on the corner and passed Bunners, which looked like a really splendid hardwear shop, in Arthur Street (why Arthur, she wondered, was that a reference to the King?) and then swept out along the Chirbury road which she had crossed a couple of hours earlier.

What had been pleasing was to discover that Shrewsbury boasted a Prince Rupert Hotel. Rupert would probably never have heard of the Prince but he would be flattered to be compared to that Stuart mobster. It was one way to shut him up, curiously, to talk English history at him. He despised everyone in the present but tell him about the past and his guard dropped.

There were two stories about how the wretched East Anglian king, Ethelbert, met his death. He was either murdered by Offa in order to gain his kingdom, or by Offa's Queen who felt jealous of Ethelbert's love for her daughter and sat him on a chair over a trap-door through which he was precipitated down to waiting assassins who stabbed him to death. Well, no matter, here was a nice moral question for Rupert: who would he say was justified in his actions, the

King or the Queen? "Neither, of course," said Rupert, "neither." But Offa murdered for the sake of his kingdom and his wife murdered for love, love of her daughter, an incestuous love maybe but still a genuine love.

From there it was easy to draw Rupert into the lore of the Dyke – or Celestine's lore of the Dyke, her love of the boundary; she could even get him to listen to some poetry about the border before she took him to bed:

> They hear
> way below and far away
> the so-various singing of small free birds
> hidden in green hills
> in a district no longer shown on maps
> and no longer represented
> in the national legislature.

Random Walk

Jonathan had told her there were not enough genes to programme all the nerve cells. There must be therefore activity, he said, random activity, in the brain. It was that random activity that constituted human genius, human activity, it created the men who fought and it created the men who lived in peace, one beside the other. Celestine realised she had used the word 'men' excluding half the human race but, *pace* the Amazons and those ghastly modern armies which encouraged women to join them – some of her feminist friends approved of that – her own feminist feeling was that whether by compulsion or whatever custom, the fact that women had escaped bearing arms was in their favour. So what did her random thought create?

It created the walk down the Dyke. Like peace and war it was a non-random activity, she had a detail of where she should go, where each swing of her leg would take her.

The Dyke itself was non-random. Set out in a predetermined way. The Dyke varies from absolute straightness between two mutually visible points to a winding trace governed by the relief of the countryside. There are three types of method of setting-out:

Type I: Parts of the earthwork which are demonstrably straight between mutually visible points.

Type II: Parts of the earthwork which between two mutually visibly points are sinuous but which at no point markedly diverge from a straight line.

Type III: Parts of the earthwork which, within the broad limits of general direction, are sensitive to the relief of the countryside.

The overall designer and his engineer had a clear purpose,

which they achieved. Celestine's expedition down the Dyke also had a purpose, even though she was unsure what that purpose was. At least she had a predetermined route carefully set out for her in her Offa's Dyke notes. She checked her day's route and slipped them into the outer pocket of her rucksack where they nestled comfortably beside Martin Gardner's *Annotated Snark*.

The poor crew who had accompanied the Bellman on his quest had no such help. The Bellman's travels were random. The Bellman, who they all praised to the skies, with his carriage and his ease and his grace. Indeed his solemnity. Indeed his very face looked wise but his navigation on the famous trip was completely random:

> He had brought a large map representing the sea,
> Without the least vestige of land:
> And the crew were much pleased when they found it to be
> A map they could all understand.
>
> 'What's the good of Mercator's North Poles and Equators,
> Tropics, Zones, and Meridian Lines?'
> So the Bellman would cry: and the crew would reply,
> 'They are merely conventional signs!

All this was quite charming no doubt but as the crew very shortly found out, the captain who they trusted so well had only one notion for crossing the ocean and that was to tingle his bell. When they landed at last on a wild shore with a view consisting of chasms and crags the Bellman was certain they were in just the place for a Snark. This allows the reader to be certain that the Snark in fact is a common creature to be found anywhere and could be achieved by the random journey the Bellman's crew had undertaken. Celestine was seeking something rarer, she was seeking consummation – something she much desired and which no-one had yielded to her yet.

Rupert, of course, had thought that he was going to be that consummation. Celestine needed to sleep but he had woken her at four or five wanting to talk and hoping that his summoning by Celestine meant that she had changed her mind. He didn't even know that she had divorced Jonathan. He had tried to get her to stay on in New York, of course, and marry him. She had refused, gone back to London to Jonathan. Ironically, Rupert's attitude to Jonathan had been one factor which had made her uneasy with Rupert, while Rupert, of course, had led to the break-up with Jonathan. To Rupert, Jonathan was a mere technician. He had no real time for scientists, engineers and doctors. "Experts – you can hire experts!" Celestine was unable to get anything of the excitement of Jonathan's work over to Rupert. "They're unravelling the whole human genome." But that was nothing to Africa; and Rupert, he seemed to feel that the rest of the world should pause while Africa was succoured and Celestine could not get him to see that creativity like Jonathan's mustn't, couldn't stop. She couldn't handle the ambiguities of his attitudes. He did not mind when she went to hear some African rap poets at the Y but when she spent an evening there listening to Fred Voss, he was furious. But Fred's a great poet, she said, he writes about work. He comes out of an environment.

And here was Rupert, convinced that she had asked him to meet her because she had changed her mind and understood she was designed and ordained to be Rupert's help-mate. Why else had she summoned him? She tried to explain she had summoned him for his presence, to help her decide her plan for association, for consummation, in the rest of *her* life, not for the rest of *his*.

Celestine was going to miss that sleep; today was her longest day. She needed to be at the Bluebell Inn early if she was going to make Knighton by six or seven that evening. Rupert she deposited at Shrewsbury station at 8.30am where her friendly Welshpool taxi driver had arrived to take her back to the Bluebell. She kissed him (Rupert, not the taxi driver) and told him to forget she existed. Allow me to disappear. *Consumatum Est.* Rupert stood perplexed, unsure, watching the taxi nudge out of the station as it headed along the river to the Welsh Bridge.

Celestine bade a more friendly farewell to the Welshpool taxi man who expressed willingness to pursue her down the Dyke as her ferry car. But tonight she would be in Knighton and was staying there.

Celestine stood for a moment by the disued petrol pump in front of the Bluebell. She rather wished the friendly landlady would pop out. When she had arrived last night the taxi had been sitting outside the pub, but the driver had been inside. He had grinned at Celestine, "It's alright, I'm only drinking juice, but do you want a drink first?" and the ever-thirsty Celestine had drunk a quick shandy. She had time to be introduced to the landlady, Helen, and her sister, Alice, who was behind the bar and, Celestine suddenly realised, had something wrong with her. "One of them Down's Syndrome children, see, and Helen looks after her," the driver had informed her.

Now Celestine would have been pleased to see either of them. For the first time, she found herself lonely. It was because she had dismissed Rupert; her other lovers she had parted from but Rupert she knew she would see no more. She pressed through the gates of Mellington Hall and found her way to the Dyke itself which climbed up through the woods for a little. There was a curious moment here when she passed a caravan site only maybe fifteen yards away through the trees. There were children shouting, dogs barking, parents calling instructions, all unaware, Celestine thought, of her passing them. Almost she could have been one of Offa's own people, looking through time into another century, another age.

Time was another factor in love, thought Celestine, there was her great friend the retired architect, Raymond, living so comfortably with his wife, Sylvia. He had driven her to the train and on the way there he had been telling her tales of the drovers' roads (*infra vide*) and she had suddenly interrupted him and said, "Raymond, how old are you actually?" and he had said, "Nobody will believe how old I am, I'm eighty."

And Celestine had thought to herself, if you had been born in my generation, I would have married you because of your kindness, but we are in the wrong time.

It was steep, steep again but she also detected (as she had indeed yesterday) that the character of the Dyke was changing. All along that bit further north there had been faint signals of the Dyke. She had displayed an old-fashioned timidity, a bashfulness. But here, in mid-Wales, there had been that long stretch yesterday afternoon with a firm line on Celestine's left all the way, of the Dyke herself, and today she was on it, big and strong as it swept across these deserted hills. There were groups of packers passing her to greetings and discussion as always about their progress. They had spent the night at Middle Knuck. Four pairs of packers she passed. Two boys together first going hard and fast, then two girls steady, and then two couples. No singles, thought Celestine.

When you reached the top of Kerry Hill you came to the Kerry Ridgeway which Raymond had been telling her about. The present Ridgeway cuts through the Dyke but beyond it a few yards south, the Dyke abruptly terminates in what is manifestly one flank of an original but very narrow opening. The Ridgeway, more ancient surely than the Dyke, was a high path out of Wales into England. More time had to be spent here because of what Raymond had told her about the drovers' roads. This had been one of the main roads along which the drovers had taken their charges slowly (because you mustn't rush sheep, cows, geese) out of Wales into England, to Oxford and to London, where the animals had of course been slaughtered.

The drovers must have been substantial men. And honest they had to be – they brought back with them to the farmer his money. Here, though, at the narrow passageway on the Dyke what a mewling and bawling there would have been. The terrified animals beaten and driven until at last everybody was beyond the Dyke. And when you got beyond the Dyke yourself finding that some of your animals had scattered and you had to search and round them up again.

Of course you ate well but you worked hard for it. On days like today, with the weather that Celestine was favoured with, it would have been a great life, but when wet and windy, not so good. And what had they worn? Celestine could only imagine the trappings of Royalty, and dressed her ghostly company in the contents of an acting box drawn from Shakespeare's day. On this lonely, empty day she found it hard to envisage the great crowd of animals and people streaming through the narrow gap in the Dyke on the Kerry Ridgeway. But they did get through, Wales communicated here with England. Independent free peoples talking to each other.

Independence. When you got into the sixth form at Easthurst, you were told now was the time you learnt to be independent, self reliant. Now you learnt who you were. "In these next two years you are going to stop being a child and you are going to become an adult. That adult will be a distinctive person and with that personality you will make your mark on the world. You will find what your vocation is going to be in life. That is what we want you to achieve here at Easthurst."

One didn't feel much freer. There was now the possibility of going out on bicycles in pairs to the local village shops – if that was independence. There were far fewer regular lessons scheduled, there was more reading on your own and suddenly there was a great deal of work to do – history texts to read and essays to write – if you were going to do well in exams and get onto college and university.

There were discussions about relationships, relationships to do with men, but little was said about the fact that in your search for identity you achieved some sort of *sexual* identity. But passion now was part of your life and in their study bedrooms girls had up photos not only of their family but of stars, pop stars mainly, who they related to. Celestine listened to pop music but never formed a passion for a singer; she secretly admired, loved, some of the tennis stars. She wanted to be just standing by those fair young Australian knights, she wanted to be rewarded with a glance and selection from the crowd, to be the one to walk off holding his hand. There were long fantasies of conversation when you told him how splendid he was and he told you how beautiful you were and you were still just holding hands.

The girls of whom one was aware but not really jealous, were those girls who had real boyfriends who wrote them letters, who went out with them in the holidays. Girls who had been kissed by boys. Now in the Christmas holidays at Bournemouth there was going to be a dance and it was no longer just John, the cousin, who chatted to you so easily, but boys who were quite different people, from another world, another planet. How did you talk to them, what did you talk about? Actually, same old things – what school you were at, what exams you were doing, what games you played, where you lived, what your dad did. But there was going home in the car, being squashed up to a boy who had his arm around you and was kissing the side of your face while you just looked straight ahead and he lacked the courage to bring his face round and kiss you on the lips.

At school there were now meetings of various sorts with boys from nearby boys' schools. Because of her liking for the teacher Celestine was doing biology in the sixth form along with history and English. She became Secretary of the Natural History Society and, greatly daring, suggested meetings with the local private boys' school. It was approved and after teacher-contact she was instructed to write off and make arrangements with the Secretary of the Biology Society. She felt she was corresponding with one of those handsome blond tennis players but when they met he was short, dark and barely an adult, a late-maturing boy who constantly took on and off his spectacles, seemed to sweat a lot and talked about bugs.

"How did you get on with ghastly Specs then?" her friends asked. But there were other boys – there was a tall fair boy who 'Specs' told her wasn't really interested in biology – he's really into games, tennis, all that – and on a field trip she was walking beside him; they were supposed to be watching out for trees with mosses on them. They didn't see any and they didn't talk much but at the end of the afternoon, he suddenly said,

"You're not at all like Specs."

"You all call him that too!"

"Yes, of course."

For years Celestine could never understand how anyone could want their children educated in single sex schools when they needed, wanted, so much to have those contacts, and she could hardly bare to remember her own embarrassed early conversations with boys. But at least Aunt saw to some of that, and in the summer now, John's Friends, Gilly's friends, meant that by the time she went to college she was able to talk and approach men with some degree of ease.

It wasn't only men you admired but there were women you wanted to be like. Celestine's father had taken her to the ballet and she had seen Margot Fonteyn. She dreamt of that elegance, that composure, even though she was already too tall and beyond any chance of becoming a ballerina; but she could try and stand still and tall, stately, step carefully, not as formerly with her eyes held down, but now looking steadily ahead with her arms moving slowly and gracefully. At least, she could when she remembered! She saw few films, there was no television, so she didn't have more icons to emulate, but there were the heroines of fiction. Elizabeth Bennet, that incredibly sensible girl, who achieved marriage to this handsome, wealthy stranger; Celestine could sit for hours and go over the mannered conversation not reported by Jane Austen when she talked to Mr Darcy, after she had finally accepted him. There was the unresolved problem, what did she call him? Surely she must have stopped saying Mr Darcy at some point, but Fitzwilliam was an awkward name to develop into any pleasant romantic diminutive. (Fitz?)

Darcy was in her rucksack: there because Celestine had suddenly thought that since that repetitive reading at seventeen she had never looked at the book and she had wondered whether it would retain its magic for her – but she had not read it at all on the walk. Her attention was given to her guide books, maps and lovers. This section of the route, with the Dyke so splendidly prominent, was easy to follow. She had dipped down into one valley bottom where there had been a large bull who she had skirted round but after one look he had just returned to his grazing. Then there was a very steep climb beside a wood across Edenhope Hill and down into Churchtown.

Reading the name on the route plan she had searched the map for Churchtown thinking it must be a town but when you reached it there were two cottages and a splendid little church which she visited. The roof was said to be home to a large colony of rare bats and she peered up at the beams with the binoculars she carried but she could see nothing of the famed colony. So on up to Middle Knuck.

There is a little problem around Middle Knuck. From Middle Knuck the Dyke presents a nearly straight alignment down the slope to Hergan (a cottage holding) and Ffynnon-y-sant, which wells out of the bank. Though damaged near the house beyond it is in good condition, as large as it ever is on a steep slope. It crosses open pasture on a new alignment, direct but not quite straight, but then abruptly turns round a spur. There is no clear immediate reason for this abrupt turn, a right angle not usually seen on the smooth and sinuous Dyke. But Fox has the answer to the Hergan angle.

There were two gangs at work between Middle Knuck and Hergan. The gang which carried out the Hergan section had its own way of doing things: it finished on the Hergan col as instructed and left the gang to the North to join up when they got there. The Hergan men were building the Dyke on a west-ward-facing slope and they continued on this work to the bitter end. The connection was the affair of the Middle Knuck gang and not theirs. The Middle Knuck gang turned their banks through a right angle and made a neat job of it before downing tools. No mention again, of course, of who was in these gangs that built these defensive Dykes, these borders for the Mercian king.

The Scenery

Scott wrote all those long paragraphs about the scenery in the glens. One did look at views but what to say about what you saw? Above Prestatyn the whole sweep of coastline going round, round to that huge Mersey haze and seeing some towers – were they the Phoenix towers in Liverpool? – anyway you felt like an astronaut viewing the world from space, knowing it really was round. Or the domestic view coming down the Hollow Way from the Long Mountain and pausing to lean over a gate. Foreground of fields (with sheep) and oddly shaped fields, no grid system here, and across the valley nestling on the hill, Powis Castle, hard to find even with the binoculars.

Coming down onto Hay-on-Wye, a map in front of you spread out. Looking out to see – the blue with the haze, the sea is always a view, the blue, the battleship grey. Yes, these are views.

But chiefly the Dyke. The steep rises, the rolling mid-sections, the steep drops down, and beside you or under you this whale-back-hump traversing the landscape, drawing your eye inwards towards it, not outwards to the distant hills or the sea or the river basins but inwards to the Dyke, the Dyke.

Celestine was a re-entrant when she came back from her three months in New York. She hoped to re-establish herself with Jonathan and for a period she did; at least she was back in their flat and if there was an uneasiness between them neither let it show. But Rupert and New York had other effects on Celestine. She felt her life was too easy, she had drifted into publishing, and ESL had become her subject and suddenly it was growing at a huge rate. She was part of the boom.

But did she deserve to be? That puritan Easthurst vocational bit came through. Here she was, over 30, already expert in her field. And she had never even taught, let alone taught English. She was restive in London, restive in her job, restive with Jonathan. Maybe she was over the Rupert affair, maybe she was, but she could feel the pressure building up on the baby front. Did she want a child? Yes, she did, she had a great desire for a child, which she wanted to fulfil, but at the same time, she did not feel that the consummation she was looking for – simply achieving one's biological potential – was enough: the random walk had to lead her somewhere else. It had to take some non-random direction.

So what did she do? Something sudden of course, a deliberate change of direction. She came to the flat one night where Jonathan was quietly working, cooked a meal for them, and after two glasses of wine, said suddenly to Jonathan,

"Next month, I'm going to Zimbabwe."

"How long for?"

"A year, at least; I'm going to teach English in a school in Harare. I have to get out of my rut. I have to do something different to what I'm doing."

It was later that night that Jonathan, after several more glasses of wine, lost his equanimity and called her a slut.

"But I'm going to teach. But you don't have to wait for me. Do what you like while I'm away." It was a way of saying their marriage could end.

Celestine recognised in herself a need to nest. She believed that the lark might be the bird who best expressed her need – her need to nest and her need to sing. As she walked, alone on the open Dyke, larks rose up beside her to sing. The larks hovered in the air beside her pouring out that song that attracted the poets. Truth to tell, Celestine had always found the singing rather disappointing, a fluted whistling on a narrow range of notes. Yet look at the sauciness of the tiny bird, attempting, or so it seemed to her, to produce in these wide spaces all the blossom of an orchestra.

The sound was lost but look at the occasion; the lark rose to protect its nest, to distract the invader, to offer some defence against an intruder. And for that defence it had no armament, it had no weapon, no rockets, no guns, only a song – that was what she tried to offer with her body. Something to distract the stranger from the bitterness the world had to offer. She offered to sing, she offered some *joie*. She did not wish to tell him that what she wanted was a nest and not a song. But if he wanted to nest could she still sing?

I now wonder why the Wyoming whippoorwill
The Shropshire lark, the glittering Oxford tree,
Jangle boughs no more and no more execute music
Near me or for me or to me...
....

I recall the advent of my right hand
Fluttering with olive branch like dove
I recall that the Shropshire lark alighted
Like love on my lips, and went within.
....

But until I hear the whipperwill lark sing again,
Or the dove revisits my right hand, and the tree
Springs like a branch from my finger, I continue.
Inclining my ear to the bosom of evenings,
Listening like water diviner for words,
Wondering why the heart's decay
Makes me no pearls, no lovely bubbles,
What have I done that takes my birds away?

Further on, Celestine had word of other life on the Dyke: somewhere between Clun and Knighton, she had found a little notice saying teas, and hastening up the small road the Dyke was crossing, she had found a cottager who willingly poured her a cup of tea while she rested on one of his garden chairs and drank it there, not wanting to take her boots into what seemed to be a traditional little front parlour.

Round the side of his cottage friendly hens came pecking, and mindful of her encounter two days back, she asked if his hens were troubled by foxes. "Not usually," said the man, "there's an earth up on that hill and one over that side too but they don't come near me or my birds. They know me, leave me alone; hunt outside this area and I'll leave them alone. But I'll tell you, two months back, I had to shoot four, five foxes and I'll tell you the way of it. One day, late afternoon, a couple of young women stopped like you've done for a cup. They had a young driver and a van they hired. They tell me what they'd been doing. They'd been helping foxes. Over in the city, Birmingham, somewhere like that, there'd been these city foxes, rubbish sacks, odd kittens I dare say, well people had been for killing them but they said no, they'd release them in the wild. So council had trapped five foxes and they brought them up here; they just driven in a field and let them go."

"Well, what happened?"

"Well, I tell you, those city foxes they had no sense. Started taking my hens, and at the farm up the road. Well we couldn't have that. And they were running around in broad daylight. So of course, we had to get 'em. I shot two. Him up the farm, he shot two, that was the end of them city foxes. So I reckon those ladies did no good with their Green Party – that was what they were.

"Do you know, I'll tell you something else that struck me as funny. That van they had hired with the driver. Well, where did he come from? I'll tell you, he was a Turk, had lived in Germany but had moved out of there, and here he was driving a van and bringing foxes out to the borders here. I bet he thought that was a funny one. I reckon these Turks the sort of people that might eat foxes. Anyway, he wasn't complaining, seeing he got paid for the job."

A *Gastarbeiter* for Celestine. Her press had done books for them, or rather she had sold some of their titles to a German publisher. The German publisher did *German Made Easy*. But some of them, like the young van-driver, had wanted *Easy English* and Celestine had sold them ESL books. There were over a million Turks living in Germany and she had seen some of their communities. The Turks had made previous attempts to get into Germany but this invasion – peaceful and tolerated on the whole (the average German attitude is one of polite indifference or grumbling contempt).

That first wave of Turkish invasion was after the Teutons and never got as far. The Turks approached Europe from south of the Caspian Sea. In 1063 the Seljuks had crossed the Euphrates and in 1084 occupied Asia Minor; Jerusalem was captured in 1071. After the lapse of two centuries, the Osmanli or Ottomans began a fresh advance from Phrygia, gradually establishing themselves in the Balkan Peninsula. Macedonia was occupied in 1373; in 1385 they extended northwards and took Sophia, and in 1453 Constantinople. Nearly a century later, they conquered Hungary which was under Turkish dominance from 1552 to 1687. That was the Turks that was!

But the Turks living in Germany now are invited guests. Around rail stations you find them, in small shops, running restaurants. First they came to work only, intending to go back home but, then, when recession came, if they left Germany, they couldn't come back. "German money being sweeter than Turkish honey," one Turk is reported as saying. So instead of going back to their Turkish homeland, they sent for their wives and daughters.

There they are on the front line in Germany. The girls do smell, said one teacher, because the Koran says it's immodest for girls to be naked so they only take one bath a week. They tend to take menial jobs such as sweepers and refuse collectors or in mines or on building sites. Always they have to think about families. Very few Turks let their daughters, once aged thirteen or more, go swimming with boys. "My father would never let me marry a German, it's against Islam."

"I'm second generation, I came here as a small girl with my father who makes furniture. I'm married to a Turk who is culturally integrated so he doesn't try to dominate me. I'd never stand for that."

Most second-generation Turkish marriages split up, however, simply because the women have become emancipated in Germany, they earn their own living and won't accept the usual role of a Turkish wife.

"In every way things were tougher for my father's generation: they had language problems, and the Germans were more xenophobic in those days. For us it's easier but we have a new problem of identity. Are we Turkish or German? We cherish our own culture and religion but we see positive things in European society, especially for women. Many women who go back to Turkey just can't cope anymore with the restrictions, at least not in the provinces – it's easier in Istanbul or Ankara. We, who plan to stay in Germany, intend to work out a middle way between Turkish female subservience and German excess of liberty."

It's called living on the borders. When the Dyke gets up above the valley of the Teme, you are looking down on the valley with Knighton in it, a Saxon town started behind the Dyke. The Welsh came to it because they gave it a name, Tref-y-Clawydd, 'Town on the Dyke'. Panpunton Hill you skirt along, and slowly below you Knighton appears, and down in Knighton Craig would be waiting for Celestine.

Craig was someone her father had met in some part of the world but he was now a lecturer in Zimbabwe. Celestine had thought of him therefore as an old man – by definition one's father is old. But Craig was younger than her father, not that much younger, so he was older – ten, fifteen years older – than Celestine. He was approaching fifty, she just past thirty.

The notion of the aid agency was that Celestine would spend two months in Harare and then would be dispatched to a village secondary school. But Craig said, "You cannot do that, you'd be destroyed. If you teach, teach here in Harare." Celestine, of course, said no, she wanted to teach in a rural area where the people really needed her help. So Craig arranged for her to go out and spend a week teaching in such a school. He sent her to one where there was already an expat, Peter from Minnesota, who would show her how things went. Craig drove her there in his old Ford Transit, a luxury, a car which went and didn't belch black fumes.

And after a week, Celestine had to admit that she felt

Craig was right. The living was hard: the Blair toilet which kept the flies down but had this long drop (you were supposed to hit the frogs); the insects attracted by the hurricane lamp; fifty miles to the nearest phone; the tiny room; the bats at night. All that would have been bearable but the teaching was so hard.

The pupils had often walked many miles to school, they were keen, wanted to learn. They wanted to achieve an 'O' Level (an important examination from Britain); with an 'O' Level in English, they could maybe get to the town, get a job, become a teacher themselves. Indeed some of the African teachers here had only an 'O' Level in English and came to her to get her to teach them to get an 'A' Level. But the students were most depressing to her because 90 per cent of them would not get an 'O' Level in English, as Peter pointed out. Men of twenty were in her class seeking the elusive exam. But coming from an illiterate background, speaking Shona as their main language and English poorly, barely writing, with no idea of composition, what use was her English degree to them? And the Head teacher stealing the money for the library books and sleeping with his female students.

"The Mashona, the Mashona." They were there when the Matabele came. They were there when the white men came. They were the people of the border (they crept out to watch as the Bellman landed his crew; they knew what was to come). They were the people who Offa found when he looked to see who he could drive out of their huts (women and children too) to build with antler pick and wooden shovel his great earthwork. The earth loaded into buckets up on the hills and hauled up by hand to the top of his great Dyke. What did he offer them? Food? Drink?

And the white men? They came and they took land – Mashona land of course. They wished to farm but the Mashona (lazy niggers) wouldn't work. They had their own work to do, and besides, the white man was only offering them money. Money? What was that for? The Mashona had no money and needed none. Ah, but white men in a big city solved that. They put a tax on each and every Mashona hut. A Hut-Tax which had to be paid. There were soldiers: so the Mashona worked by day. By night they cared for their huts, their cattle, their people.

So Celestine went back convinced, and ended up in a secondary school in Harare, teaching students who had more chance of success. Many were children of government people, politicians or civil servants, often themselves corrupt but still believing that the secret of life for their own children was education. There was some semblance for Celestine of the teaching that she had had herself fifteen years before.

So then some sort of social life in Harare, mixing inevitably with ex-pats, university people, and finding herself fending off young local teachers who would declare passionate love to her, so that social gatherings around the school became a pain. Leaving her in consequence spending more and more time with Craig. His wife had half left him, gone back to America with their children to get them a proper education. But she sensed (although Craig never spoke of it) that when his family were over for holidays, his relationship with his wife involved no intimacy. Craig was endlessly kind to her, kindness personified.

Kind. Forms: *secynde, kynde, kynd, kuynde,* with ten definitions to choose from. Naturally well-disposed, having a gentle, sympathetic or benevolent nature, ready to assist, or show consideration for others, generous, liberal, courteous. Or affectionate, loving, fond. Or acceptable, agreeable, pleasant, winsome. Or soft, tender, easy to work with. Craig fitted all of them (except was he winsome?). He worked incredibly hard in the English department at the university and found time to help many of the young teachers who flooded to him for advice. And he worked with the book agency which tried to get books into Africa. *Kind: benevolent, fitted with general goodwill* (the Doctor).

He was away for two weeks down in Cape Town for some meeting of the Book Trust. And when he came back, he had called in advance and said let's have supper together at my house. It was such a relief to know he was in town again. Someone dependable. When she went round that evening, she fell into his arms embracing him, so pleased to see him, but suddenly realised that these welcoming embraces were giving a message to Craig which she had not intended or planned but which was pleasing to her. He was a gentle lover, saying as he slid into her, "Does that please you, Celestine?" and when she unveiled her eyes and said, "Yes," that alone was almost enough to bring him to orgasm.

She didn't move in with him, she maintained her room; but nor did they bother to conceal they were lovers, perplexing for the Africans who thought if you were not married you were a prostitute – but then they accepted Europeans did things differently. The fact that she was Craig's mistress gained her a curious respect and afforded her some protection from the enthusiastic young men who had crowded around her.

Her father came out to visit her at Easter. She wondered if he guessed at her relationship with Craig; if so he kept his guesses to himself. He stayed with Craig and Celestine went dutifully home every night during the fortnight he was there. The judge was a constant in her life and it was on his visit that she realised what an affection she had for him and realised how important her existence was to him. Of course, he would never say anything of that but the last night of his visit, he did say, "I hope you won't stay more than your year, Celestine. I worry about you here. All the diseases, and politically... I'm getting back to London more often too." And Celestine suddenly thought, when I'm not there my father is lonely. He is a solitary and I'm his only real lasting relationship.

The publishing company had given her a year's leave of absence, encouraging her to get this teaching experience but holding her job open for her. And she missed her friends. She found it difficult to form close friendships here because people saw you in transit. She missed the intimacies of talk with Joan, Sylvia, other friends, which Craig, for all his kindness, could not replace. There were intimacies that developed between women which were different, Celestine thought, than those which developed between men. There were concerns about each other which could be displayed and discussed that excluded men from the conversation.

Craig and she had parted sorrowfully. He had given her a beautiful garnet necklace which she loved. She longed to see him again and was glad that tonight she had her most sympathetic lover. The Dyke made a most unusual turn which brought you onto a crest which led along Panpunton Hill where you looked down at Knighton. It was a very steep descent and then you crossed the River Teme and made your way along its bank before turning up into town. She found then that there were two steep flights of steps to climb – quite short, but suddenly she found herself exhausted, and when she entered the field it was wonderful to see Craig strolling and then catch sight of her and hurry over. Once again, to fall into his arms with relief and to allow him to take off her rucksack and carry it for her down to the hotel.

How curious to find that the past can reassure the future. Talking of all those old friends and acquaintances in Zimbabwe suddenly made that whole year one of pleasant adventure. Here was her Prospero again and she could with honesty love him.

> O! Never say that I was false of heart,
>   Though absence seem'd my flame to qualify
>   As every night I from myself depart
> As from my soul which in thy breast doth lie.
> This is my home of love: if I have rang'd
> Like him that travels, I return again.

Violence in the Family

The good thing about Craig was that now you were no longer lovers you could talk to him about your affairs. Perhaps it was after all possible to have intimacies with a man, a thing you had previously regarded as impossible. Any rate, you could talk to Craig about Rupert and his demands and Craig thought it was funny which was a curious relief. The mismatch between Rupert and Jonathan amused him, the Black African Knight, he said, with the White English Bishop. And he said seriously, "They held you in check. It was good you got out of them." "There was nothing wrong with Jonathan." "But he wasn't right for you."

Knighton took little exploring in the morning although they paid a visit to the old school which was the headquarters of the Offa's Dyke Society and paced round the exhibition. They each bought Society badges. Craig was keen to walk on the Dyke and Celestine encouraged him to climb Panpunton Hill from which she had descended yesterday. The opening of the Southern Route which she would take today was wooded and she thought she would not find the magnificent views which she had had the evening before. Craig walked her through the back streets of the town and watched her set off up up through the trees as she headed on south to the Newcastle Rings, Burfa Camp (both of which earthworks Offa ignored) and Kington.

In any event, it was time to let Craig go. He had been a lifeline and a comfort while she had been accepting that she had let Jonathan go. Before she went to Zimbabwe, after she had told him she was going, she had 'cracked up' she supposed was the only way to describe it. She had found herself constantly weeping, waking Jonathan at night saying, "I do love you, I do love you. I'm sorry about Rupert, I was wrong, wrong, wrong." Jonathan had not been very good at that. There seemed to him to be nothing to say. Joan was sharing a flat at this point with Sylvia. Joan had explained that Sylvia was butch and "that's good, puts men off" and "I have some time to myself." Sylvia was a tall, strong girl, she did weight-lifting to keep herself in shape and she worked in that most male of environments, a garage, where she was a fully trained mechanic. But her presence made Joan less available as a comforter and advisor.

She even went once or twice to a church. Her father had been a non-believer and had bred into Celestine a good deal of cynicism about church and church-going, while sending his daughter off to schools where a 'Christian upbringing' was part of the agenda. That famed biology teacher at Easthurst had also influenced her never attending chapel, commenting airily to Celestine once: "I could never believe that beetles or any other animal for that matter had souls and I can't conceive that man is anything but an animal. It seems there will be nothing left of me therefore to go to heaven or hell and I remain therefore essentially uninterested in the landlords of such establishments."

But Celestine went into a church one Sunday thinking maybe I'll talk to the parson afterwards. But he seemed to Celestine a fool with his text for the day and such a lot of bowing and scraping to various religious objects in such a way (she had walked into a High Anglican service) that the whole performance disgusted her and she slid out before the service ended to avoid the embarrassment of having to meet the man. So she had left for Zimbabwe tearful about Jonathan but unresolved. He had written to her formal little letters enclosing mail, finding himself unable to write about their relationship.

So, thought Celestine, what did I do? I really bitched him. She sent him a postcard on which she wrote: "I am having an affair. Do you mind?" To which Jonathan had not replied. He forwarded her mail without comment.

She didn't tell him when she was getting back and went straight to her father's flat in Victoria. But on the first Saturday she went over to their apartment: Jonathan's and her apartment. She stood outside the door for some time and then, greatly daring, got out her key and went in. It was about half-past three in the afternoon and there was no-one: but there had been recently. They had eaten some pasta for lunch and drunk two-thirds of a bottle of Spanish Rioja. The glasses on the table were her glasses, some she'd seen in a shop in the Loire Valley long ago and her father had given them to her. She went to the bedroom, two people had clearly slept there, indeed there were a skirt and blouse tossed on the bed. A dirty bra and pants mixed in with a pile of dirty shorts of Jonathan's.

On Monday she went to the Post Office and put in a Re-direct for the mail of Mrs Celestine Jones as well as the mail of Celestine Quareine. She was tempted but did not take the glasses. A month later she sent Jonathan another postcard simply saying she was back in London and "I can be contacted at the Victoria address." She did not expect a reply and got none. *Finis*. Was that why this ten-years-or-so later she was walking the Dyke?

Walking, travelling, moving, those were all activities she liked. She didn't really like to be stationary for long. She liked her own long legs, liked to use them to walk. She walked fast, she always had, taking those long paces, and here she was, climbing as ever, up Frydd Hill between the Great and Little Frydd Woods. The Dyke constructed on a grand scale in Knighton is scarcely more than a hedge bank in the wood but at the south corner of field 40 the Dyke is a little larger and the improved scale continues in fields 41 and 42. On the boundary between these fields the Dyke is irregular and spoil holes are seen on the west side. The end of this is a crest line and is marked by pine trees.

On passing it the Dyke presents a completely altered character, both bank and ditch being on the grand scale. The contrast is dramatic; a patch of scrub separates a bank and ditch so small that it might easily escape notice from a high rampart and a deep west ditch 60 feet overall and 28 feet on the scarp. That this change – both of scale and character – takes place on a crest line, a spot as easily recognised as the col at Hergan is significant; and it is most fortunate that the junction has escaped serious damage. The stretch from the valley to this point was undoubtedly the work of the Cwmsancham-Panpunton Hill gang as the east ditch shows.

Craig had been curious about her trip; unlike the others, who had thought only of themselves, Craig had wanted to know what she was up to. He had questioned her about the books she was carrying. "Travelling light, I know, Celestine, but you never go anywhere without a book. What are you carrying?" And Celestine had to confess to her two slim volumes, *Pride and Prejudice* and *The Annotated Snark*. "An ill-assorted pair," had been Craig's comment. "They are both travelling somewhere: one eminently sensible and one absurdly insane. The *Snark* is the first truly modern poem – people talk about Hopkins with all his technical skills but the content, the content; the *Snark* is about the future."

There were dangers on the trip for all members of the crew. Not only external dangers from the Bellman's incompetent navigation but dangers within the crew itself. In particular there was the situation that involved the Beaver and the Butcher. What was the Beaver aboard for anyway? The Bellman said that it had often saved them from wreck though none of the sailors knew how. The Beaver paced the deck or sat making lace in the bow. In the end the lace was the only product from the whole trip. Indeed initially the Beaver went on making lace when the others had actively started to seek for the Snark. The Barrister was shocked by this and tried to appeal to its pride and vainly proceeded to cite a number of cases in which making lace had been proved an infringement of right.

In addition to the incompetent Baker who was unable to bake them any useful provision, the Bellman had engaged another provider who was to prove incompetent and who needs especial remark – he had just one idea, but, that one being 'Snark', the good Bellman engaged him at once.

> He came as a Butcher: but gravely declared,
> When the ship had been sailing a week,
> He could only kill Beavers. The Bellman looked scared,
> And was almost too frightened to speak:
>
> But at length he explained, in a tremulous tone,
> There was only one Beaver on board:
> And that was a tame one he had of his own,
> Whose death would be deeply deplored.
>
> The Beaver, who happened to hear the remark,
> Protested, with tears in its eyes,
> That not even the rapture of hunting the Snark
> Could atone for that dismal surprise!

The Beaver advised that the Butcher should be conveyed in a separate ship; the Bellman refused this proposal. The Baker suggested the Beaver should procure a secondhand dagger-proof coat while the Banker offered for hire excellent policies, one against fire and one against damage from hail. However, whenever the Butcher was by, the Beaver kept looking the opposite way and appeared unaccountably shy.

The Beaver, Celestine had always noted, was referred to as 'it'. Was this another example of Carroll's avoidance of anything sexual in his work? She had even laboured through *Sylvie and Bruno* (and *Sylvie and Bruno (Concluded)*). The childish couple were half fantasies of an adult couple who did indeed marry but their courtship was conducted as if they were children and their bodies didn't intrude into the relationship in anyway. Celestine thought she would like to add ten women to the crew that hunted the Snark. All the names of the crew began with B and the girls' names would begin with C. Joan used a four letter C word pretty freely though it was a word that some feminists would not use. Celestine liked it as a term of abuse, liked it as a term for part of her body.

Ralph had called her cunt all the time and she had loved it and he had meant it too, partly to imply that she was simply his sexual object – and for a time that had been what she wanted. Nothing more. She had been for him the truly compliant lover feeding the ego-trip he was continuously pursuing. She couldn't conceive now how she had behaved in the way she had. Well she would meet him tonight and maybe he would explain himself. She feared what he would do.

It was difficult sometimes to appreciate the Dyke when her mind became occupied with her life. Sometimes she looked later at the guide book and saw she should have seen 'magnificent views' again, and yet in the evening she couldn't remember if she had looked. The walking itself, of course, held one's attention; the placement of the foot avoiding muddy places, searching the next field-hedge for the stile; sometimes it would have an accompanying post with the Offa's Dyke Path symbol on it. Her binoculars, a present that year from her father, were invaluable in this, helping to distinguish a farm post which looked like the OD post, or a doubled piece of fencing which might be a stile.

There was a tendency, too, to spend a lot of time studying the guide book, the *Offa's Dyke Society Route Notes*, the strip maps the society provides, and then of course the Ordnance Survey map. There was the constant calculation of how many miles you had done and how many more there were to do. Would she get to her destination in time?

There were interruptions. Like here today, in the middle section of the Dyke, suddenly she had heard that strange cat-like sound, the mewling of buzzards. She swung her glasses up and soon located the pair gliding, as ever, so high up that they didn't look the big birds she knew them to be. There were buzzards all up and down the Dyke, sentinels patrolling this boundary, seeming not to be the hunters they were (Celestine had never seen one dive for prey, but thought rather they had some custodial role, watching to see that no-one damaged the property – the Dyke – which lay below them).

And apart from the views there was her constant need to

understand what the Dyke was doing. Changes from major mounds to what seemed, even originally, to have been quite a slight mound needed explanation, as did the variation between straightness and irregularity. There was no doubt that these changes had a physiographical character. It is in this area that the Dyke was first built. In heavily forested areas – and much of this area was heavily forested – the engineer essentially threw up a mere boundary bank made from a succession of spoil holes. In his maturity further north he cast off these defects and even in forest he built the Dyke, even if, on the steeper hills, it was more like a platform or berm. But the berm was a sign of his maturity.

The Easthurst brochure which her father had shown her emphasised that the school aimed to turn out mature young women. When, thought Celestine, did she become mature? One wasn't mature ever, but there was a time when you were grown-up. You couldn't be grown-up unless you knew who your mother was or at least something about her. Over and over again, during the last years of school, Celestine had conversations in her head with her father, when she said, 'I must know about my mother,' but over and over again when the holidays came she couldn't bring herself to mention the subject which she knew he didn't want to talk about.

The nearest she ever got was to say to him one evening, "I would like to see a photo of my mother." He said nothing for perhaps five minutes, sat there having allowed the paper he was reading to drop to his lap. Then he went over to his desk which was in their sitting room and got a key out of the top drawer and got out a framed photo and gave it to Celestine.

"Put it back and lock the drawer," he said, leaving the room. Celestine thought he had left her to look at the picture alone but in a moment he was back carrying a jewel case. "These are your mother's jewels. They are for you. Don't wear them in my presence. I'm going to bed." And then he did leave her alone.

Celestine stared at the mute photo trying to get some feeling, some response. It was a young woman – 23, 24, she guessed, with her hair cut short with a fringe. The photo was black and white of course but Celestine judged the hair to be a darker brown than her own. Otherwise she simply stared straight at the camera not quite smiling but with her lips looking as if they could easily move. She stared back at Celestine giving her no message. The jewel case contained a good string of pearls, a gold chain with a cross, two or three quite nice brooches, some thin silver bracelets; Celestine thought they might be English and she slipped one on and liked it. It was curious to think that the last person to have worn it must have been her dead mother. She was struck by the fact that there were no rings in the box.

The only other person she could enquire from was her Aunt. She was of course her mother's older sister but there had been a big gap between them, ten years separating Celestine's grandparents' only two children. Her grandmother had been over forty when Hazel – Celestine's mother – had been born. Celestine had no memories of her grandmother, who was dead by the time she first came to England.

Her Aunt had talked about her childhood and her little sister but then she had, at eighteen, left home to become a nurse and had married herself when she was 23 and become immersed in the 'practice' and later had her own children to worry about and she could tell Celestine very little about Hazel as a young woman. "She trained as a secretary and worked for a law firm, that was how she met your father I think." The summer she was eighteen, Celestine said to her, "You must tell me how my mother died." But her Aunt didn't really know. "Your father would never tell me the details. She was killed, murdered I think, in some sort of robbery."

That summer Aunt was busy. Gilly was getting married. It seemed to Celestine that this was the first of a rush of summer marriages. Old school-friends, college friends, new work-friends; there was this scene on English lawns in what always seemed to be the Home Counties. Driving in a car with new clothes and wearing a hat (that last item seemed to be *de rigeur*) to an English country church.

Then there was the quaintness of the English vicar delivering a homily to bride and groom. Some of them were truly awful, with arch remarks about going forth and prospering and bringing forth the good seed. The services were epicene, they lacked all passion and commitment. Afterwards there was the photographic scene which as the years passed got longer and longer with video to add to flashing cameras. Celestine sometimes wondered if the young couples spent all their married lives examining all these mementos which they had collected in such volume.

But Gilly's wedding was the first of these occasions, and it had a strange sequel for Celestine. She and her father had stayed on in Bournemouth for a week after the wedding and were there to see the local paper's report of the marriage – 'Prominent Bournemouth G.P.'s Daughter Married' – followed by a list of misspelt guests. But Celestine suddenly thought that newspapers covered not only marriages and births but also deaths. She made a casual enquiry of her father about Indian newspapers; were they in English? "The *Times of India*," he said, "modelled on the *Times* but a very good copy." Then from her Aunt, the date of her mother's death: early March, she remembered.

Where in London did you find the *Times of India* for eighteen years ago? She thought of the Indian Embassy but went and asked first the local library and they told her: "Colindale, they keep every paper there." So she went out. There was some resistance from the librarians there at first. What research was she doing that required her to have access to the paper? So she told them; "My mother died and I'm sure there was a report of it in the paper because she was killed and I want to know about it." That last remark she forced out, almost crying as she said it. Then they helped her.

She was sat down in a little room and brought what she asked for, the *Times of India* for February and March. She didn't know whether there would be a headline or whether she would have to look in death columns but she thought if she was killed there must have been a news report.

It had been a leap year. February, the 29th. 'Young British Lawyer's Wife Missing. Fears for her Safety.'

> Mrs Quareine had formed the most unwise habit of walking by herself after dark in parts of old Delhi. She had left her house in her car at nine o'clock. The car was found near the Red Fort but Mrs Quareine was not in it. A distraught Mr Quareine said, "I begged her not to go out by herself. I was working. Midnight I found I was alone. The Bearer told me her car had gone."

Then nothing for four days. Monday, March 4th: 'Lawyer's Wife's Mutilated Body Found'. At least at that time the detail was muted, Celestine didn't know whether she wanted more detail or less. The naked body of a white woman found in a ditch. 'Police believe she had been held prisoner for three days and killed Sunday night.' Sexually mutilated and repeatedly stabbed. No clues as to the killers. Two weeks later there was a report of the inquest but again no details and verdict of 'Unlawful Killing by Persons Unknown'. That night she did ask her father a direct question.

"Did they ever find the people who killed my mother?" Startled, he replied, "No, nothing was ever found out about them." Celestine said, "I read the pieces in the *Times of India*." "Ah," he said, "I had asked her not to go out. I had to work in the evening." And he very deliberately picked up the book he had been reading, adjusted his glasses and turned his head and the book away from Celestine. So Celestine was left with the horror of her mother's death and the question mark over that remark of her father's. Why did her mother go out at night leaving her father and a six month baby, Celestine herself, alone? That would have to be further pondered.

It was not exactly crowded but the further south one got it seemed to Celestine the number of walkers on the Dyke increased. Today she had met one group of six who were on their last day, they were doing the southern part of the path but finishing at Knighton. The Dyke too, which in its northern part passed through no towns, in fact barely a village, occasionally a hamlet like Broadtown, now in the south passed through towns, Kington, Hay-on-Wye, Monmouth. Visitors to these towns walked out of them along the Dyke to sample it. Celestine and the long distance walkers rather despised them. 'Transients,' one serious minded rambler had called them.

It had also occurred to Celestine that the walkers were Saxons in general. She hadn't even met many Welsh, perhaps they took their border for granted. But here now coming towards her was a little family, who were transients in a way, but they attracted Celestine's admiration because they had two young children. One child, who she guessed might just be walking, was in a carrier on his father's back, while a scrap of three or four had been half-carried, Celestine guessed, all the way up Rushock Hill. She stopped for a chat, and to congratulate the little boy. The couple too interested her because they were of mixed race, the father a Saxon clearly but the mother an invader new to the Dyke. Celestine guessed she was West Indian. They seemed very relaxed and glad, as was Celestine, to sit and chat for a bit. They were driving up the Dyke, stopping here and there to walk bits depending on how much they could manage with their kids. Soon Celestine felt relaxed enough to ask the woman whether she'd been born in England: "Yes, my parents came from Jamaica, though – although I'm supposed to have a Scottish great-grandfather," she laughed. "No Welsh background though." "You're an invader, like me," said Celestine, "I come from India but my name is Welsh."

The new wave of migrants – drawn not, as of old, by expulsion or a shortness of food, but by the promise of work, money, fortune, life like *Dallas*. Celestine wondered how the Dyke would deal with this new group of borderers. They were, she realised, the re-entrants.

Woman 1.   I'm going to England because my mother sent for me. I'm staying five years.

Woman 2.   I'm going to England because I hear that other people are doing good. I'm going to stay about three years.

Woman 3.   I'm going to England because there's no employment here. I'm staying two years.

Woman 4.   I'm going to England because my fiance is there. I'm staying five years.

Woman 5.   I'm going to England to do nurse training. I'm staying three years.

Woman 6.   I'm going to England because it is my mother country.

Woman 7.   I'm going to England to make money. I'm staying one year.

Woman 8.   I'm going to England to join my husband. I'm staying four years.

Woman 9.   I'm going to England because they said they needed me. I'm not sure how long I'm staying.

Woman 10. I'm going to England to insure a better future for my children. I'm staying for as long as it takes.

We used to sing songs about England. You know like: (she sings) "Rule Britannia, Britannia rule the waves" and we used to chant "Red, white and blue, what does it mean to you? Shout it aloud, Britain's awake. These are the chains that nothing can break." Those are the songs we grew up with and we had to dress up in blue skirt and white blouse when they having these coronations, or when they crowning Queen Elizabeth and King George. Yes we felt very much involved and we had to sing: (she sings) "There'll always be an England and England shall be free, if England mean so much to you as England mean to me."

Ralph (*infra vide*) was manic about selling (of course). "We are not selling enough here in England. All those bloody immigrants – the schools will pay, get out amongst them," so she had struggled to this bit of North East London and to a local meeting of ESL teachers. Her host seemed to be a lady of tremendous energy – Elyse Dodgson, who had said on the phone, "Of course, most of the kids in my school are of West Indian extraction – come early, I'm rehearsing *Motherland* with them." So there was Celestine amazed at the abilities Elyse had got out of these 'kids.'

"Come early", but she had set off late. Raining, and the directions (two changes on the underground and then a walk) sounded difficult, so a taxi on expenses and then negotiating the way into the school through its various gates, and finally a school secretary: "Elyse, of course, she said you were coming," and into the welcome and warmth of this active group of 'kids' and Elyse treating her as an old friend.

The rehearsal had been the last lesson of the afternoon: the children left, then there was tea laid on in the hall and in ones and twos the teachers of ESL arrived, damp, bedraggled, each telling her of their main group. Here years later on the Dyke, she thought suddenly that all those children they described, Bengalis, West Africans, Turkish cypriots, Greek Cypriots, the Eastern Europeans – they were all borderers, and she imagined all these groups of children flooding past her talking their own languages, crowding down the Dyke to the crossing at Crow's Nest,* their new language giving them a new country.

But then, she was suddenly being asked to speak, show the books, scatter her leaflets, talk about special offers from her company, offering free sample books to teachers but feeling inadequate and spoilt, with her job much better paid than these teachers. Ducking out rather exhausted before their formal talk from some specialist academics. Different ages – different approaches.

Back outside not to the sun on the Dyke but to the grey cold damp of a late November day in London. Hoping to get back to the peace of the flat (but that was not to be – *infra vide*).

* One of the few deliberate gaps in the dyke

It was a cold, cold November day. People were so cold. I wanted to turn around and go back; it had all been a horrible mistake. I don't want to do nursing, I don't want to be here. I didn't realise it would have been that cold and it was misty. Now I can look back and say it was misty; at the time it was dense fog. One of the things that shocked me was looking around and seeing English people doing manual work. It seemed so depressing, the picture that I had built up in me mind. It wasn't that I thought it was the golden land but the streets, the space, the accent, the strange accent... There were curious onlookers standing around looking; anxious black people and curious white people...

We thought because we knew all about them, they would know all about us. We had been taught about that country in our lessons, all their kings, all their history. When I'd been living here for five years or so, I went to Scotland to look for MacDowells. Of course I was married by then. We went to this small town looking for MacDowell graves. Local people asked us why we were doing that. I'm descended from a MacDowell, I said, and they just laughed and laughed and laughed. But I am, I am descended from a Macdowell.

The West Indian girl on the Dyke laughed. "Scottish blood – same as Welsh – maybe I'm a bit of a Celt."

Celestine left the friendly family and pressed on to the top of the hill. Just here were the famous three yew trees, the Three Shepherds, on the Dyke itself. They were called this as they were thought to represent the souls or bodies of three shepherds who died in a winter blizzard. Above them, on the shoulder of Rushock Hill, there is a definite lower ditch and upper spoil ditch. Here too are the last views of the Welsh mountains, for now the Herefordshire plain opens out widely East and West. At the yew trees the plateau begins to narrow and the hill to have a definite ridge. The yew trees are visible from all parts of Radnorshire. Yews are frequently seen on earthworks in southern England but Fox had not yet seen them in Wales. Perhaps for this reason he ended his 1930 season of work here. At these secular trees his survey was suspended until 1931. Celestine had a further two miles to walk in her season down to Kington with Ralph awaiting her no doubt at the Burton Hotel.

As she became a more senior editor in publishing she became aware of the powers behind the industry. Up 'til the mid-seventies publishing still had something of a gentle-manly (or ladylike?) flavour to it, but then the moguls moved in thinking there was money to be made. One thing they thought of as potential money was ESL publishing, so Celestine was in a protected bit of the business. But she also began to meet the Managing Directors, Chairmen, people who actually talked to Robert Maxwell, had connections with senior civil servants in the Department of Education, would go off to talk to prominent politicians, back bench whips. Name-dropping at having met these eminences began to be part of her life and she found meeting these people gave her a curious frisson. She liked to be able to name-drop too. She wanted to be seen in their company. Why, she couldn't say, but she wanted to know famous people. She never saw herself as becoming famous but she wanted to be associated with these Gods.

Nasty

Buy-outs, mergers, suddenly the old Managing Editor of their Trade division was gone. We're getting Ralph Edgehorn out of Random House. He's coming. Ralph had started in broadcasting, started publishing Books of the TV Series, made a swift move to a senior post with Penguin, at 35 had suddenly been head-hunted to New York. Now, at 43, head-hunted to do many things, but one was 'to turn the Trade division around'. He'll do it in two years, everybody said. *Publishers Weekly* gave him a whole-page profile.

So here he was suddenly in the lift, "Hullo, hullo, good to meet," and although Education was part of the Technical division it was also part of Trade. Celestine represented

Education at Trade sales meetings, trying to push a book of theirs over to the Trade representative. There was Ralph: "Volume is too small, we have to double it this year, we must scavenge titles, titles that sell. We'll try to buy from outside." Then suddenly, "Some of those Teach-Yourself-style language books, we've got some good ones. Why don't we develop something? Cut some of our old texts down to something simpler. Digest them, that can be done quietly in-house..."

Celestine was soon running this Teach Yourself list. "We want twenty titles by next spring, Celestine." Ralph would pour into her office, sit on her desk, ruffle through mss. she was reading. Stir things up. He was always in the office hours after everyone else. People started staying later to catch his eye. If you didn't catch his eye, you might find yourself fired over a weekend. "New wood," he said, "prune, prune."

"You're here late, Celestine. I'll take you to eat. Hurry while I call the White Tower, they can usually fit me two downstairs." On first-name terms with most of the staff and the other diners.

"I'm still living in Claridges, haven't had time to get anything sorted out. Must get an apartment – flat, of course – here soon. Come round."

Claridges' rooms – or at least the one that Ralph had – seemed to Celestine like an apartment already. There was a little ante-room and a separate sitting-room with a bedroom beyond. Take a brandy. Ralph disappeared into his bedroom to re-appear five minutes later wearing just a slight robe through which his erection was clearly visible. He embraced her and kissed her hard then said, "Go into the bedroom and come back naked." Celestine did as she was told.

There began a strange period of her life. Her phone would ring both at the office and at home with not invitations but instructions. "We're having dinner with Lady Anscombe," or "We're taking Jeffers out tonight," or "We're going to the opera, I've got the Arts Council box." There was some generosity, like a gift of a diamond-studded brooch. "I picked it up at the airport." And once when she said, "I've nothing to wear, I haven't had time to do any laundry," he reached into his pocket and gave her £500 in notes and said, "Buy yourself some new ones."

The demands to join him in bed were as peremptory. "Hi, cunt, there's a car on its way for you." She got used to walking through the lobby of the hotel and up to his suite watched by the eyes of the night staff. Celestine went, saying, "I'm exhausted, Ralph. You never really sleep." Whatever time he got in, Ralph was up every morning at six o'clock. When he went to the States for a long weekend she stayed in her own flat and slept the whole weekend away.

She told him that she was dining with Joan and Sylvia on Thursday. But mid-morning there was a call, "Dinner with Jeffers: important, you must come." But she had to resist. "No, Ralph, I can't, won't come." She could feel the fury down the phone. Friday the car was sent for her around ten at night, and she found Ralph in his robe awaiting her, and she was ordered straight to bed. "Lie on your belly, Celestine, you are going to be whipped; when I say come to dinner, you come."

Once she had submitted to this humility, it began to happen that she would fail him on a regular basis: she realised he would plan her failures. Afterwards she realised that although he published, promoted apparently, the Arts, and said various opera stars who he knew were marvellous, she never really heard him enthuse about anything other than people and their importance. It was manipulations, it was possessions, it was money. It was owning people like her. It was months before she remembered that she had not given Ralph a word: and by this time she knew what the word was.

Nasty: *gnastie, naustie*: origin obscure – what language would want to claim the word? But five meanings, the nicest related to the weather. Others: foul, filthy, dirty, indecent, obscene. Or offensive in some respect, disagreeable, unpleasant, objectionable, annoying, ill-natured. Difficult to deal with, dangerous, bad. Dr Johnson added a curiously more modern word: *polluted.*

Down Mexico Way

Rain, gentle rain but causing gutters to drip, was what woke Celestine in Kington. You could hardly expect to walk twelve days on the Welsh Borders and have it dry every day and so far it had rained kindly. It had drizzled at Chirk and rained hard the night she was in Welshpool but looking out today she could see grey skies and what looked like a day set to raining. Grey skies, she thought, looking at Ralph, sleeping beside her although it was after six. What happens to aging whizz kids? Grey skies, and in the rain, things, possessions, slipping away from him.

Celestine had thought it would be hard to get Ralph to come. But he had come willingly – surprising after their abrupt rupture. He was waiting in her booked room in his robe alright and Celestine came to him peaceably. But he had a surprise for her. "Celestine," he said, "I want you to marry me." Celestine thought: if you hold on long enough you win. And she smiled at him. ("Your little smile, Celestine," Ralph had said, "how I long for it when I'm away.") "Ralph," she said, "you may whip me if you like but you may not marry me, and first you can help me off with my boots." He even did that humbly enough.

Able was a male friend. She had been working with him almost since she started in publishing. It was one of those relationships which for some reason never went beyond work but at work they were greatest friends. She'd been able to tell him all about her marriage and he had listened over a series of sympathetic lunches. A listener, and not an advisor, although when she started going out with Ralph he had said to her: "I hear you're seeing a lot of Ralph. Watch out, he's a tough customer." Later she realised that he had been going to say *nasty* but substituted tough so as not to offend her.

But six months later, Able had information of a different kind. He called her into his office one Friday lunchtime, and said: "You might be interested in this letter. I had it by special delivery this morning." It was a curt note saying the company had decided to close the Educational division and Able's services would not be required from next Monday morning. There followed the terms of a not-very-generous financial settlement.

Celestine couldn't speak, she found herself wanting to shout but no words came. And Able, seeing her astonishment, said: "Your friend Ralph hasn't mentioned it to you, clearly. I thought you must have known." Then Celestine was able to focus at least on one issue. "But you've been here for years. You've built their list. They can't dismiss you like that. Where will you go? Our list is doing so well. What will you do?"

"I'm alright," said Able, smiling. "I knew what was happening, one of the University Presses is interested, they'll buy the division. I've already talked with them. I'll take most of my authors with me. I assumed you knew. Everyone else, except you, in this division, has had a similar letter this morning. For the juniors like Sally and Anne, it's going to be hard, there's not much hiring of Junior Editors at the moment."

"Why haven't I been sacked?"

"ESL is being retained. You are going to be absorbed into the trade division. He looks after his own."

"His own! I'm not his! I'm not his! I won't be called his own. He can't treat people like that. I won't stay, I'm leaving too."

Ralph was just leaving for New York; he was quite impervious to her anger.

"It was only making five to seven per cent, all our companies have to do fifteen. Yours is the only bit that's useful. You'll be fine."

"But you never told me."

"No point in disclosing things until decisions are made. We only finalised last Friday; haven't had a moment to tell you since."

She looked round his office for something to throw at him but there were only huge bowls too big to heft so she had to content with slamming his door and banging down the passage shouting, "Bastard, bastard, bastard."

She wrote a letter of resignation and like her colleagues spent the afternoon clearing her desk. She got no severance money at all, Ralph fixed that. But she spent Saturday writing a hate-letter to Ralph and telephoned her somewhat astonished father to say she was coming to the islands for three months.

Piles of books, now as an adult able to lie on the beach by herself, and enjoying evenings with her father, re-organising his domestic arrangements so that meals were more interesting. Then in three months a letter from Able offering her a new job.

She left a gloomy Ralph for a second time that morning at Kington, he was still drinking coffee. The rain was steady – wet. It was rather tempting to wander round little Kington and not set out on her wet tramp. It was not a Saxon town but Norman with a fine tower representing their presence, still they were a murdering lot too. In the church a tomb commemorates a knight who was killed in battle; his wife subsequently participated in an archery contest at a local fair but swivelled away from the target and planted an arrow neatly in the chest of the man who had killed her husband.★

The main trouble with walking in the rain was that you got wet not from the outside but from within. Celestine was soon sweating freely as she started uphill out of the town. Why was it always uphill to start with? She tried undoing her lightweight plastic mac but the rain got in and she was soon thoroughly damp. Any rate the uphill was fairly short and then there was a good two mile walk along Hergest Ridge to Gladestry.

There weren't any walkers today, Celestine noted; they had all waited in, or they were behind her, in Kington. The

★ 'Lewis Carroll-style Death', Gavin Ewart: "I saw my son without his head, I saw the tortured and I saw the dead – 'Why, this is most peculiar,' I said."

biggest surprise for her in the shops in Kington had been a Mexican café, the entrance was being cleaned as she passed, by a short dusky man. "Are you really Mexican?" she had asked and the man smiled back with an, "Of course, *Senorita*."

"Are you open?" she asked.

"Not really," he said. "What do you want?"

"I was thinking of asking you to fill my flask with coffee."

Usually Celestine carried juice or water in her flask but the damp weather suggested coffee.

"Come in," he said, "we have the best Colombian coffee."

She had a cup while he filled her flask. "How did you come to be living here?" she asked. He had thick dark Mexican hair; he had already lit the inevitable cigarette.

"When I get up into California" (the dream of every Mexican) "I get a job driving for Mr Morris; he's a business man. Then maybe two years later he gets sent to run his firm in London. He asked me to come with him. Then in London there is this Mexican restaurant I go to in Covent Garden. I get to know them there and sometimes I help out. One summer they hire this girl who comes from Wales. So now we're married and have two little girls. My wife says London no place to bring up children, so we come back here and I start this little restaurant. People like Mexican food."

"You miss Mexico?"

"No, I like it here. Mexico City, it's a filthy place. No work there, no space. Soon my sister, she come to help me here. Maybe she marry a fine Welsh boy. Then 'poof', who wants Mexico when you can work and live easy here."

"You come from Mexico City?"

"No, I'm a country boy from a Zapotec village."

The Mexican's smiling Welsh wife brought the flask of coffee. (Had she been washing dishes, wondered Celestine, or was her husband a good dishwasher?) The man took the flask and passed it on to Celestine:

"Here's your coffee *Senorita*, have a good day."

"You speak English very well," said Celestine (tempted to

add but deciding not to: 'for a Mexican'). "Next time I come you must tell me about your mother."

Celestine paid the modest charge and set off. Then after the pull out of Kington and her general dampness she stopped under a tree to sample some more of the Colombian coffee. Coffee at breakfast, the cup in the Mexican café, another now – soon she would need to pee. There was always the slight embarassment (for which she despised herself) that a walker would suddenly appear as she crouched for relief – it was a feeling akin to the embarassment of wetting yourself as an older child, which got her back to her childhood and her absent mother. If she did ask the Mexican about his mother, he would ask Celestine about her mother. His mother in her village (alive or maybe dead now) of Zapotec. But Celestine's mother across some quite different border: it had led to another of those abrupt interruptions to the quiet evenings she spent with her father in Carlisle Mansions.

'Where is my mother buried?" (she somehow assumed burial not cremation)

"In Delhi."

"You didn't bring her body back to Britain?"

"No." (A pause)

"Where in Delhi?"

"A small Anglican church; there's a graveyard round it. The embassy staff use it – they made the arrangements" – a pause – "I pay annually for the upkeep. It used to be an Englishman who was the parson but now a new name, he must be an Indian" – a pause – "I'd like to know it's well looked after."

"I'll go and have a look one day," said Celestine – a pause – "I think I'll go to bed now."

The duties of the daughter to a father. Perhaps if she'd been a son he'd have been asked to go, but Mr Quareine was circumspect with Celestine as fathers are with daughters.

In California

In my parents' house, the altar is probably completely adorned with zempoolxochitl flowers, turkey-crest flowers and rat flowers, and with bunches of bananas of all kinds, with oranges, lemons, candies, mescal, tortillas, red mole, tamales, cookies, soft drinks, water, chocolate, beer, breads made in the shape of people, and, in the middle of it all, a cooked chicken. Everything is arranged around the images of the saints so that at the appointed hour, the dead can come and savour these delicacies, because they won't be served like this again until next year.

Dear Maria, my desire is to find you well and in the company of your family. We are all fine here in Mexico. I hope you will pardon me for sending these lines but Faustino and the son of Don Alonzo, along with several others, are in jail in San Diego. They have been there for two weeks. Can you tell the officials that you are a relative so that they will release them? Write to me. Greetings from Pedro, Felicia and Rosa. Sonia is going to be the queen at the fiesta. Your friend who never forgets you.

My esteemed friend, Maria, I hope to find you well in the company of your family, as are my desires. I am very grateful that you called to the jail, Faustino used the name of his brother. He and the others got out of jail on the thirteenth of August and are now in Chicago. Greetings from Pedro and Felicia. With the affection of your friend.

Some guess that 1,500 illegals are here, at Tijuana, on any given night. Some guess that 90 per cent of all illegal crossings occur here. Some guess there are four to twelve million illegals in the United States but no one is certain. There are no reliable bases for any of these numbers. The Border Patrol cars give numbers of illegals they catch but some are caught and released two or three times in a matter of hours.

Beneath the illusion created by numbers, two facts about the border have real significance. The first: bringing people across is a major service industry with juicy profits for both countries. The second: the simple fact is that everyone who wants to cross, does. The wetback and the mother, they both cross. The baby crosses. "Yes, little one, I am going to save this sock so that when you're big you can say, this is what I wore when I came to the United States."

Finally my friend found me a job as a busboy in an Italian restaurant. I worked two days a week for four hours each. They paid me the minimum, something like $2.25 an hour, and I began to work hard because I wanted to earn more. My dream was to make money, come back, and start a business. Little by little, I got more hours and finally a complete shift. After being a busboy I became a dishwasher.

Then I made the daughter of my boss my girlfriend. Her name was Linda. I think that my boss thought, I'm not going to want a dishwasher for a son-in-law because one day he came to see me and said, "Joker, learn a little English and go into the kitchen and learn to be a cook." I was so happy. Within days I became responsible for the kitchen – even with the right to invite a friend to have a pizza without paying.

You know North Americans are very funny about their dogs. Once we saw a woman who had her hair cut and dyed to match her dog, or, maybe, it was the other way round. I remember one time – this was the craziest but it's true – we took a trip to San Francisco. We were waiting for a cable car at Fisherman's Wharf and a woman ran by completely nude. Can you imagine? She didn't have a stitch on. Miguel and I couldn't believe our eyes. She was a 'streaker'. "No," I thought, "if my grandmother knew this, she would die."

For those of us who were raised in a *pueblo* in Mexico, here we find a life that is really nice, beautiful. One becomes accustomed to the life and doesn't want to return. If someday they send me and my family back we will return because I like living here so much. My oldest daughter is four years old and goes to pre-school. She can speak various words, count to thirty and say the days of the week all in English. At times she surprises me; she says, "Poppy, you have a happy face." She can sing in English too. My youngest daughter was born here. She is from the United States.

No, no, no! I was afraid of the negroes and the houses were so ugly. In Mexico they were brightly painted, here they were so dark. I kept telling my father I didn't like it. He didn't say anything and after two months or so I became more accustomed to things and liked it better. My grandma came and took me back to Mexico but papa came to the rescue and I said I wanted to stay in Chicago.

There are many things I like about the United States. You have rights. You fight for them and the law supports you. If there is a law you obey it. Not in Mexico. If you buy something at the store and they don't deliver it the day they say they will, you can make a claim and they don't ask whether or not you have papers. You can make a claim. In the United States you sue someone if they don't complete something. And they pay attention to you. In the United States everyone is equal, everyone. If you have work and you want a car you can buy one just as new as your boss's.

In a faceless society there are people who are bigots. There are people here who still have certain images about the Mexicans, about Mexican Americans, about non-Anglo-Saxons. You affect the people you can, you try to change them, and for the rest that's their problem. It really comes back to what my dad used to say to us. "*Asi son los americanos.*"

This is what the great trek has always been about. Indelibly etched in the very earth they travel, after more than one hundred years, this greatest movement of a people in human times rolls on. Like a river responding to the land, it gains momentum, with gravity's pull, is nearly bought to a halt by some massive blockage, but it moves again, if only at a trickle, until a break is found. Only when it finds parity with its surroundings will it halt.

A river may act as a pull but it also may serve as a barrier. At Kington the Offa's Dyke Path leaves the possible line of the Dyke keeping further west as it heads down to Hay-on-Wye. Fox was busy however in the Herefordshire plain which is drained by the Wye and its tributaries the Arrow, the Lugg and the Frome. These and other streams meet to form a wide alluvial plain in the neighbourhood of Hereford and thus determined the position of the Bishop's see and the county town. But where was the Dyke?

Fox had problems. The most southerly position he found, it fades out on a bluff above the River Wye at Bridge Sollers. From Bridge Sollers onwards, Fox saw the river itself as forming the boundary. Celestine would catch the borderline again tomorrow when she reached Monmouth. But what of the huge gaps that exist north of Bridge Sollers? The Rushock Hill segment ends on Eywood Brook and is picked up a mile and a half away on the right bank of the brook. This suggests that the Eywood drainage line, the belt of marsh and jungle through which water meandered, was the boundary. It suggests too that this lateral re-entrant was not cleared by the Mercians.

Northwest Herefordshire, in the eighth century, was all woodland and the Mercians lacked the manpower and the economic bases to make an effective advance beyond the Wye. But in the forest, if any boundary was marked it took only the form of felled trees or a small mound. In a dense forest in a rich lowland, the Mercians and the Welsh were not actually in contact. A border or a marriage yet to be achieved. The dense forest is tied in with the geology, for here one passes into an outcrop of old red sandstone. This formation provides in these lowlands one of the richest soils in the country, a soil which in natural conditions is densely afforested. There are evidences of this heavy afforestation. Records: in 1233 an order was issued to the Sheriff of Hereford to cause a breach to be made through the midst of the woods. Existing woods in their plan and distribution are manifestly remnants of an extensive forest. The names of farm and hamlet show that in this area, pre-Domesday area settlements were clearings in woods – wood (*wude*), ley (*leah*), field (*feld*). The damp oakwood forest was a complete barrier.

Celestine despite her late start reached the Royal Oak at Gladestry by noon. It was still raining but the landlord was happy to let her sit in his bar, take off her dripping mac and backpack, eat her sandwiches and enjoy a pint of his beer. She had not been drinking midday; she avoided publishers' lunches because they made her sleepy in the afternoon but she had ten miles to go and the necessary walking should keep her awake. The landlord was anxious about her dampness and found a small electric fire so that the bottom of her jeans dried out. She got fresh dry socks out of her pack to replace the sodden ones in her boots and was informed by the landlord that the rain would give over soon and if she just waited 'til one o'clock she would have a dry walk that afternoon. Meanwhile why not have a little extra in her sandwiches, a slice of his wife's homemade pork pie, why not? "You kill your own pig?" she asked. "Yes," said the landlord.

The Butcher and the Beaver were the success story of the Bellman's expedition. They started if not enemies at least suspicious borderers but ended as firm friends, returning from a frightening expedition when they had heard the cry of a Jubjub. Just as proceeding through the northwest Hereford jungle a Welsh warrior might fear he had heard a Saxon hunting horn, the Butcher, hearing the cry, declared: "'Tis the voice of the Jubjub" and repeated this statement three times. The proof is complete, he said, if only I've stated it thrice.

But the Beaver here was in difficulty. It had recollected with tears how in earlier years it had taken no pains with its sums. It was unable to add to three, a task that the Butcher was not only prepared to undertake but also to demonstrate how it could be done. "Bring me paper and ink. The best there is time to procure."

The Beaver brought paper, portfolio, pens
And ink in unfailing supplies:
While strange creepy creatures came out of their dens,
And watched them with wondering eyes.

So engrossed was the Butcher, he heeded them not,
As he wrote with a pen in each hand,
And explained all the while in a popular style
Which the Beaver could well understand.

'Taking Three as the subject to reason about –
A convenient number to state –
We add Seven, and Ten, and then multiply out
By One Thousand diminished by Eight.

The result we proceed to divide, as you see,
By Nine Hundred and Ninety and Two:
Then subtract Seventeen, and the answer must be
Exactly and perfectly true.

Although this method is certainly long-winded it does give the answer three. The Butcher then proceeded to give a lesson in natural history – forgetting all laws of propriety. Phyliss Greenacre thinks that the ten members of the crew represent the ten children of the Dodgson family (Carroll was a Dodgson). "This part of the poem where the Butcher gives the docile Beaver a lesson in natural history," she writes, "is probably [analysts have difficulty in writing possibly] but a thinly disguised picture of the consultation among the little Dodgsons regarding the mysterious [sex] life of their awesome parents."

There is another feature of the lesson that is important to note. In Holliday's illustration the reference book that the Butcher has under his feet is a Colenso's *Arithmetic*. John William Colenso became Bishop of Natal where the native Zulus badgered him with embarrassing questions about the Old Testament. The more Colenso pondered his answers the more he began to doubt the historical accuracy of the Old Testament. He used arithmetical arguments to buttress his attempts to prove the nonsense of various Old Testament tales. How, for example, he questioned, could 12,000 Israelites slaughter 200,000 Midianites? This atrocity, the Bishop argues, could only have been carried out on paper.

Colenso argued his case in a book (also in the *Snark* illustration) called *On the Reductio Absurdum.* Gardner argues that Colenso reduced the literal interpretation of the Bible to absurdity as Carroll reduced the old Sea Ballad to absurdity. Is that what the *Snark* is? Celestine had woken aged ten crying with terror after her father had read it to her. Later in her dreams the men who had killed her mother became the insane members of the Bellman's crew. Note too that the Zulus from Natal were those who later trekked to Zimbabwe (*supra vide*). Colenso defended polygamy among his Zulu converts.

Celestine knew now that although the poem was about nothing, it was also intimately connected with her mother. Her first copy (a first edition) had been given her by a woman called Bridget Hope. Every Christmas a present would arrive for Celestine from Bridget who was a godmother (represented by proxy at her christening in Delhi). She was her mother's best friend. Dutifully Celestine had written and thanked her for the presents. She had written at birthdays and invited Celestine to visit. Her father had replied on Celestine's behalf that it was not convenient. Bridget lived in northwest England and Celestine in childhood had the impression imparted to her by her southern-bred cousins that the north of England was far away.

But she lived nearby, in the town of Shrewsbury. When Celestine had failed in her questioning of her father and her aunt and had gained all she could from her newspaper search – 'Her body was found naked and it is to be noted that the jewellery she was wearing, including her valuable diamond engagement ring, was missing' – she thought of her godmother and said to her father: "I want to go and stay with my godmother." He had looked up and said, "She may not want you."

But Bridget wrote kindly at once to say she would be delighted to see her and that summer – the summer of the *Times of India* – Celestine took the train by herself to Shrewsbury. The train had been very fast from London to

Birmingham but then it crept slowly north and west through the industrial waste of that part of England. And then as the train swings more west it gets into the English countryside and became suddenly full of local people who'd been shopping in Birmingham or Wolverhampton, crowding in with parcels to take back to smaller towns like Wellington and the villages of Shropshire.

Celestine had been thinking that this friend of her mother's would be a young woman like the woman she had looked at in the portrait but of course she was older than her mother would have been; she was in her late forties and was one of those whose hair went white at an earlier age. She was stout, dressed in firm tweed skirts with thick tights and strong 'sensible' walking shoes.

"I'll be carrying a red rose, from the garden," she had written, "I'll wave it."

So there was this comfortable placid lady standing in front of the beautiful Victorian Shrewsbury station, waving her rose.

The next surprise for Celestine was her voice, which was soft and lilting with quite a pronounced Welsh accent. "You come from Wales," said Celestine. "I was born on the borders," said Bridget, "my father had a farm above a little place called Buttington outside a town called Welshpool, that's where I went to school. Do I still sound Welsh? No one ever tells me." She and her family lived in a small village about five miles from Shrewsbury called Yockleton; her husband was a solicitor in Shrewsbury, an affable George.

"Celestine says I sound Welsh, George, isn't that nice?"

"You've always sounded Welsh to me, my love."

"Well, you never told me."

George laughed and gave her an affectionate hug. "I thought you knew."

They had two children, to Celestine's surprise younger than her, ten and twelve, but on that first visit, to Celestine's relief, they were away, staying with Bridget's sister. "I ought to work but I don't," said Bridget, "I never got properly educated, I rode ponies and became a secretary, that's where I met your mother and that's where I met George eventually. I said I'd marry George as long as I never had to type his letters again." Bridget drove Celestine round the country and talked quite easily and happily to her about her mother. "Hazel, your mother? Well, we shared a flat, there were three of us but the others came and went. Your mother was there with me for three years, but of course, I didn't know her that well. Never visited her family, though she came up and stayed with mine one summer. She loved to read all the time. Then she was going out with your father. Is he still as handsome as he was? Hazel was bowled over by him. Then him going abroad. You see Hazel's parents never travelled much. Your mother thought that alone was romantic, she adored him."

"But then," said Celestine, "why did she go out alone at night?"

"She was restless, a bit bored. She wrote and told me that your father worked most evenings. I don't think she minded but she loved the streets of Delhi, the bazaars, the smells, the strange people. Of course, I don't really know, she wasn't a great letter-writer. But they came back when she was pregnant with you and she stayed a night or two in the old flat when your father was visiting an aunt or something. So we had great chats about India, she loved it."

"It killed her," said Celestine.

"Yes, dear, I suppose it did. Now, this is where my father's farm was. Of course, it's gone now but shall we get out and walk a bit?"

Celestine was glad to 'walk a bit' and followed Bridget up through gates to peer from forty yards off at the farm she had been brought up in and to stare at a house where Celestine's own mother had stayed. They walked on up the hill past the house.

"This has become," said Bridget, "since my childhood, an official path, you know. It's Offa's Dyke Path. Your mother, when we were here for two weeks in 19__, became fascinated by the Dyke and we had a plan – which we never carried out

– of walking it together. I shall never do it now. Maybe you could."

She would break off talking about Hazel and move to other subjects but then she would come back again and suddenly in the middle of some quite different exercise, she would drop a remark to Celestine about her mother. "Of course, she adored your father but I think perhaps she was beginning to wonder what else there was... I mean, for her. She had, when I last saw her, a restlessness."

"It was a pity she didn't go to a university, she was intelligent but, of course, we girls were quite prepared to just get little jobs and then get married. But she did love books and do you remember when you were ten, I gave you *The Hunting of the Snark*? She loved that poem. She read all the books she could about Carroll and she said the great thing about the poem was that Carroll didn't mean anything but nonsense. But that it welled out of him, out of his brain, his subconscious, so you could take it seriously and at the same time know it was absurd. Of course your mother was quite a frivolous person. She didn't often talk seriously about things and I believe *The Hunting of the Snark* was the thing she felt most seriously about in the world. There was something still quite childish about your mother, I used to think – as if I will ever be grown up!"

Although one was not on that bit of the river which had formed part of the boundary, one did, for the last part of the path, go along the river, at first actually on a level with the river and then climbing up above its banks so as to swing left over the bridge into Hay-on-Wye. And leaning, looking over into the water, was Jacob. She had known he would come here to the famous bookshops of Hay-on-Wye. Actually, most of the specialist bookshops seemed to have disappeared. There were simply these vast emporiums which held millions of books that no-one needed. The famous cinema contained innumerable books but you never saw one you wanted. Only the poetry bookshop retained some specialist interest; Celestine bought a copy of Galway Kinnel's *The Avenue Bearing the Initial of Christ into the New World* (that was some border). Then she was able to get to their hotel and shower before their dinner, and then to rest beside Jacob.

When she got back to London, summoned by Able, she had found him happily ensconced in the University Press. "The good thing," he said to Celestine, "is they actually recognise that books exist for time. Not just for now, like (if I can mention him) your friend, Ralph, thought. So you can plan to produce a list which may not sell a lot today but that people will want to go on buying. That really is something."

This move out of commercialism was satisfactory. There were other changes about town, of which a brief letter to the islands informed her. Bachelor-girl Joan was married to Peter. "But you'd known Peter for years." "Yes," said Joan, "he has been about, and then him being a civil servant – but somehow I kept going back to him and then I got pregnant by him and I suddenly wanted to have the baby. And I suddenly said to him, let's be respectable, let's have the baby and you marry me. And he said he would."

Able, with some glee, had been busy making-over not only those bits of the company that had been formally sold to the University Press but also acquiring those bits that Ralph had wanted to retain. All those authors who Ralph wanted to make Trade, themselves wanted to be respectable – "They want to come to us, so Jacob said, well, hire Celestine if she can get them."

"Jacob, who's he?"

"You know," said Able, "MacQuire."

"Oh, the famous MacQuire."

Jacob MacQuire, that's who Jacob is. The first thing that struck you about Jacob was that he really was clever. He had edited the new edition of Gibbon. He had gone over every footnote in every edition there had ever been and really checked them out. He had faulted Gibbon on ten dates and was able to footnote his own reason for the suggested change. "The time you must have spent," said Celestine.

"Well, I was at Harvard with this fellowship, and those American academics, they really want detail."

He was like Able and wouldn't show off his learning. He would sit and listen, let other people do the talking. The first time he came to dinner, John, the great talker, was there, and, of course, he held forth as usual. Shakespeare, the Italian painters, opera... But she doubted John knew much about the Graeco-Roman world and she wanted to hear Jacob talk about that. But he seemed content to let John talk. "It was interesting to meet him," he said afterwards.

He was so reasonable too. Once Celestine had been there eighteen months she was moving up towards board level. There were late meetings: "I know it's not easy for you. You choose the day and we'll fit the others round you." When you went to his house, there was his lovely relaxed wife, Cecile. There would be good company and (Celestine still had her penchant for the famous) you suddenly found yourself talking to Dennis who had directed the Ballard Ballet of Vermilion Sands.

When he asked Celestine to help him copy-edit a reprint they were doing of Carlyle's *French Revolution*, she was really pleased.

"Me?"

"Well, you did history, didn't you? Someone told me you did the French Revolution."

"Yes, but I haven't looked at it for years."

"I have too much really in my job [he was a director] to take it on although I'd like to be involved if you could do the donkey work."

So there they were, working late at night.

"I think we can squeeze an assistant to help you with your list; that'll give you some office time to do it. But I'm afraid there'll be a lot, you'll have to give time outside to it, but you'll be First Editor."

So in the evening she would stay on late to discuss text with him and then he would say, "Cecile will be late tonight, what about some wine and a bite?" Give him a little drink, he would go on being his urbane self, but give him a little more and he would suddenly reveal anxieties. He had been brought up by his emigre parents from the Ukraine who had retained their orthodox Judaism. Of course, he had fled that, intellectually, at his Scottish university, but he had concerns about his two boys – he thought they should have gone to Synagogue, and he should have arranged for their Bar Mitzvahs.

"But if you think they should have had that it means that you half believe it yourself."

"Well, one does look for an underlying structure, some sort of organisation in life and really of all the old religions, the Jewish makes most sense."

"Sense, Jacob? If I'm going to have Gods," said Celestine, "I'm going to have those naughty old Greek gods, at least they believed in fun."

Once you start revealing your religious doubts, that was an opening for revealing other problems.

"It is good to talk to you, Celestine. Cecile somehow doesn't understand what I feel about it. She's not a Jew you see."

"Nor am I," said Celestine.

"Well, you know what I'm talking about."

Once you had started admitting your wife had disadvantages it was easy to go on.

"She's a lovely mother of course, but she's just not interested in what I do. I mean, I try to keep up with all her worries about the legislation on Social Services which she has to teach but if she'd occasionally ask me a little about what I'm editing, it would help."

Then hastily backing off from these confessions and chatting easily, affably, about the publishing world, making her laugh with his encounters with Ralph when he bought the Education list; "He sent a car for me late at night to his suite in Claridges. He was in a robe. I think he had nothing on under it."

After Jacob had been deposited home that same car had

probably picked up Celestine. One night she had to confess to Jacob about her affair with Ralph though she'd sworn she'd tell no one. But Jacob could understand her fascination and laugh about it with her. They had so much going together that when they went to America, to the New York office (Able holding the fort at home), she knew they would sleep together. The Algonquin too, somehow, as they both admitted, had a seductive air about it.

Jacob was the first man she had related to, to whom she had had no immediate physical attraction. He had hair that slid way back off his forehead and he had a lank lock which he vaguely combed across his extensive baldness. He seemed to have a permanent slight stoop and he peered short-sightedly about him. He seemed to have never developed any way of taking daily exercise and she found he worried about it and did boring press-ups every morning. Sexually he was nervous – not an eager bull, but with worries about whether he would sustain an erection. He seemed only to have mounted his wife and other mistresses in the missionary position and Celestine had to show him how she liked to kneel and encourage him to explore sexually. But she quite enjoyed this. He was older than her but somehow socially and sexually retarded. He had never known anyone (he said) who was interested in the shirts he wore. "Let's buy each other shirts in Saks," said Celestine in New York. "Shirts!" said Jacob, "you buy me a shirt!" Why did she like him? Because he was clever, Celestine supposed, *clever.*

Clever was another obscure word. It was in local and colloquial use long before it became a literary word. A single example occurs in middle English but it does not appear in general use until the sixteenth century, and Sir Thomas Browne specifically mentions it as an East Anglian word. It meant things like nimble, which was not Jacob at all; perhaps handy, convenient, agreeable, 'nice'. Nice was Jonathan's word. He was not a Jonathan. Johnson allowed dexterous, skilful, but then added, 'This is a low word, scarcely ever used but in burlesque or conversation and applied to anything a man likes, without a settled meaning.'

He was good to be with because he would talk knowingly about books. He would not want to walk with her tomorrow as she set off for the fringes of the Black Mountains. He was not really a man, a man for King Offa; he was not a hill-man, he was a plainsman, suitable for this town on the edges of the Hereford plain, but clever, too clever. She would look for the hill-man tomorrow.

Certain men stand out like hills
Rising above their fellow men
To see the future from afar
Better than they see today
Clearer than if it were the past.

River Boundary & Roman Roads

There were obviously problems about relating to Jacob. But he was all for pushing it along. He was telling her he would leave his wife; together, Celestine and he would be the great publishers of the age, with marvellous editions of the great historical texts. But the age, the age, what was the age? It was curious how the English (*infra vide*), a rather insignificant race, put their name on ages. So even in America, most sensitive to colonial influence, the latter half of the nineteenth century – objects – things – lifestyles – is referred to as *Victorian*, after the rather insignificant little lady who dressed in black for half her life.

In the late twentieth century there came a mood and a time which Celestine was party to. It might have been named after the sham President who at least had an economic policy named after him, Reaganomics; it could be named after the nonentity who was his follower. But that was not how the age came to be named. Nor was it named after the Germans, so powerful in the Old World, nor the Japanese from the New. Or any other contenders. It didn't define all the age but it defined a mood and a behaviour: *Thatcherism*. After another lady, not dressed in black, just dressed badly, probably because the body underneath was designed for a suit of armour rather than feminine clothes (*infra vide*), a loud, arrogant, bossy, harsh-voice, wishing to queen it without warmth; a handbag lady, an essentially very, very unattractive lady, but still the creator of Thatcherism.

The thing about Thatcherism was that there was a whole landscape full of closet Thatcherites. They didn't like to admit they agreed with her, let alone vote for her, but they did. They didn't come out like gays or lesbians; they remained concealed.

"Awful lady, but I do believe on this particular issue she may have something."

Jacob was a closet Thatcherite.

"If she cuts grants much more, we won't sell any books; the poor students will have nothing," said Celestine.

"The loan scheme has quite a lot to recommend it, look how well it works in America."

Or "There are a lot of people who just live on the dole, they don't really look for jobs."

"But there are no jobs, Jacob. We are not hiring any staff, we used to take on three or four juniors a year, now nobody moves, only Ralph's."

Or "When you had such high taxes it didn't really mean much when you got a pay rise – now it makes a difference."

Or "There's lot of empty property in London; if the housing market settles and people begin to rent again, there won't be the homeless."

"Jacob, they are poor kids from the provinces, they will never rent in London."

"All those hypochondriacs cluttering the GPs' surgeries."

Celestine had not entirely ignored politics. She had done political meetings. She had been Green, paid her subscription against the Bomb. She disliked the feeling she was being preached at and that seemed to her what politicians did. But on the whole they didn't really change your lifestyle, they didn't invade you. But Thatcherism did. There were Management courses which told you how to do things as you had done them before, only writing everything down on bits of paper. There were audits – superficial research with an emphasis on money – and no auditor knew what it was they audited. And there were the people, the accountants and the lawyers, the boys who had done the Business Administration course at Princeton: all arch non-producers with no imaginations, revelling in their new technologies, the dull screens glowing green with flow-charts and numbers serving to confuse the mortal whose hand was not quick at tap-tap-tapping on the keyboard.

Jacob was one of the first into pocket data-banks. He gave Celestine one; she never used it. "It's got all my addresses, everything in it, so compact." Celestine liked her old blue address book. She liked its mess, the names crossed out of people who had actually died; the repeated address changes for her father as he moved around the world; the changed name for Joan which she had to keep under her old surname because she could never remember what Peter's surname was; the spilled coffee that crept on to some pages from the cup she knocked over at her desk as she tore up the drafts of the letter she was writing (not typing) to Ralph the night she resigned from the firm.

"You're simply anti-technology, Celestine," said Jacob.

"Nonsense," she said, "I'll love new technology when it does useful things for you. I can sort my car out which you can't – you wouldn't know how to handle any of those tools in the tool-kit I bought from Sylvia."

Sylvia had a garage of her own and most of her mechanics (not all, there was Matteo, the lovely Italian) were women and she had acquired a lot of female clients: she ran courses on How to Look After Your Own Car and Celestine had gone, and loved it – taking down the engine, admiring the beautifully-tooled parts and wishing she did more with her hands. But not the tap, tap, tap at all those boring, linked computers. How did they help you edit Carlyle? OK you did literature searches with them but in the end you had to sit and write.

What it all amounted to, as Celestine saw it, was a secret, unrecognised dishonesty. You could run everything – a health service, an education service, a publishing company, a shoe factory. But you couldn't actually do anything yourself. You couldn't make a shoe, you couldn't edit a book, you hadn't stood in front of 30 nine-year-olds and tried to get them to think, feel and understand. You had never helped a surgeon saw through a diseased femur. "Never become an expert," said Arthur Rank, whose son wanted to expand into film, "you can hire experts." But you couldn't! They just appeared, and where did Apollinaire, Borges, Chaucer, where did they pop up from and where were they laid? How would those Celts, the Welsh, the Irish, fare?

> Sing the lord and ladies gay
> That they were beaten into the clay
> Through seven heroic centuries;
> Cast your mind on other days
> That we in coming days may be
> Still the indomitable Irishry.
>
> ...
>
> Under bare Ben Bulben's head
> In Drumcliff churchyard Yeats is laid.
> An ancestor was rector there
> Long years ago, a church stands near,
> By the road an ancient cross.
> No marble, no conventional phrase;
> On limestone quarried near the spot
> By his command these words are cut:
>
>> *Cast a cold eye*
>> *On life, on death*
>> *Horseman pass by!*

Learned, scholarly, successful, nice, perhaps even charming – but boring when you came down to it, Jacob was boring. He had to go. He would never leave his settled home, his books, his mannerisms. But still Celestine had summoned him, a bit of her past which she had to recognise although it was hard sometimes to have any understanding of why she had been like that. Celestine allowed Jacob (who was no walker anyway) to escort her as far as the first kissing gate which led into the first fields of the day. She made him kiss her in the kissing gate. "Get safe home, Jacob," she said mischievously, "and be a little more romantic." Jacob looked puzzled and turned to go back into town.

Celestine had a long day ahead, seventeen and a half miles and further; all the guide books and the route notes agreed that this was the worse way-marked section. (The Offa's Dyke Society produces the way-markers, usually very well.) The route book even had a bracketed note: "(To sum up this confusing area: the clearest route is Ben-y-Beacon and directly up Hatterall: this is used by most walkers. The official route is clear up to the gullies but from here to under the Hatterall is faint)" While her guide book said: "There are some confusing and misleading paths mostly made by sheep."

Fox was east of Celestine, floating down the Wye. Mostly there is no Dyke, only at the English village of Bicknor does the Dyke rise up big and strong on the left, Mercian side of the river. On the north east side of Trump hill overlooking the Wye Valley a high bank begins the scarp which still measures sixteen feet although the west ditch is occupied by a trackway. On the south west corner of field 14 the bank of the Dyke reappears at a point where the plateau is breached by a steep sided re-entrant. It is a striking walk here but lost later as it hits the hill known as Rosemary Topping. From Rosemary Topping southward to Symond's Yat the scarps fronting the river Wye are very steep and precipitous and the plateau edge forms a natural boundary.

Across the river from English Bicknor is Welsh Bicknor and Fox concludes that here the two races were in contact across a ford.

They were in contact too in this lower section of the border where two Roman roads are known to cross the Dyke. They are 37 miles apart and no other Roman road survives in use or indeed whose exact course is known. One road is in the Upper Wye Valley, one down above Chepstow. It is a curious fact that the only place in the entire stretch from Highbury to Sedbury, where no Dyke or natural obstacle is present on the east bank, is the easy slope opposite Chepstow Castle. There is every reason to suppose that the Roman bridge or a ford was still in use in the eighth century, the piles are still in the river bed. But elsewhere the Roman roads died out, the Mercians did not push along them and when they were not used in the Dark Ages, they disappeared while those used survived. There was an absence of Anglian or Saxon pressure on the Middle Wye. The country made it too hard to move forward.

The track down to Hatterall was broad and on very boggy land and one could easily avoid other walkers if one wanted to. Celestine decided, however, she would encounter the single walker carrying a heavy rucksack with tent attached; clearly a man who was doing it seriously. He was wearing those long, now unfashionable, khaki shorts which reached to just above his knees and he had a full walking stick.

"Hello, hello," he said. "Where do you come from?"

"I'm from all parts of the world," said Celestine. "What about you?"

"Oh me, I am the original Anglo-Saxon. English of the English, that's me. I even live in Winchester and here I am walking the Dyke."

"You're a school teacher," said Celestine.

"How did you know, but yes, you are right. I teach history at a little school down near Brighton. So done a bit of history here, walking the Dyke. What about you? Have you come all the way down?"

When Celestine said she had, he made a bow. "Stout girl," he said, "stout girl. Sorry we aren't going the same way, but we must head on, each our separate ways."

An Englishman, well, they were half the borderers, and who were the Anglo-Saxons anyway? It was Alfred who had started calling himself King of the Anglo-Saxons. The Saxons, Teutons, were pushing around from the second century onwards (Ptolemy mentions them); it is doubtful if by the time they reached England there was any distinction between Angles and Saxons – they were the settlers, Teutons, if you liked, who pushed the Romano-British and the Celts west. As for the Mercians, that was another obscure word and it seemed likely that it meant borderers because that was what they were, people who pushed at borders – north into Northumberland, south into Wessex, but mainly, persistently, pushing into Wales.

"What are the English like?" Rupert had asked Celestine. "Surely you are not English yourself. Aren't they stiff and awkward, very formal in their manners, arrogant, thinking that breeding matters. Aren't they all those sort of things?"

And Celestine had replied, "Well, I am English, although I was born abroad. I've always felt that the country is one I visit, I've never been exactly sure where I come from, where I fit in, where I would find myself and say this is home."

Celestine hated people who did things in crowds; she was not a solitary – she wanted companionship, but she abhorred some of the scenes of the English life. She hated the crowds at football matches, the behaviour of the fans, their vulgarity, their yobbishness. Then felt guilty for those opinions; they were the working classes she sought to protect from the outrages of Thatcherism. But she hated it, she hated loud-voiced people on trains drinking their six-packs of lager. She hated noisy crowds on beaches; she liked, not solitude, but small companies of people, and she thought loud behaviour might be a feature of the English.

But you know most of the English are now middle class. What sociologist friend had told her that? There are more white-collar workers than there are manual workers; if you had wanted to tell Rupert what the English were really like you should have thought of all those nice people you were brought up with in Bournemouth, all those well-mannered young men who escorted you to your first dance. *They* were the English.

They thought they had a right to live without too much effort. They worried about housing, a neat house with a garden. They cleaned the car on Saturday morning, they might exercise on Saturday afternoon. They played tennis in the summer. Celestine remembered those hours at the tennis club all day, flopping about there. "Right, oh yes, why don't we make up a four then, if you'd like a game." The club

Professional with his constant tired jokes to the older men: "You look fresh as a daisy; me, I'd be exhausted."

Then the jobs, one third of them working in the south east of England. A country of clerks, people who did rather well in the civil service with no very pronounced views; that was the men; and the women, with more marginal jobs, earning a little less money. Perhaps doing something more... exciting? Well, less contained. Their talk, college gossip, friends, sex leading to marriage and then managing their babies and where they should go on holidays, decisions being taken in January about those valuable two weeks in August. "Are you going to Spain this year?" Then the children's schools, their careers, and round and round again.

In middle age and in old age the partners realise
that however fond they may be of one another
the thing they worry about most is: the children.
Everybody must die, but how will the children get on
In such a world, there must be great anxiety –
a nuclear war, a kind of fascist state
and/or Direct Rule from the Oval Office?

There are possibilities, if you're going to be anxious.

Children in the past have fought their way through.
Children become adults. They have talents and qualities.
They don't think of themselves any more as children.
As we have been, they are grown men and women,
able to take the new responsibilities: children.

"What are you going to do about the old people, your parents? Are you going to have them living with you? My husband can't stand my mother but we shall have to have her, she just can't manage on her own any longer. I hope I die decently young. The children, their jobs, what are they going to do? He has no idea of a career."

Then there were all the people who spent hours and hours on their gardens, weeding, pruning roses, creepers, hedges. Watching Wimbledon, millions of them and of course knowing about all the American soaps. But serious too. "You are so lucky in London, you have all that wonderful theatre, more people go to the theatre than watch football." But what did they go and see? The longest running play in the world, Agatha Christie's *The Mousetrap*, or *No Sex Please, We're British*. Hamming it up in what were called Whitehall comedies. Down at the other end of Whitehall was the parliament – they *really* hammed it up.

Grey men, the clerks of Surbiton writ large and become the governors of a country which had boasted Offa as a king (a man who sent cloaks to Charlemagne). But now couldn't decide whether to live as part of Europe or not and seemed to have no concept of anything except economic growth, when there were too many cars, too much food, no need for many people to work. All the men wore grey suits and discreet ties. They lacked style, conscience, imagination.

They, the English, had to live alongside people too. Which they didn't really like doing – like the West Indians (*supra vide*) who they had invited into their country to drive their buses but had not really expected to stay and multiply. They weren't sure they liked their habits. After all the English had had to suffer for years from the Irish, the Scots and Welsh. But they had pushed them to their borders. *The West Indians were invaders, immigrants within.*

Sitting on a stile, Celestine had been scribbling as hard as she could for ten minutes about the English; she had no real compulsion herself to become a writer. But the man in shorts had started her on this train of thought that had led to thinking of Rupert and trying to write down for him all that she knew about the English. She could go on writing more. She didn't know how different these people she had tried to describe were from the Americans (*infra vide*) or from the Germans (*supra vide*).

While you were becoming English – if that was what Celestine was now – you were also still growing up. Trying to sort out all the unfinished business with your parents.

Celestine had certainly had to do that, but many adults, she thought, had all sorts of problems to worry about in their past. There was also growing up and living in the present, being a girl, a woman, in England. The Head saying to them, "When you leave us here, you will know who you are."

Some girls, Celestine knew, felt they were girls from a very early age. They wanted to be dressed at three and four in dresses. They were neat and tidy at school, already grooming their hair meticulously, looking to see that the band they had put round their hair was in place exactly right. But Celestine had not been like that; she supposed she had been what was called a tomboy. At ten and eleven, at twelve, still just wearing teeshirts and jeans all the time and thinking about games. The Aunt used to nag her, "Brush your hair out properly, Celestine."

Even when you were excited about your body, how big your breasts would be, what it was really like to bleed once a month, you didn't actually want to look – *pretty*, she supposed that was the word. To Celestine it happened quite suddenly. She saw in a shop a green silk (as it turned out) blouse and she went in and touched it. She felt the sheen of the silk and she wanted to feel it on her. She was in London staying in the flat and she had gone out to get some fruit; there was a good barrow-boy near Green Park Station. She and her father were what he called 'pigging it', which meant they made supper together. They had lovely Mrs Welsh who 'did for them' when Mr Quareine was in town and looked after the flat when they were away. Often she left something prepared, but that night she hadn't. Her father said,

"There were some lovely peaches about today, I should have bought some for supper," and Celestine had said,

"Let me go and get them. I love walking along that bit of Victoria Street, I bet the barrow-boys still have some."

"Don't be too long."

It was in a window of a boutique on the south side of Victoria Street that she saw the blouse and she suddenly wanted it very much. It was a Thursday night which in

London is late opening, so Celestine went in and looked at it. The shop assistant came forward, "What are you, love? 38, I'd say?" Celestine didn't even know her bust size. "Yes, that would fit you lovely. Have to have a rich boyfriend to buy it for you," and she named its price which astonished Celestine. But she said to her father that night, "Dad, there was a silk blouse I really want." Next day, he went with her and said, "If you really want it," and, "I am going off next week."

Up until that point her aunt had helped her buy clothes – for school it was blue skirts and sensible tops and in the holidays jeans and teeshirts. It was funny, sixth-formers were allowed to wear what they liked; she and her friends had spent hours discussing what the older girls wore but somehow she had never thought that she would be buying clothes for herself and enjoying trying to find something that made her feel good and, she hoped, look good.

Now instead of being happy to go down to Bournemouth, she would beg to stay longer in the London flat and invite a jealous schoolfriend to stay. Then the two fifteen-year-olds would spend hours in Oxford Street looking, wondering what they could afford in clothes, in bangles, in cheap rings.

Celestine did well because her father gave her more money than most of her friends got and he also in a rather haphazard way would pick up for her at airports in foreign countries, scarves, accessories, which he hoped his daughter would like. Then there was make-up. Can I try your lipstick? Doing your eyes which could take hours and "Do you use rouge, powder?" Hairdressers suddenly became very important people to Celestine. You had to have your own special hairdresser and she would no longer go to her aunt's hairdresser in Bournemouth. "I want to have it done by Timothy in London, he's super." Scent, terribly expensive, but toilet waters which you could spray on yourself so that you smelt beautifully. And again she was lucky because now when her father went off and asked her if she wanted anything when he next came back, she was able to say, "Get me some scent at the airport, Daddy." She would have been even more spoilt if he had been there more often but it might be six months before he got back to England again. And meanwhile, Celestine had left school, had suddenly grown up, had suddenly become an adult.

Grown up, but still being looked after, still with people controlling you, still with people telling you what you had to do. Like the Bellman organising his ten-member crew on the boat and then actually himself carrying them ashore.

'Just the place for a Snark!' the Bellman cried,
As he landed his crew with care;
Supporting each man on top of the tide
By a finger entwined in his hair.

'Just the place for a Snark! I have said it twice:
That alone should encourage the crew.
Just the place for a Snark! I have said it thrice:
What I tell you three times is true.'

This established the rule that caused the Beaver so many problems which the Butcher so kindly solved for him. After successfully landing them the Bellman noted that the spirits of his crew were low and even when he repeated some jokes he had kept for a season of woe, the crew could do nothing but groan.

He served out some grog with a liberal hand
And bade them sit down on the beach:
And they could not but own that their Captain looked grand,
As he stood and delivered his speech.

'Friends, Romans, and countrymen, lend me your ears!'
(They were all of them fond of quotations:
So they drank to his health, and they gave him three cheers,
While he served out additional rations.)

It was in this speech that he first described the five unmistakable marks of the Snark following which he moved on to delineate their particular characteristics: some have feathers and bite while others have whiskers and scratch but the next piece of information he gave was the vital one. For, although common Snarks do no manner of harm, Yet I feel it my duty to say, Some are Boojums. It was at this point that the Baker fainted because of his Uncle's warning, that if the Snark was a Boojum he would softly and suddenly vanish away.

Dark clouds began to mass around Celestine as she reached the top of Hatterall Ridge. There were still four miles to go and she sped on as thunder began to crackle round her but the rain miraculously held off. The Pen-Twyn hill fort she did not have time to explore properly although you walk right through it. It is small compared to Beacon Ring, the hill fort on Long Mountain, but it has very extensive banking as you head south towards Pandy. It seems as if the hill fort men were expecting armies to come up on them from the south. Offa thought the Welsh might come on over the river at Chepstow but who the hill men thought would attack them is much more murky, their lives and religion really unknown, whereas the Mercians were Christian (one of their kings abdicated to go to Jerusalem), not that the Christian religion had bought peace to central England.

More Kissing Gates

At last she was able to see Pandy and find that two kissing gates ended the walk, just the right symbol for her meeting with Charles. The Lancaster Arms was waiting to receive her and young Charlie. She thought it was sexist to feel that women were doing anything unusual in having intimate relations with younger men. It was all very well to think that, but nevertheless she couldn't not enjoy the flattery of this young (as she thought him) man falling for her.

Charlie was a new sort of animal for Celestine: he was political for one thing, had a degree from Bangor in Political Science; not a first class degree but with it somehow he had got a job with some American Research mob (was it the Ford

Foundation?) and was assisting a member of the shadow cabinet who was jointly chairing a committee with a Labour politician. It all had to be cross-party. It annoyed Celestine to discover her name had been passed onto the MP by Ralph. But then she realised Ralph wanted to keep all his political options open and he probably wanted this MP as a friend and thought he would like Celestine (she never knew if he did).

This committee had been set up to organise dissemination of information to ethnic minorities about British life and culture; and vice-versa too: the dissemination of material about the ethnic minorities to the 'Brits'. The committee was formerly associated with the Department of Education and Charlie and a girl from the Department were the Technical Secretaries. Celestine with her (vast!) experience of publishing and teaching abroad was invited to be on the committee with the specific task of saying something of the role of publishing.

The whole thing was a shambles from start to finish. First of all a time scale had been put on the operation of six months. Then there were some thirty people on the committee, as everyone had to be represented. That meant every ethnic group had to be there. The chairman was determined that everyone should have a fair chance and asked everyone to make an opening position statement in three minutes each. Well, some managed three minutes but some went on much longer. Some had axes to grind. One gentleman from Birmingham said nothing really could be achieved until Salman Rushdie's *Satanic Verses* had been banned.

Celestine had sat down next to a West Indian poet she knew, Archie. He had edited an anthology of West Indian poetry for her and he taught at some Midland university. After a day of unfocussed discussion, Archie was asked if he would draft a document about what topics might be published to present English culture to the ethnic groups. Archie immediately asked if Celestine's experience as an editor might be involved and she found herself, with Archie, responsible for producing this ill-defined document.

Charles, as staff member, was to assist them. It all had to be ready in three months.

Both Celestine and Archie were madly busy at their work. But Archie was in Sheffield so although he was supposed to be main architect of the document, it was Celestine living in London who Charlie called constantly. She had foolishly given him her private phone-number. She was back at this point in the Carlyle Mansions apartment; Charlie conveniently had a room in Pimlico.

He was shorter than Celestine and had a huge unruly mass of curly hair. He bounced around like a teddybear on a string, Celestine told him. He had boundless enthusiasm, felt the project they were involved in was very important (which it was in a way, if only it could be handled more sensibly) and turned out to be highly efficient at finding material, collecting material, writing and producing reasonable drafts of what they were doing.

He was also great fun – he loved jazz and dancing, he knew several little clubs around Covent Garden and he was always dragging Celestine off there. Celestine had just re-joined Able and was as usual under frantic deadline-schedules at work. But she did love dancing and she loved jazz. She also found the clientele at some of the clubs fascinating. There were girls who danced and were, Charlie maintained, half hostesses, half prostitutes. Their draft document had been submitted but Celestine still found herself being dragged out by Charlie twice a week. Long enthusiastic phone calls about the committee punctuated her working day. Once, when he had gone to take a pee, Celestine found herself being asked to dance by a friend of Archie's named Bernard, a little man with glasses: "Madam," he said, "will you dance?" She did. He tried to bury his nose in her cleavage. Charlie turned up to rescue her but her new acquaintance hung on.

"You should come over to the Jazz Festival in Amsterdam," he said. "The jazz clubs there are marvellous, and the dancing."

"Come on Celestine," said Charlie, "let's go."

"I'll get tickets," said Bernard, "for the flights tomorrow, hotel and all, for the weekend, £150."

Charlie and Bernard soon had it together.

"I've got a lovely Dutch actress, Martine, coming with me, you'll love her," said Bernard. "She's my minder."

Celestine and Charlie eventually climbed aboard a taxi, committed to the weekend in Amsterdam. "Bernard thinks we're together you know," said Charlie. "Celestine, couldn't we be, I mean, you know, I think you're wonderful; please, please, please," and he turned his cherub face towards her and she couldn't resist putting her finger into that mass of curly hair and saying, "You're very sweet." 'Child'-like, she thought to herself.

Childlike, of course, simply means belonging to or becoming a child. But *child* itself has much more to it: *chylde*, or the old Northumbrian, *cildas*. A youth of gentle birth used in ballads and the like as a kind of title. When used by modern writers in this way, commonly archaically spelt – *chylde*, *childe* – for distinction's sake.★ *Childe Charlie*, she thought.

"Come in then," she said taking his hand, and adding, "Child Roland to the Dark Tower came." A remark which mystified Charlie who was desperately embracing her as she found the key. Charlie was desperate for her and as soon as they were naked, he had spurted on her belly before he had entered her, while they were still standing naked, embracing. Charlie sank back into a chair and said, "I suppose I'd better go now." Celestine said, "Charlie, don't be silly, get into the bed and lie down. I'm going to come in beside you." And a little while later as she helped him into her she added, "Second time around, you won't come so fast." Charlie proved a very energetic lover as she might have expected. Celestine found herself moaning some days later at him. "You're insatiable, Charlie," to which he replied, "You made me that way, Celestine."

★ Johnson has in addition: "Any thing the product or effect of another – Macduff... child of integrity."

They loved Amsterdam. Bernard was right about the clubs, provided you could keep away from the drugs you got offered all the time. Then there were the tiny Rembrandt etchings in his house which Celestine thought were the best pictures they saw. Little tiny representations of the man who painted the vast glamour of the Night-watch, choosing to picture himself so small and innocent in his eye.

In the Old Kirk his wife is laid (Horseman ride by); surrounding the building in sordid streets, the prostitutes stand in their windows, smiling, waving at their potential customers. Celestine and Charlie passed slowly by and Celestine made Charlie pause while they turned to look at a girl in very short denim pants lying over a chair so that her long legs could be admired; her window was down three steps so that they peered down at her and she peered up at them, smiling not only at Charlie but at Celestine as well. And she beckoned them both in.

Charlie tugged Celestine on.

"Would you like to go in, Charlie?" she asked. It was funny, she could see that the suggestion was shocking to him.

"I have you, Celestine, how could you think I could dream of any other woman?"

"Do you think if you married me" – he had begged her to marry him several times already – "do you think you would never, ever fancy another woman again?"

"I wouldn't want them, Celestine, I only need you."

Celestine leant over the bridge by Rembrandt's house (there is always a bridge in Amsterdam) and said to Charlie,

"Walk round a bit, I want to be alone here."

She didn't add that her mind was wandering/wondering about all her past lovers.

Back in London, Celestine was at work but poor Charlie wasn't when the report was submitted – it was, as Celestine had predicted, a total muddle. Charlie was out of a job. It was not a good time to be out of a job in London. He applied here and there and spent much of his day (and all his nights) in Celestine's apartment re-typing his very slender CV, reading the advertisements, calling his friends who would give him the depressing news that there had been four hundred applicants for that job.

The trouble for Charlie was that he had no real idea about what he wanted to do. Celestine knew that what one did was also part of who one was – developing that identity the Headmistress had talked about. Charlie as yet had only half an identity; he had nothing that really interested him, there was none of the passion that Celestine (although she never thought about it) brought to publishing, brought to identifying people who could do books on the boundaries; books for people who were not native to the English language. She tried to explain all that to Charlie and he listened but thought she was trying to tell him something about their relationship. "If only we could get married," said Charlie. But actually Celestine sent Charlie away, the judge was coming back for a month and Celestine wanted to devote time to her father. She was never going to marry Charlie and quite sadly she just told him they must stop seeing each other. He was the first lover she had so dismissed. Perhaps she was becoming English, just as Rupert had said – "cold and passionless."

Child Roland to the Dark tower came,
His word was still, Fie, foh and fum,
I smell the blood of an English man.

Seek it with Thimbles, Seek it with Care

They sought it with thimbles, they sought it with care;
They pursued it with forks and hope;
They threatened its life with a railway-share;
They charmed it with smiles and soap.

The Baker engaged with the Snark – every night after dark –
in a dreamy, delirious fight: "I serve it with greens in those
shadowy scenes, And I use it for striking a light."

There are eight sections, or 'fits' as Carroll calls them, to
The Hunting of the Snark, and her father divided the reading
into two parts. His little daughter listened the first evening
with rapt attention and made him repeat the stanzas about
the Baker leaving all his luggage behind. "We left lots behind
in Africa," she said, closing her eyes for sleep. As she grew
older, her fantasy that the world was being enacted for her
took on a more sinister dimension: if the actors stopped
playing their part, what would happen to her? The clear possibility was that she herself would disappear. They might
decide that she was not worth preserving in which case they
only had to stop playing their roles in her play and Celestine
herself would stop existing.

Her cousin John had been fifteen that year. Twelve-year-
old Gilly was already at her boarding school, while Celestine
still had another year at her Bournemouth school. John was
appearing in his school play at the end of his term. Gilly was
back from her school two days before her brother and was
mad for them to go. Celestine couldn't be left at home. "It's
King Lear, she may not like it much," her uncle said, for once
contributing to a discussion.

"What a strange play for a school to do," said the Aunt.

"Are you sure that is what it is?"

"Yes," said Gilly, "he wrote me about it. The English master is retiring and this is his last production and *Lear* is his favourite Shakespeare play so he decided he would do it. John plays a servant who gets killed. He has to fall – dead man's fall – he says it's jolly difficult."

Gilly was at the stage when her fifteen-year-old brother seemed like a God.

Lear it was. The knowledge that her cousin John was the servant who Regan stabs did nothing to abate the horror of the scene for the ten-year-old Celestine.

As flies to wanton boys are we to the gods
They kill us for their sport

As Gloucester's eyes were torn out, Gilly whispered to her: "They're not his eyes, it's grapes she's stamping on." But for poor Celestine, Gloucester's eyes were out.

I have no way, and therefore want no eyes;
I stumbled when I saw, and our mere defects
Prove our commodities. I have heard more since.

So one month later, having nightmares, or rather night-*thoughts*, still about Cordelia, whom she saw as someone identical to herself: no mother and a father who she adored but who was constantly away. But here he was, back again, reading her the final fit, 'The Vanishing'.

'There is Thingumbob shouting!' the Bellman said
'He is shouting like mad, only hark!
He is waving his hands, he is wagging his head,
He has certainly found a Snark!'

They gazed in delight, while the Butcher exclaimed,
'He was always a desperate wag!'
They beheld him – their Baker – their hero unnamed –
On the top of a neighbouring crag,

Erect and sublime, for one moment of time,
In the next, that wild figure they saw
(As if stung by a spasm) plunge into a chasm,
While they waited and listened in awe.

'It's a Snark!' was the sound that first came to their ears,
And seemed almost too good to be true.
Then followed a torrent of laughter and cheers:
Then the ominous words, 'It's a Boo–'

The Baker was gone and great was the astonishment of Mr Quareine when, as he finished the absurd and comic tale, to see his daughter burst into floods of tears. If his wife had died in childbirth he might, he thought, have rejected the baby, but Celestine was six months old when that tragedy happened and he had already been caught by those hazel eyes staring at him and then breaking into delighted smiles so that all he had thought during those horrifying weeks in Delhi was, I must look after Celestine, I must make it alright for Celestine. Then as she got older, not so many smiles, but this slim (he worried she didn't eat enough), slight, but tall little girl, staring at him with her bright little eyes.

Here was his ten year old weeping and seeming bereft when he read her a nonsense poem about nothing. (Only it wasn't about nothing.) He comforted her as best he could, kept on saying, "It's only a story, Celestine, it's not true, it's just made up." He didn't know of poor Gloucester's eyes being put out a month before the Baker vanished.

Her father went to discuss the matter with his sister-in-law. It was not helped by the fact that she never read anything, knew nothing of the Snark and indeed had the notion that books might be at the root of quite a lot of problems. Her husband spent all his time with his books, her little niece always had her head buried in a book (which at least meant she was no trouble) and now her brother-in-law, of whom she was secretly rather frightened, drove his daughter to hysterics by reading her a book.

"Why did you read it to her?" she prevaricated.

"Her Godmother sent it to her for Christmas."

"It was probably something else she read today. Peter *will* let her borrow all his books. Then it's been raining and she's been in all day. Moping about. She needs some air, take her for a good drive tomorrow by herself, leave John and Gilly here and run her up to Salisbury. I don't believe she's ever seen the cathedral. An outing, is what she needs."

Celestine sat silent by her father in the car next day but she held his hands as he led her round the building. She loved it.

When they got back that night, the Aunt had asked her father how she'd been.

"Fine," he said, "fine. She didn't say any more about crying but I wish I knew what went on in the child's head."

In the turquoise-coloured fields of childhood there's nothing except childhood.

Nor is there anything in the yellowing sky, nor
on the bare ochre wall, nor behind the bare ochre wall,
nor on the oriental horizon, nor beyond the horizon,
nor in the little house, nor on the target, nor in the mirror,
nor behind the mirror.

Except childhood.

Objects are strange and unfamiliar because they were there
before and will be there after. So far as I remember,
childhood is solitude amidst
a confederacy of things and creatures which
have no name or purpose.
Names or purpose are thought up by us afterwards. Then we
believe
that the wall divides something from something else,
that the house provides shelter from stormy weather and
that the nightingale spreads happiness by song and
fairy-tales.

That's what we believe. But it probably isn't so.

For the emptiness of houses is boundless, boundless
the fierceness of nightingales, and the path from gate
to gate has no end anywhere.

And seeking we lose, discovering we conceal.
For we are still searching for our childhood.

Celestine thought, when she saw Charlie: 'I'm something
of a mother figure to him. I seem organised, composed, and
he thinks me beautiful; while all the time here I am walking
down this Dyke to ease the muddles of my mind.' Charlie
hoped, of course, that he was being recalled, but Celestine
told him it was (sadly) a last farewell, she was going to work
in America and she didn't know when she'd be back. "But
say goodbye to me nicely, Charles," she said, putting her
arms round him again, "like you did that first time, remember, the night we met Bernard."

Charlie was bustling as ever, hustling I suppose you might
say, but he still didn't have a job or any clear idea of what he
wanted to do in his mind. Celestine thought maybe he never
will, maybe an unknown future (and God knows, hers was
unknown enough) was all he could wait for. With a bit of luck
something would fall his way and he would embrace it just as
she hoped some other girl would fall his way and he'd
embrace her. Somehow she found herself feeling guilty that
she had enjoyed his company, taken something of his life but
given, she thought, nothing very much back.

Bustling and Hustling

Charlie was bustling in the morning, and she let him set out
with her to another lovely little hamlet (the village of
Llangattock-Lingoed – how did you pronounce all that?)
"Go and have an early drink in a pub, Charlie, I've got to get
onto Monmouth." He was reluctant and came into the

churchyard with her and they both admired the rood beam in the little church of St Cadoc's but when he tried to follow her through the metal gate on the far side of the churchyard she pushed him back through it and firmly shut it with herself on the far side. "See you someday, Charlie."

These two days without the Dyke beside her made Celestine feel that Fox had got ahead of her. He had no work to do on that middle stretch (although actually he had passed by madly investigating mound and bank looking for traces of his Dyke.) But in the end, of course, except at Bicknor, he had settled for the river boundary. At Symond's Yat there are some well-known earthworks, says Fox, and these might have been utilised by Offa's engineer, but they are older, the characteristic defences of a promontory, early iron age fort. Today, therefore, he was below Monmouth looking at the Dyke on the hillside above the left bank of the river.

Suddenly downstream from Monmouth the Dyke appears again in lower Redbrook. It is on a flat topped spur four hundred and fifty feet above the River Wye and it is a very large work – a broad bank with a berm and necessarily with an upper (E) spoil trench on the edge of a very steep (W) slope. This start at Redbrook is an original feature and from here the Dyke runs on virtually uninterrupted until it ends on the sea at Sedbury.

Fox had to use a bill-hook for the first time to force a way through the undergrowth to get at the Dyke, but the Dyke is there following the contour above the river. At Creeping Hill it follows a curious course to allow for continuous visual control of the Wye Valley. At the Devil's Pulpit – a jutting crag of limestone immediately below the line of the Dyke – the earthwork has a high ridge beyond it and is broad and flat like a causeway on the edge of a very steep scarp. At Plumweir Cliff the Dyke makes an acute angle like an elbow – another example of the determination shown by the builders to maintain complete visual control of the Wye Valley. Why did they need that visual control?

There is abundant evidence that limestone outcrops are

the most favoured dwelling places of man in Britain. They were well drained and virtually free from forest. The outcrop bisected by the Wye and Mercian frontier is an important one, the larger half of it, measuring nine miles by two to four miles, is in Welsh territory. Centrally situated in the limestone belt was the cantonal town of the Silurians, Venta Silurum; and the population in Offa's time was still considerable. Across this limestone country the Mercians needed a well-defined boundary and this they obtained. It may be doubted if anywhere in these islands can be found a historic frontier so adequate, so dominating as this plateau edge overlooking a swift river in a windy gorge – a gorge which is often narrow and precipitously flanked and in places six hundred feet deep. The Dyke along the Wye extended further northward than would appear to be geologically necessary. The limestone belt borders the Wye from Chepstow to Tintern only but the Dyke on the left bank extended from some five miles beyond Tintern to Highbury (or Sedbury).

We infer from the clues provided by the Tidenham Charter there were two hamlets outside the Dyke. One was Lancaut (Lancawef), the other unnamed was on the Beachley Peninsula. Part of the peninsula was let to Scipwestan. *Divisiones et consuetadines in Dyddanhomme* (and this was two centuries later). At Kingston (now Sedbury) there are five hides including thirteen yards of rent-paying land and one hide above the Dyke that is now also rent paying land, and as regards that outside the enclosed land some is still in demesne, some is let out to Welsh shipowners.*

Thus the frontier was drawn and the Dyke built on the plateau edge above the Wye. Because of the trade along the lower reaches of the river being in the hands of the Welsh, it was inconvenient to make the river the political boundary; sailors must be free to moor their boats on either side. Coastal shipping requires free access to the head of the tidal waters of the river. The high water mark of ordinary tides is

* Fox acknowledges the work of Miss A.J. Robertson on the Tidenham Charter.

at Llandogo but on exceptional occasions the tide reaches Redbrook which is under the high plateau where the Dyke ends. Northward the peculiar privileges granted to the Welsh in the tidal reaches ended, and the river was the boundary – except at English Bicknor where the Welsh were granted rights on both banks of the river to trade in wood and iron. Elsewhere, higher up the river, they could traffic if they wished but their liability to English as well as Welsh taxes and dues began.

Offa decided that the push west (go west young man) had ended and the people below him on the river should be allowed to go about their business of peaceably moving logs of wood up- and downstream. Offa's frontier was the result of negotiation, a treaty between the Welsh and the English. Immense labour was undertaken by the Mercians so that the Welsh might have untrammelled use of their river trade and their seaport. The Mercians built their border above them so that they could look down and survey their neighbours but leave them to live in peace. *Vivere en pace.*

Later the Normans were about here. Fox says that Offa was wiser in removing causes of friction than later rulers were. Celestine, still well west of the Dyke, was climbing up from St Cadoc's to the chapel at Caggle Street and climbing then on up to the White Castle. Roofless, it stands as a monument to conquest as a way of proceeding. "Hatless, I take off my bicycle clips in awkward reverence."

Celestine had moved fast, she was in the Hestry Inn at Llantilio-Crossenny by half past twelve with still nine miles to go to Monmouth so she had her now usual, in these cultivated areas, pint of beer, but was on the road again by a quarter past one. Because tonight was a night of the future, not a night of the past, she had invited Max to join her. Max who she would not meet for three months. Max who would pursue her through her future and who might be a man for more than one season.

Time and dreams went with her in the afternoon. Time past stayed with you, it gave you the haunted memories of the evening when Regan stamped on the eyes of Gloucester, when your mother ("Heavily Mutilated Body" – what had been done to it? – breast cut off?) was being murdered. But dreams evoked something else. They evoked your fears, anxieties, and maybe you had to have them that way two, three nights a week. Night dreams gave you a future in which you never participated. Day dreams might give you a future which happened. If it did, what then? In dreams begin responsibilities.

Meanwhile from Llantilio-Crossenny to Monmouth is nine miles. It would be good to be in Monmouth by six. The better weather had brought out the walkers again and Celestine had had several friendly pauses. At three she was at the Abbey Bridge over the Trothy river and she could sit and talk.

"Hello there, where do you come from then?"

"Ourselves, we're from Aberystwyth."

The Welsh at last, and here out on their own borders. She moved along a little to allow the couple to sit beside her. They were a comfortable couple, she was a teacher – the Welsh exported more teachers than any other product, but she was a teacher in Wales. He had started on the railways, but that had all gone now so he managed a bus company. "Trade's not so very good," he said.

What was strange about the Welsh was that they actually seemed to have grown out of the Romans and the Romano-British. But where did they get that language, all those double 'l's? They made it themselves and the Saxons left them alone, so that by the time the Saxons really started pressing west, the warlords and kings who popped up to oppose them were Welsh. And squashed and pressurised, conquered and re-conquered, they went on popping up, persisting. And the king who recognised that right to exist was not a Welsh king, it was Offa.

Lying beyond the Dyke were the Welsh alright but who were they? They were talkers; the poet Skelton reports that in the fifteenth, sixteenth and seventeenth century, heaven was suddenly overwhelmed by an abrupt influx of the Welsh; they drove everyone crazy with their incessant talk. The keeper of the keys arranged for an angel to stand outside the gates and to shout in a loud voice, "Caws Pobi." On hearing these words all the Welsh promptly thundered out in a stampede once the gates were slammed shut behind them. The secret, of course, is in the meaning of the words Caws Pobi – a romantic call from the heart of the Welsh poet? A cry from the great Owain Glyn Dwr to join the last Prince of Wales in his revolt against the hated English? – no, none of these things. The words 'Caws Pobi' mean 'toasted cheese'.

> His intimate friends called him 'Candle Ends',
> And his enemies 'Toasted-cheese.'

It becomes clear that the Baker in Carroll's poem was a Welshman, and the disappearance of this hero takes on a wholly new significance, indicating as it does the disappearance of the Welsh nation (this story, rescinded from Williams, also indicates that the Welsh, not the Americans, were the first foodies).

What was going on west of the border while Offa stood and watched was no less than the invention of a people and its history, a people who didn't exist in fact but lived in fantasy. In their monasteries established by over a hundred Welsh saints, their scholars were elaborating a history for their kingdoms. They were joined by the poets and story-tellers who erected a hypnotic and fabulous structure of memory, legend, myth and history into a perception which was Welsh; and they did it in a language which had been Celtic but was now unmistakably Welsh.

The world they created was a world which took them straight back into the other world of Macsen Wledig and Vortigern and Germanus and Ambrosius, a world dominated more and more by the giant mythical figure of Arthur. Thus a few and fragile people took the whole inheritance of Britain on their shoulders. And late in the eighth century they were confronted with an imperial Offa, King of the Mercians, who had the effrontery to score his Dyke across their land and shut them out as foreigners.

In a valley right under Snowdon, near Beddgelert, a dramatic, rocky outcrop dominates all passage through; here in these dark ages rose a typical hill-top fort settlement, the nucleus of some little king of the *bro*. It had its imported Mediterranean pottery; it smelted its own iron; it made its own jewels, working gold, glass and enamel. It called itself Dinas Emrys, the fortress of Emrys, but later this Emrys would become Emrys Wledig, Emrys the Emperor – and under Dinas Emrys was the great lake, that magic lake where Arthur's unsheathed sword was hidden and where the Red Dragon of the Britons and the White Dragon of the Saxons fought for dominion over the island of Britain.

Particular in its Welshness was this secular work of the poets. Gruffydd ap Cynan organised the eisteddfoddau, the bardic schools and apprenticeships which were long and arduous in the strict metres allowed. This was the age of *gogynfeirdd* – the court poets, the *bardd tueta* – the household poets. They organised a complex and powerful tradition – like cathedrals, architectural in structure.

'Lo! The long hillside and the valley were full of sun. In the Mathrafal the sods are trampled under the feet of proud horses. We are welcomed with drink under stars and moon by a generous blood stained warrior.' The Old Song of Taliesin, welcoming them with the 'tall powerful eagle on the long mynd', glimpsed by Celestine, now east of the Dyke when she was up above Broad Town. The lower caste *cyfarwyddion*, the story-teller, knew several hundred tales orally transmitted. As the hated Normans ride in, some genius finally writes down the Four Branches of the Mabinogi. What followed was the transmission of all this material from this Welsh Xanadu into Europe. Gerald wrote, 'when a choir gathers to sing, which happens often in this country, you will hear as many different parts and voices as there are performers, all joining together in the end to produce a single organic harmony and melody in the soft sweetness of B flat.'

The Lords created whole schools of translators within

Wales particularly in Glamorgan and Monmouth. Flemings were some of the earliest to transmit stories of Arthur and Merlin into Europe along the clerical network. Peter Vostaert produced a Dutch version of *Gawain*; clerics made Latin versions with their Celtic origins acknowledged. William of Ghent, a troubadour who produced the Dutch version of Reynard the Fox, spent time in Wales and was a friend of Walter Map, a racy jongleur whose Arthurian romances were translated by a Brabantine.

Then in the early twelfth century came the *History of the Kings of Britain* written by Geoffrey of Monmouth, who lived in Gwent, Wales, west of that busy Wye water-way which the Welsh boats were busy plying up and down. Geoffrey's classic view of British history is dominated by the great hero Arthur bestriding Europe and the northern seas of the northmen; it broadcasts a compulsive history, a rich, mythical, compulsive history, and a prophecy of redemption when Arthur would once claim the throne of the whole of Britain.

This matter of Britain swept the French-language universe and dominated a continent, it entered the discourses of Christendom and emerged as something rich and rare. By 1180 Arthur was a hero in the crusader states of Antioch and Palestine. The Eastern peoples speak of him as do the Western though separated by the breadth of the whole earth. Egypt speaks of him, nor is Bosphorus silent. In the old empire at Constantinople, Arthur was honoured. The Welsh were assiduous in translating their world hero back into the language he had started in.

Wales is an artifact, writes Williams, which the Welsh produce. All nations are artifacts, the Welsh have the distinction of being aware of it. They push back across the Dyke no longer with bloodied men with long-swords out on night raids of Merino sheep. They were granted by Offa enough peace to build themselves, not just their own language, but a poetry out of which, at a time when nationalism dominated states, the broken ghosts of Welsh history allow a little light to break through:

Light breaks where no sun shines;
Where no sea runs, the waters of heart
Push in their tides;
And, broken ghosts with glow-worms in their heads,
The things of light
File through the flesh where no flesh decks the bones.

"Do you sing?" asked Celestine.

"Oh, yes."

"Like all Welshmen!"

"We've a very fine choir in Aberystwyth. As soon as I'm back we shall be starting. Always give a big concert at Christmas. This year it's Messiah. So we've a lot of work to do."

"It's alright for the men," said his wife. "They just sing, we have to do the teas. Choir nights, the men just sing but we sing and do their teas."

This sounded like a Welsh feud that Celestine did not wish to become involved in so she hastened back to the music and enquired whether they sang other sacred music.

"Oh, yes, we've done all the great ones. We did Haydn's Creation Mass last year and we've done the Mozart too. They're trying to get us to do a modern piece by an American, David something, next year. But I'm not sure if those Americans really know how to write music. All that jazz and stuff they do. Summer concerts, we sing songs: some of those negro spirituals. I like them."

"What's the American piece, then, sacred music?" asked Celestine, thinking of her musical friends in Manhattan.

"No," he said, "this piece is about Alice in Wonderland. That's a funny thing for an American to try and set to music. Anyway Jones (that's our choir master) says it's a great work, and the young man who wrote it, he's going to come all the way over and hear us sing it next summer. So... I suppose we'll be singing it. But I don't know as I'll like it."

"Go on with you," said his wife.

"We better be going on," said the Welshman from

Aberystwyth and they smiled a goodbye and off they went.

There had been music in all her schools but Celestine had never got into the piano-lesson bit; probably a mother would have seen her daughter had music lessons but her father had too many worries to think of planning extra music for his daughter. Choir at school had been quite fun and outings to sing in Salisbury Cathedral were exciting and then (and still) she had listened to popular music, although never with quite the excitement of other teenagers; she had had enthusiasms but nothing substantial.

It was Jonathan who had started her listening, with a show of aggression unusual in him ("But Celestine, you *must* listen to music") and he had made her listen to his records. They had gone Sunday afternoons to the Festival Hall and sat and listened to the Beethoven Quartets. She had half got into it but it was Stravinsky who made her compulsive. She had been taken to see 'Petruska' by her father when she was quite young and Nureyev was dancing. The ballet started with the marionettes hung up on the racks and Celestine had no idea that they were to have life. Then the music: the dead marionette that was Nureyev moved, the music waking him to life and flowing into Celestine too.

On her first visit to New York, she had made friends with Linda who taught English at Columbia but was very involved with music in New York. Celestine had found herself listening to performances of musicians like Glass, Liberman, Tredici. She began to be able to make some judgments about new work. She never dared tell any of them that she listened to music as a background – all serious musicians disapproved of that, but Celestine could not concentrate on it all the time, her mind just wandered. But when Petruska came on she always had to stop what she was doing and listen.

Wandering in the mind was a mistake on the Dyke path; without thinking, after climbing the hill by Hendre Farm, she had swung right, going on with the road instead of taking the enclosed track, and wasted a good twenty minutes. Then there was another steep climb through a forest before her walk down into Monmouth where Max, her lover-to-be from America, was awaiting her.

She sat for a drink when she got to the top of the wood and thought to herself, I've carried *Pride and Prejudice* all this way and never read it at all. She pulled it out and looked at the final chapter – 61 – and read that a woman may take liberties with her husband. Jane Austen had never considered what one could do with a lover.

It was awkward at the press when Celestine broke off her relationship with Jacob. He was about, inevitably, and tended to follow her dog-like out of rooms trying to get her to a tryst she no longer desired. She felt that other people knew of their past relationship and she wished to put it behind her. She started to take jobs home, saying that it was quieter than in the office, a habit she knew Able disliked – he felt you should be available and work as a team, and was doubtful if you did do more work at home than you did in the office.

There was no question that partners took up time; children too, she noticed, as Joan had had two children in quick succession. They were as good friends as ever but childcare, Celestine noted – like democracy, as Oscar Wilde had described it – took up a lot of your evenings. Celestine was realising she was not going to have children. Sometimes, when she saw a small baby, she desperately wanted to have had a child, and thought, 'That would really change my life, I would know where I'm going, I would be doing things for them.' But they were an illusion, children, she thought. If you didn't know how you should spend your life, how did devoting time to having children solve it?

It occurred to Celestine that none of Jane Austen's heroines ever had children. Sometimes they had nephews and nieces but when she hurriedly brought her novels to an end, her heroines were promised a life of the utmost happiness – the predictions of the small band of true friends who witnessed the ceremony were fully answered in the perfect happiness of the union. Jane Austen, of course, never solved the future of anyone's life beyond the point at which they committed themselves to this perfect union, but it was striking that she also avoided the easy way out of the future by not littering it with the patter of tiny feet.

Perhaps it was London that was failing Celestine. Friendly to her, a familiar place where it was easy to have friends and even to find space for oneself; but it wasn't vibrant any longer. Had it been, she wondered, in the sixties, when Ginsberg had declared Liverpool the centre of the human universe, and London had seemed to share in that glow? It was a city lacking excitement; it was a city being demoted by its governors, becoming grubby; its infrastructure declining, the underground with all its escalators constantly under repair, a hopeless lack of any traffic policy – these were minor things in a way, but they bespoke the greyness of its government which was spreading to its people.

There were bits of Britain she still had things to do in. She had to complete this walk her mother had planned down Offa's Dyke; she wanted to feel, like Fox, it – the Dyke – get into her bones, with all its details, its place names, its rises and falls, its sinuosity, its stillness. But after, she thought, perhaps she should live elsewhere for a time, somewhere where there was more bounce among the people, more energy, more excitement. Was it wrong, Celestine wondered, to like excitement?

Her father was getting towards retirement and he had just been offered a sabbatical year in some strange new academic legal institution set up with monies from the UN, mostly American, really, she supposed. It was on some sand dunes outside some capital city; was it Long Island? She couldn't remember; she had only half listened to him as he talked. But he had also heard that there was a UN Agency looking for advice about teaching languages and developing a publishing programme, and she thought she'd go for that.

It took her into the future. The future is no more intrinsically interesting than the past except of course for its unknown quality. But most future failed to live up to the past, new faces were not as nice as old, new technology might not make the planet better to live on. Old wars were not necessarily nastier than new ones. Indeed the wars seemed to be getting worse. New novels were not of necessity better than the old. Predicting the future was no more difficult than probing the lies of the past.

> We must be still and still moving
> Into another intensity
> For a further union, a deeper communion
> Through the dark cold and the empty desolation
> The wave cry, the wind cry, the vast waters
> Of the petrel and porpoise. In my end is my beginning.

So Celestine was leaving, she was flying off to a New World. Joe would tell that all the best people from the Old World had ended up on Ellis Island, and he would nod at that significantly and say, "But you stayed behind." She would nod back and say, "I'm here now, Joe, what are going to make of that, my Uncle from Rome?" He would slip some witticism out of his mouth and then add, "Well, welcome aboard, I'm glad they didn't shut you up on the Island for too long." Celestine had seen photos of Ellis Island just as it was, at the moment it was shut; it was grim. But now she hoped for a gentler entry to America, her new Border Country.

So Celestine, slipping into Monmouth, was meeting her future lover, Max. The way into Monmouth from the Dyke path is over the Monnow Bridge. The Monnow is a major tributary of the Wye and joins it here, a junction which caused the town to be built. The Bridge is one of the few remaining fortified bridges – keeping the Welsh out no doubt – but now, on crossing it, Celestine was back on her route, back on the line of the Dyke.

There was Max as promised, awaiting her at the Castle motel. He was tall with dark brown hair, brown eyes, and a full soft beard, although his upper lip was shaved. He tended to plumpness and intermittently he was worried by this and did some hasty extra exercise or made some minor variation in his diet. But mostly of course, he enjoyed eating and he particularly liked the wines of Provence. He would have the drink just right tonight.

There he was slipping delicately beside her as she entered the hotel. "I just arrived too," and, "I'll take your rucksack, all my things are safe in this shoulder bag." She was tingling as she stood by him at the registration desk. She just wanted to touch him and she kept putting out her hand and just touching his upper arm while he was filling in all those silly forms that hotels use to delay you getting to your room and your lover.

This lover was the present and future lover. He was now, and all the flatness of the past was erased. He was also her experienced and familiar lover. There were games they played as they arrived in hotels. Shall we play the undressing game, he asked, with his hand on the nape of the neck on the lift. You'd win, Max, because of my boots, it wouldn't be fair. The last naked got spanked; Celestine didn't like being spanked but she always won – somehow her feminine clothes slipped off more easily and Max was always still pulling off a sock when she was naked. She didn't really spank Max properly either, she hated to mark his body, she loved it too much, but they ended up panting with excitement (*excite*, *exit*, *excyte*, *exyte*, Fr. *exciter*, Sp. *excitar*: to move, stir up, instigate, incite, to provoke; to call forth, to quicken, to rouse from unconsciousness; excited: stirred by strong emotion; to rouse, to animate, to stir up; Max was an exciter: one that stirs up others and puts them in motion).

"Anyway I need to be clean," she said. "You have first shower quickly while I get my boots off, I want to shake out my skirt too." When she came out of the shower dry and scented, Max was naked and standing erect pouring out glasses of champagne from a half bottle.

"I picked it up on the way from the station, it was in an icebox, so it's still reasonably cool."

They held their two glasses up and toasted each other over the rims. They had two sips but Celestine quickly took both glasses and put them on the side table and threw herself on the bed saying, "Come into me, Max."

Knowing he wouldn't, for Max was the master of the foreplay with Celestine, in a way no other lover had ever been. He lay beside her, his hands beginning to explore her, she tried to roll on top and mount him but he was stronger than her and he wouldn't let her. He held her arms back above her head smiling at her and she begged him again to come in but he smiled and shook his head. "You don't really want me yet." "I do, I do, Max," begged Celestine, but he turned her over, knelt above, spread her legs and bent to tongue her delicately and leisurely, slowly moving forward from her vagina until he tongued and nibbled her clitoris. She tried to wriggle back on to her back so she could ball him and make him come in but he held her legs firmly down.

She had enjoyed the tongue with other lovers but it was Max who had slowly, it seemed, over years, played with her until she now craved that attention. When he finally allowed her to roll over she pulled her legs up straight out so that he could bury himself in her. She didn't often offer him that position because unless she was very relaxed there could be pain deep within her but today she knew there would be none. She knew too that Max would not be able to resist that invitation.

Max rested beside her for a moment. She knew she had to wait a minute before she could nestle one leg half across him and lie with her face on one side looking at his face, perhaps daring to touch his face knowing that his post-coital face was not one of sadness but of abstraction. Soon however he raised himself, walked round the bed, retrieved the champagne bottle and freshened their glasses. She really wanted to lie still but he pulled her up and gave her her glass again. They drank again and she could see him coming back to her and he kissed her again. "I love straight legs," he said, touching her breast. If she didn't watch out he would be aroused again, she had to force herself to be energetic and stand up.

"Don't start again. Max. I've been walking all day and I want to eat. What do you think of the hotel?"

"I was looking outside at their menu, looked pretty standard three star to me but I tell you what as I came along I saw a new looking Thai restaurant. What about that? I don't know what the wine will be like, but I'd like to try the food."

He had partly dressed while she went to the bathroom again but he was quickly to her when she came out, making her stand while he combed out the hair on her mound and slid his hand into her again.

"Don't, Max," she said, feeling herself beginning to give way again.

"OK," he said, "as long as you're bare."

"Max, you're the only man in the world who could persuade me to go out to dinner in Monmouth without my pants on. Celestine fastened the black silk garter belt, which had been his first gift to her.

"Anyhow," he said, "we don't want to drink too much or we'll fall asleep and not make love properly"

"We could wait 'til the morning. Max," said Celestine.

"Why?" asked Max.

Twelve Morning & Twelve Night

Celestine thought perversely that of all the folk she had met on the Dyke, from the Mongol to the Mexican, the Saxon to the Jew, she had not yet met an American, but here they came, a jambling crew of them, ten in number with names that defied invention for they were real. Who would relate Kim from San Francisco with Bach the musician or Michelle the Cook with the Jordan river. Diverse and varied, they were all round Celestine in a moment. "You've walked the whole Dyke!" Impressed, very, but unable to stop being Americans. Her four-year-old nephew, Timothy, Gilly's first child, would ask at London Airport, "Who are the Americans?" And Celestine would reply, "They don't know but they are trying to find out."

There were ten of them, I repeat this – I have said it twice – a motley crew – how they got together to walk the Dyke she could never find out. But there they were and fascinated by her. "You've worked in Manhattan! You're coming back there right after this? I must give you my number, be sure to call. It would be just lovely to have you to stay." "In publishing, how wonderful." She wondered afterwards how they managed to tell her so much about themselves so quickly, but then she thought, that is Americans; they are so keen to define themselves, they don't wait. Why, Kathy told her at once about the first time she went out with her husband and a pen leaked and it got all over her shirt. Another ten minutes on the Dyke and she would have heard all about the first night. Little Joe seemed in some way to be their leader. At least it was he who finally said, "Come on, guys, we'd better get walking and leave Celestine. She's nearly finished, we've got a ways to go." He claimed (all Americans tell you their descent at once) that his mother was Irish but that wasn't what he was. He was an Italian, he was the Uncle from Rome, the famous relationship that every Italian wanted. They stumbled in their eagerness to tell him their affairs, their concerns. Little jokes too, very simple ones bumbling out of his mouth so that when you were with them there was never a pause, never a gap in the conversation, you were born away on wings of pleasurable talk as you squared up to the Uncle from Rome.

Of course, there was a foodie, but an American foodie. What a luxury, a person who really believed that food was life. She was telling Celestine at once about her catering business in the Crimea. Celestine thought she said that, but realised this was Crimea on the West Coast. "Biting," she said, "biting into a sweet ripe apricot or a juicy grilled steak is not only a simple act of nourishing oneself but also an act of sensuality, a political and economic statement, an act of trust and courage." Celestine could just hear Max's quiet, cool, laid back, "Good food should be the *occasion* and not the *subject* of good conversation." Behind and beyond Michele there were regiments of foodies, there were guru foodies, organic foodies, home-grown foodies, religious foodies, there wasn't a foodie that hadn't been thought of, bursting to tell you about their world. Nievo had seen the world as one vast kitchen but this was the world seen as one huge restaurant. "Poor Americans," Max would say, "desperate to eat well yet you can't get a decent meal between Washington and the West Coast and nowhere to compare with a simple dinner in Provence. You remember what the waiter said when I congratulated him on the superior cuisine, "*Ils ont dit que la cuisine francaise, c'est meilleure que la cuisine anglaise.*"

But there seemed to Celestine no essential reason why taking food in should have any more attention given to it then passing it out. Her uncle had kept an eclectic selection of books in his downstairs toilet and there she had first encountered *The Specialist*, an account, fictional no doubt, of a man who devoted his life to building privies. His pride and joy was a family four-seater and here, no doubt with courage

and with trust, people had sat to review the political and economic world around them. No doubt the sexual world was
beneath them.

Elizabeth was tall, laughing, too, with the pleasure of
meeting you, "I knew it was going to be a good year for
meeting people. I had Aquarius in the ascendant." Was it
Aquarius and was it in the ascendant? Celestine could not
remember afterwards but she found herself telling Elizabeth
her birth-date and the hour she was born.

"I knew you were Leo, I just felt Leo as soon as I saw you.
Jan's got this marvellous pocket computer and we could do
you at once and then you'd know."

"What would I know?" asked Celestine, bewildered.

"It doesn't predict details of what will happen but it tells
how it's going to be for you. Do you know Kim?" pointing to
the tall girl standing by John, "Why Kim is going to have a
great year when she's 71."

"It's something to look forward to," said Kim.

"But how old are you now?" asked Celestine.

"I'm 44 now, so it's a bit of a ways off."

Celestine's hates included many of the religious people –
fanatics, intolerants – but astrology seemed too bland to rate
as a religion. Elizabeth, somehow connected with Joe through
an office, had, Celestine thought, rather a boring job, so she
poured herself into her study of the stars in their course. How
could she, wondered Celestine, when clearly most of it was
complete bullshit. But there you go. She wasn't aggressive
with it, she wasn't dangerous with it, she did nobody any
harm with it, and it enthused her with a personality; it gave
her a time and place and established an identity, the identity
that she was seeking. Because Americans have no inherited
identity they have to create a new one all the time.

These, she had to remember, were the nice Americans.
There were so many horrid ones. There were the nutters out
there, the religious sects, who holed up in New Mexico with
an absolute arsenal of arms and had some sort of stand off
with the FBI, praying all the time, while the leader abused all

the women: that was a personality to have established. Then there were so called *non-nutters*, who were in positions of power and did insane, mad things. They had this poor boy who had got into some gunfight in a robbery with some undesirables and they caught him. But he was brain-damaged, barely able to read, a confused rudderless type of guy. So they strap him into an electric chair and then 30 seconds before switch time, they take him out again because of a stay from the insane American legal system. Two or three times they put him in and out of that chair, but finally they do fry him. He is dead. Americans do that.

But these, thought Celestine again, these are the alright Americans. She was sharing a sandwich with a sombre-looking man called John, his hair brushed straight back, greying; he looked, she thought, a bit like a Norman knight. He was an Abroad American, hadn't lived in America for twenty years. He visited, of course, his old parents, who were still living in Connecticut, but he had really, he said, become a European. But of course he hadn't. It was a funny thing: meet a man in Seattle who says to you, "Hi, you English? I came here from Manchester twenty years ago," and he would be American all down the line. But take an American to Germany and dump him there and what would you have in twenty years time? You'd have an American, and of course the reason was simple: there *were* no Americans, it was a border country but one where you lived permanently and where you spent your time trying to achieve independence, an identity, some sort of self-image against the fearful odds of the nasty Americans all around you. Being nasty in their crazy different ways. When Joe gave the marching orders, Celestine was quite exhausted, felt she could barely stride on south but then she took some deep breaths, her head cleared and she was back in the sheer sanity of the Dyke, the Dyke and its border people. People like herself, identifying with the landscape, the old, old hills around her, the wide river on which Fox thought the Welsh had been so active in their boats, while the Mercians up here on their Dyke had watched them, cautious, perhaps, rather than unfriendly and had left them to live in peace.

As they were leaving she suddenly noticed that there was one man who she hadn't realised was part of the crew. He had been busy all lunchtime, apparently repairing the path, sweeping it with a broom, but now, on Joe's summons, he began to hurry after them.

"Hey," said Celestine, "who are you?"

"Sonny, that's my name, you betcha."

"What have you been doing, Sonny?"

"I drive their truck. I'm their driver. Just now I've been tidying up, sweeping the path, got to get it tidied up, can't leave these rocks and pebbles."

"But, Sonny, this path has been here a thousand years, you'll never get it flat."

"I can have a real go," said Sonny.

She took his arm, "Stop a moment," she said, "tell me where you come from."

"Gee," he said, "out there in the mountains.* Eleven, my Ma had, in one little shack. You got the hot water out the boiler by the fire."

"What did your father do, Sonny?"

"He was a hunter, you betcha. He'd bring back the squirrels for supper. Nothing like a squirrel steak. You boil him first, you carve a bit off, you got a tasty steak there."

"So do you hunt, Sonny?"

"Don't have time, I'm working all the day, then I got the cars. I got fifty cars up there, you betcha!"

"What do you do with the cars?"

"I sells a bit of them then I'm left with the rest. But I'm not so happy with it these days."

"What's wrong, Sonny, the work?"

"No, no, I just got married the second time and I guess that keeps you busy."

"You mean you don't have time for the cars?"

* Sonny was born in the Adirondack Mountains.

214

"She calls me Mr O. I'll get to the cars later. You betcha."

"You'd better go on, Sonny. Are you going to sweep the path clear ahead of Joe?"

"You betcha."

Celestine looked at him and smiled at this big, bulky shape, his massive head, his missing teeth, his mild manner. "Sonny," she said, "you betcha."

In the mornings, Max was always more malleable. Once she had handled him he was quite submissive and she could make love to him one of her favourite ways. She would ride him and then when she got too excited to move herself, she would come down on him and after a minute they would roll side by side. There she could hold and kiss him while they ground their bodies together until he flowed into her.

Max was frantically busy as ever and it seemed that they would meet again with her father at a reception at the legal institute in a month's time. Max was a psychiatrist but he was joining the Legal Institute at the UN's request to try and persuade the lawyers to have a little more understanding and compassion for human nature. He was also trying to complete his monumental work *On the Nature of Love and Peace*.

"I wish you weren't going away, I sleep so badly without you," she curled round his back, always holding him so that their naked bodies touched all night. "It's only a month, love."

Let this sad interim, like the ocean be
Which parts the shore, where two contracted new
Come daily to the banks, that, when they see
Return of love, more bless'd may be the view:
Else call it winter, which, being full of care,
Makes summer's welcome thrice more wished, more rare.

Celestine was heading south on her last full day's walking. And today too was a lighter day's walking. She had only just over ten miles to go to the Brookweir Inn. But she had known that Max and she would rise late and then potter a bit in

Monmouth, which they did, before she saw him to his train. Then for much of the day she had to decide about upper and lower routes. She could keep to the lower river route or she could climb up and pace along the Dyke itself, high up above the river. What she chose was to take the first section by the river (which was what Fox had thought was the boundary) and then swing up at Redbrook to where Offa's final impressive section of the Dyke began.

Border Peoples

Fox's survey, he admitted, had been a laborious undertaking, both in the field and in the study. It was perhaps tedious to read. But it was worth doing because it demonstrated the competence, skill and dogged determination applied through two centuries by related groups of Englishmen in the Dark Ages; and the reality and vigour of the Welsh opposition. One sees, though in a blurred outline, the England of the Mercian pioneer, adventurer, frontiersman. Here on the borders of the highland, nature was his enemy as well as man. Densely forested hills, ravines matted with primeval jungle, extensive and impassable marshes environed his way.

So Celestine was in Brookweir by soon after 12.30 and had even time to detour up to the village of St Briavels. Then she chose also to take the lower river path. She was planning already her final morning and she knew that by then she would be on or by the final section of the Dyke, which Fox had assured her was on the major scale. Tonight she had summoned no lover, she was alone in her room in the Brookweir Inn. She rose early to greet the day. So far she had dressed for walking in the customary faded jeans and sensible tops, but this morning she dressed for a lover. She forbore to wear black stockings, which she thought might attract too much attention. She wore her black silk shirt with her usual thick socks and boots and beneath her skirt she was bare, there was nothing between her flesh and the solid earth of the Dyke as she strode across it, around it, beside it. The Dyke, which she had thought of as feminine in its upper reaches, seemed here like its builder, a solid masculine figure.

She could feel flooding down beside her the people of the Dyke, the Marcher Lords. Offa's very work had led to the creation of a race of people often powerful, often violent, a boundary people. From the pivot of Chester, they stamped their imprint from north to south, a seedbed of powerful families – Montgomerys, Mortimers, Bohuns, Clares. They stretched deep into mid-Wales. Glamorgan was immensely powerful as the Fief of the Clares. They ran west along a rich and open coast, planting towns and peopling the plains with an alien people. There was a permanently disputed shadow-zone and endless border-raids but there was also a fine mesh of intermarriage and fluctuating tactical alliances. The beautiful Princes Nest of Deheubarth could play the role of Helen of Troy, precipitating wars over her person. Gerald (*supra vide*) was a grandson of hers through her daughter Angharad, while no fewer than three bishops were descendants of the evidently potent Nest.

The dramatic creation of the Welsh European culture mirrored the growth of a hybrid society in the March. The March not only survived as a separate entity, it was extended (by Edward I). Northeast Wales was handed over to Lacys, Greys and Warennes who took their place among the older families, as did the Welsh families who had taken a winning side. (Edward had to take action against the Clare whose empire as far as the king was concerned was getting out of hand).

The Marchers were involved in the Wars of the Roses. They supported York and controlled the Marches but the Lancastrians were Welsh. The Yorkists were cut down in 1469 and the Lancastrians two years later. But one Welsh lad had caught the eyes of a widowed English queen when she saw him bathing naked. Owain ap Maredudd ap Tudor and his grandson unfurled the Red Dragon of Cadwalader at the battle of Bosworth Field. Merlin's prophecy had come true at last and Henry, to ensure it would, called his first son

Arthur... The Welsh, reported the ambassador of Venice, may now be said to have recovered their independence, for the most wise and fortunate Henry VII is a Welshman.

The headmistress at Easthurst gave them a valedictory address. "You girls have become in these last two years adult young women." "Is that what I am?" Celestine asked her father. "Do you see me as an adult young woman?" And Larry Quareine looking at his tall (stately, he thought her) young daughter, said, "Yes, I think you are grown up."

Celestine was back from another visit to her godmother. The latter had suddenly said, "You worry why she went out walking at night. You'll never know – don't *you* get a bit restless at times?" This slid into a conversation about the little bit of the Offa's Dyke walk that she and Hazel had done twenty years before. "We walked from my father's farm to Montgomery and back. It took us a long day but your mother loved to walk."

Celestine had longed to know about her mother but had had no interest in the rest of her family history. She thought the obsessional interest in one's ancestors was curious and offended in some way her sense of equality. What did it matter what sort of parents you had, what your grandfather had done, you were on your own out there in the world; you might have inherited some things from your family, she supposed, but there was nothing you or they could do about that. But it did occur to her now that she had never asked or been told anything about her father's family, nor had he vouchsafed any information.

'Grown up', she should at least know something of her own father's history.

"Where did your family come from, Dad?"

"My grandfather, your great-grandfather, had a corn factor's business just north of where you've been, up in Wrexham, but it was all sold out before I was born."

"So we come from the borders?'

"I suppose we do. The name Quareine, my father always

said it was a corruption of some Norman French word – to do with the Queen, of course."

Family matters were not subjects which her father talked about for long either; it was as if his excursion into family life had opened a book which had then shut on him and he desired to keep it shut.

"How much money do you think you'll need for college?"

"Heavens," said Celestine, "I don't know, Dad."

"I don't want you to be short. I've looked at the forms and they suggest £ ___."

He went on to plan to give her substantially more than the university suggested. Celestine was going to be better off than other students. What would she spend it on? She didn't want to dress more expensively or look any different, she wanted to be like the other students. She could give some to charities like Oxfam while holding some in reserve, she thought, for things that would crop up (which they did – Rory's beer money and holiday).

As she walked bare – at least her body bare beneath her skirt – Friar William of Rubruck came to her mind: attempting to keep to the statutes of his order, he had travelled with bare feet strapped into his sandals. Up on the high Mongolian plateaus as his toes froze, his hosts had taken pity on him and provided him with some sort of fur boots to save his feet from frostbite. When Celestine had gone shopping that evening in Jerusalem she had bought herself some sandals. She had seen them as some sort of expiation between Jew and Arab. The bible was full of sandals being latched and unlatched and she had thought sandals in Jerusalem will be really well made and will be really comfortable to walk in, especially when the shop-keeper told her they were made in a factory employing both Jews and Arabs. But later her academic host told her that the factory-workers could not even eat lunch together. The Jews, of course, took out their matzot (it was Passover on the occason her host was describing, and no bread can be cooked during this festive period) but the Arabs began eating sandwiches made from bread. The Jewish workers thought the Arabs had purposely brought bread, knowing it was offensive and prohibited for Jews. The incident signalled the differences and boundaries between them. (Sexual liaisons involving Arab and Jew are highly patterned but in some cases mixed couples do continue to live with or near to one another.) Relationships on the boundaries.

In fact the sandals were not easy to walk in; they proved badly made and uncomfortable, and she threw them away.

You had to walk bare to make love. The clothed body permitted no intrusions. Now her body, which until now she had always covered, was bare. Bare to the Dyke and bare to the intrusion of man – perhaps Max when she met him would persuade her that while children were not a way of life, fertility had a function. It was a form of creativity – it certainly carried with it excitement.

Near Chepstow town now; but don't walk into it, head down for the last stretch of the Dyke. She went treading on and (surely the Americans must have rejoined here) into Pennsylvania village which stands right on the Dyke; she walked along Offa's Close and Mercian Way. Offa's Saxons had, she thought, as she tried to remember the museum at Knighton, worn almost a sort of sandal with broad leather bands wound round their legs. In Germany a man could still not put out the sign 'Shoe Maker' until he had actually made a pair of shoes. It had to be a well-crafted pair, the apprentice's masterpiece. Until he had made that he was nothing. Could a Turk make a German shoe, could he turn out a masterpiece? Celestine and Rory had gone on a Greek Island package tour which took you into Cyprus. Their chartered aeroplane had failed to show up for the return journey and they had had to spend two days in Cyprus. Celestine had decided she wanted to visit the Turkish part of the island and there she had bought her best ever sandals. So they could make sandals. The question was, would the Germans let them?

Boots. Hers had stood up well, once she had solved the sock problem (getting just the right thickness to prevent rubbing). The English in their great industrial days had been great boot-makers; Napoleon's armies had marched to Moscow on boots that had been 'Made in England', a few skeletons had marched back in them. Boots could be peaceful, could allow you to walk along the borders, but could be beastful – you could be kicked with a boot.

The West Indian, Archie, had walked home late one night in Sheffield and seen a gang of five, six, white – no doubt English – youths, kicking a black man, no doubt a fellow West Indian, on the ground. What to do? He had run on quickly to his home and called the police but rang Celestine the next day in much distress because he felt he should have gone across the road and tried to intervene. "They'd only have kicked you, Archie, and I want to keep your bright head intact. It has its uses to me." Who else could edit the Anthology of Caribbean Poets in England?

The Welsh wife yesterday had reminded Celestine of the Wife of Bath. Mavis had interrupted her husband at one point by suddenly asking Celestine: "Don't mind me asking then but how old are you?"

Celestine was a bit vague about her birth date.

"Oh, getting on forty, is it, have you had any children?"

"Oh, you should be having a child soon then, but you're walking alone."

"I'm meeting a friend tonight."

"Oh, good then."

They went back to the problems of singing Messiah.

Ever since the David and Jonathan episode, Celestine had rather naughtily taken to looking back at her fellow walkers and she had turned round to see how that Welsh couple were faring. She had left them with Mavis retying her boot and when she turned to stare, Geoff was extending his hand to pull her to her feet. They stood for a moment, one hand clasping another and Mavis planted her second hand over Geoffrey's and he clumped his remaining hand on top so they were standing facing each other with a four handed hold. They threw their heads back and laughed, Geoff having made some joke no doubt (sexy, Celestine wondered?). They leant out from each other, for a moment, supporting each other with their four-hand hold, and then turned and went on along the path hand in hand.

Now forty years after
They're still meeting
Across borders
Their hands like the four wings of two doves
Folded together
Unable to fly away
From each other
Very capable hands
Capable of a lot of things
But not of saying goodbye.

In answer to your question, 'What did you mean the Snark was?' Will you tell your friend that I meant that the Snark was a Boojum. To the best of my recollection, I had no other meaning in my mind but people have tried to find the meanings in it. The one I like best (which I think is partly my own) is that it may be as an allegory for the pursuit of happiness. The pursuer of happiness betakes himself as a lost and desperate resource to some wretched water place and hopes to find, in the tedious and depressing society, or the daughters of mistresses of boarding schools, the happiness he has failed to find elsewhere. Words mean more than we mean to express when we use them.

The whole tale of the Snark moves from one beach to another, indicating where Carroll's fantasies lay. Little girls on beaches (the daughters of mistresses, he had no interest in the mistresses themselves). Celestine had been a little girl, she felt, on many beaches, but she had never been drawn in the nude. Carroll assigned Henry Holliday the task of illustrating the *Snark* after they met on January 15, 1874 and Holliday gave him a series of exquisite drawings of nude children. We can make a good guess they were little girls. Carroll planned to duplicate them in photographs from life.

He pushed these photographs of nude little girls to the oldest age he dared, offending a lady whose daughter he wanted to photograph beyond an age which she felt appropriate. But Carroll gave up his little girlfriends as they grew up – all of them with the exception of Gertrude Hathaway, the dedicatee of the *Snark*. Seeing her aged 27, he preached a sermon that Sunday on 'Lead us not into Temptation'. Behind and beyond Carroll was the whole of adult life, the Welsh Baker disappearing when he encountered the adult female Snark.

His companions – nine of them left on the beach – all male, one mad – needed, Celestine felt, female company, and she selected nine woman to be their companions. There names were Celestine, Cressida, Cassandra, Cordelia, Cleopatra, Celia, Constance, Calpurnia, Charmian. Cordelia was a match for the mad Banker but the tasks of the others were to bring these heroes of childhood into the adult world, a world which poor Carroll never entered. He was left behind, a poor entertainer on a beach.

For Carroll, happiness was a little girl on a beach. For most men, Celestine thought, happiness was in bed with a big girl. Nightmares of her childhood, of her mother's disappearance, were banished by her fertile body as she strode along the Dyke.

In these last sections the Dyke, as it ran to the cliffs at Sedbury, was a large structure. It runs a little back from the line of the Wye to allow a re-entrant which was formerly a pill or creek. There is on the west flank of the re-entrant a small defensive earthwork which makes it highly probable that the creek was important in Offa's time and he was once again giving space to Welsh shipmen.

In these last two or three fields Celestine found again a real strong piece of Dyke beside her, a good fourteen feet in height. And as ever it was undulating ups and downs, then quite suddenly at the end of the slope you saw a large stone, and almost obscurely, the Dyke ends, 'on the cliffs at Sedbury.'

There were trees and bushes surrounding the little mound but you could force your way through some bushes and look down across the mud to the Severn with the Wye coming in and to the right the Bristol Channel and the sea, the sea.

Notes towards an Ending

Offa's Dyke is a treaty, a written statement in earth of a border between two peoples. Boundary: that which serves to indicate the bounds or the limits of anything material or immaterial, also the limit itself (*boundari, bundary*). Bound (of *boane, boen, bune, bonne, bunne*, also *bunde, binde*); in mediaeval Latin, *bodena, bodina*, earlier *butina*. Bound and Body; Celestine's body was a boundary. Her body was the Dyke; the ridge of bone that centred her body was the height of the Dyke, but behind it, under it, was the softness which she gave not only to men but also to herself. From it sprang her vigour, her beauty; Celestine was offering to be a partner in the world, a lover to the world. Her body she offered as a boundary which you had to cross in order to redeem yourself. You had to seek re-entrants, ways back to friendship, back to Celestine.

These are all mere work-rules, mere jottings, seeking for what Celestine was achieving. She was achieving a consummation. Consummation has in it *finality, completely accomplished, supremely qualified, perfect, of the highest quality*. From Consummation, consume – to burn up, waste, destroy. There are further notes I should insert here – for example, where is Reverend Kilvert who patrolled these borders, marching along them to meet some wispy muslin-dressed Victorian girls to whom he was unable to declare his passion?

A further note: a feature of vital importance in the history of Anglo-Saxon law is its tendency towards the preservation of peace. Society is constantly struggling to ensure the main condition of its existence – peace.

An Ending

You reached the end of the Dyke. Beside the mound stood a man, tall, antique. She knew his face well from the silver coins which remained, his rather globus eyes, the almost receding chin, the somewhat prominent nose. He stood there and turned towards Celestine, towards this intruder who wanted in some way to make his achievement her own.

He was standing there, tall, fair, his sword at his side; he was a king who had ruled for 39 years. His predecessor was murdered by his own bodyguard and Offa fought, no doubt, to establish his position. He was a man who killed men. His sword was famous and was named; it was called 'Skree' and was given to Edmund Ironside 219 years later, so it had some potency and had presumably also killed some men. Offa was involved with Wessex, with Northumberland; some he dealt with by force, some by treachery, some by guile, but he stood four square as King of Mercia.

He stood there looking at Celestine, nearly eleven hundred years younger; and she looked at him. His eyes encompassed her body in a glance and then they returned to her face. "How," she, Celestine, asked, "did you behave? How did you treat the women who you came in contact with? Your Queen is mentioned as a murderess too but how, in the long reaches of the night, did you treat her?"

You controlled north and south, you had friendly relationships east into Charlemagne's Europe, but you were faced with a problem west. You had farmers pushing along the river valleys towards the Kings of Wales. Mischievous, menacing sometimes, but individuals; and at a certain point you decided to stop and let them be. That did them good – it left them murdering, slaying each other no-doubt, but also trading, writing poetry and frantically developing a culture which was archaic but in a curious way, noble. You created the Dyke, from which you could watch the curious Welsh and keep them peaceably and firmly at bay. To do this you had a stern task. Look at the middle of the Dyke. It is difficult to imagine anything more indicative of strenuous purpose and successful achievement than the straight course of Offa's Dyke in broken country.

But now he was looking eleven centuries ahead at a woman standing up to him at the bottom of his boundary, his great peaceful achievement. He could see her loose flowing clothes that made her open to him. She stood offering herself to him but he knew that she knew that in the morning, just as she had been his to take at night, he would submit to her caress, her touch. There would be equality in love.

She had been born in a world of which he knew nothing – the Indies – which he had never heard of. She knew murder from that land. She knew of other lands where his sword, Skree, was unsheathed and killing races like the little Silurians, the innocent tribes of the Gwent valleys, the wandering heathen of Dinas Emrys, but now called by different names: Armenian, Croat, Thai. He knew those religious wars, too. All she had to oppose those forces was her person, her body, with its perception of men who had failed her and who she had failed; with its language which he had allowed to develop (not Welsh, impossible to speak), a language of the mind which was a frail bulwark against the wars, the aggressions which she knew too well.

It seemed a weak weapon, as was his Dyke. But his will, his work, had stood for all those years, holding together the border people – people who would venture across the border into each other's territories, yet intruded in peace. That was what he had intended; that was what she intended. He held a hand out towards her; she held a hand towards him. They embraced; they kissed, gently but firmly; they turned to look south, towards warmth, towards re-entrants, towards friends, towards where the tide flowed in and the sun was glinting off the sea.

Acknowledgments

First to Yaddo, who gave me a residency which allowed me to write the first draft of this novel, and to my colleague and mentor there, Joe Caldwell, who gave much support and good advice. Secondly, to my good friend Peter Porter, for his encouragement. Thanks also to Nicola Gray, who has the ability to read my handwriting and provided me with a type-script; and to David Crystal, for encouraging the use of dictionaries.

Acknowledgment is due to the following, for permission to reprint work in this novel:

Offa's Dyke: A Field Survey of the Western Frontier-Works of Mercia in the Seventh and Eighth Centuries A.D., Sir Cyril Fox, published for the British Academy by Oxford University Press, 1955, reproduced by kind permission of Mr Charles Scott-Fox; 'That Beauty, That Beast', Edwin Brock, originally published in *Ambit 100*; 'Calamiterror', George Barker, from *Collected Poems*, published by Faber and Faber; *A Guide to Offa's Dyke Path*, Christopher John Wright, published by Constable; 'Our English Cousins', James Laughlin, from *Ambit; Four Quartets*, T.S. Eliot, published by Faber and Faber; *African Laughter: Four Visits to Zimbabwe*, Doris Lessing, reprinted by permission of HarperCollins Ltd; 'On the occasion of the enthronement of Charles as Prince of Wales', Stevie Smith, Uncollected; 'Over All the Obscene Boundaries', from *At the Gare Bruxelles Midi*, Lawrence Ferlinghetti, published by New Directions; extract from *Motherland*, by Elyse Dodgson and Company, originally published in *Ambit 91;* 'Under Ben Bulben', from *Last Poems,* W.B. Yeats, published by Macmillan, reproduced by permission of A.P. Watt on behalf of Michael B. Yeats;

'The Children', Gavin Ewart, from *Ambit 107*; 'Brief reflection on childhood', Miroslav Holub, from *Poems Before & After*, Bloodaxe Books, 1990; 'Light Breaks Where No Sun Shines', Dylan Thomas, by permission of David Higham Associates; *Mexican Voices, American Dreams*, edited by Marilyn P. Davies, published by Owl Books.

The author particularly wishes to acknowledge the use made of the following material in this novel:

The Uncle from Rome, Joseph Caldwell, published by Viking; *The Annotated Snark*, edited by Martin Gardner, published by Penguin; *The Mission of Friar William of Rubrick*, published by the Hackluyt Society; 'Maiden Castle', Naomi Mitchison, from *The Hostages*, published by Parrish; 'The Confessions of Golias'; the Arch Poet of Cologne, from *The Goliard Poets*, translated by George F. Whicher, published by New Directions; *When Was Wales: A History of the Welsh*, Gwyn A. Williams, published by Penguin; *Germany and the Germans: An Anatomy of a Society*, John Ardagh, published by HarperPerennial; *Cyril Fox: Archaeologist Extraordinary*, Charles Scott-Fox, Oxbow Books; Offa's Dyke Association literature and maps.

Every effort has been made to contact copyright holders; the publisher and the author regret any omissions, and will be pleased to rectify them in future editions.

RECENT FICTION FROM SEREN

Mr Vogel
Lloyd Jones
£7.99pbk | ISBN 1-85411-380-1

★★★★★

"A manuscript, allegedly discovered in an old pub, provides the
focus for this extraordinary tale. Mixing fact and fiction, Jones
shoehorns elements of the detective novel, a great deal of
mythology and some uncommon history into what must be one
of the most dazzling books ever written about Wales."
INDEPENDENT ON SUNDAY

"Surely one of the most remarkable books ever written on the
subject of Wales – or rather *around* the subject, because it is an
astonishing mixture of fantasy, philosophy and travel, expressed
through the medium of that endlessly figurative country."
JAN MORRIS

"A sprawling, genre-hopping stew of a novel that will absorb
anyone with any kind of interest in Wales."
DAN RHODES

"In the spirit of Sterne (trapped on a wet weekend in
Aberystwyth) or Flann O'Brien (enduring the final cure), Lloyd
Jones delivers the tour-guide Wales has been waiting for: warped
history, throwaway erudition, sombre farce. Stop what you're
doing and listen to this mongrel monologue."
IAIN SINCLAIR

"A rambling, redemptive mystery, stuffed full of all things Welsh:
rain, drink, wandering, longing, a preoccupation with death and the
life that causes it. A bizarre and uncategorisable, and therefore
essential book"
NIALL GRIFFITHS

www.seren-books.com

RECENT FICTION FROM SEREN

Totes Meer
Dai Vaughan
£6.95pbk | ISBN 1-85411-338-0

"One of the most skilful writers of our age."
REVIEW OF CONTEMPORARY FICTION

"Dai Vaughan, one of the most imperiously intelligent fiction-writers alive, has constructed a novel of complete originality. It is a pattern of voices debating their lives and their worlds, sometimes in lonely soliloquy and sometimes in dialogue with others. The voices of a man facing death, of a Palaeolithic humanoid reflecting on hunting, power and the origins of music, of an ageing artist returning to solitude and her own memories of creation and grief, of a boy wide-eyed in a new place... among others. The voices at first seem unconnected. But the reader soon grows aware of the subtle skill which gathers them all into elements of a single composition. And this is also a polemical book. It is a novel of many ideas: about memory, about politics (above all, Vaughan's recurrent theme of the impunity of the powerful, never reached by the vengeance of their victims), about art, prehistory and classical myth. But its underlying strength is the sheer quality of Vaughan's writing, 'poetic' in its fastidious freshness and economy of word-use. This is a book to keep, to re-read and to give."

NEAL ASCHERSON

RECENT FICTION FROM SEREN

The Land as Viewed from the Sea
Richard Collins
£6.99pbk | ISBN 1-85411-367-4

SHORTLISTED FOR THE WHITBREAD FIRST NOVEL AWARD

Richard Collins' beautifully-wrought debut novel is a dreamlike
evocation of land and sea and the places where the two meet.

Two friends work together on the land: one allows the other to
read the novel he is writing, 'The Land as Viewed from the Sea'.
Slowly, as both novels unravel, fiction begins to intrude upon
reality, altering their relationship, and threatening to change
their lives forever.

"A gripping tale that unfolds with immense narrative skill."
WHITBREAD AWARDS PANEL

"A compelling read, dreamlike and lifelike at the same time."
GUARDIAN

"An evocative story of dislocation and loss"
TELEGRAPH

www.seren-books.com